Scoundrel in Disguise

Other Five Star Titles
by Annette Blair:

The Butterfly Garden

Scoundrel in Disguise

Annette Blair

Five Star • Waterville, Maine

First Edition
First Printing: May 2006

Published in 2006 in conjunction with Tekno Books.

Set in 11 pt. Plantin by Myrna S. Raven

Printed in the United States on permanent paper.

Library of Congress Cataloging-in-Publication Data

Blair, Annette.
    Scoundrel in disguise / by Annette Blair.—1st ed.
      p. cm.
    ISBN 1-59414-483-4 (hc : alk. paper)
    1. Railroads—Fiction.   2. Great Britain—History—
Victoria, 1837–1901—Fiction.   I. Title.
PS3602.L333S38 2006
  813'.6—dc22
                                       2005034661

All my love

To our best Thanksgiving gift ever

Dressed in ruffles and lace, smiles and grace

Kelsey Elizabeth Mullens

A blessing and a joy

MY LOVE IN HER ATTIRE

My love in her attire doth show her wit,

It doth so well become her:

For every season she hath dressings fit,

For winter, spring, and summer.

No beauty she doth miss,

When all her robes are on;

But Beauty's self she is,

When all her robes are gone.

—Anonymous

One

Newhaven, East Sussex Coast, England, Spring 1847

At first breathtaking sight, Marcus Fitzalan was willing to wager his membership in the Society of Scoundrels that the Lady Jade Smithfield was proud to be a scandal.

Black leather breeches embraced her long sleek legs. A matching waistcoat caressed her lush, ripe breasts and nipped at a waist smaller than the span of his hands. Her pirate's blouse laced high enough for modesty, but low enough to tantalize.

She kept him standing in her study, as if on the auction block, circling him in a way meant to intimidate—like a buyer examining a stallion's fine points—not entirely unaware that her perusal afforded him the same enticing opportunity.

Hair of rich sable silk fell in loose waves down her back, pointing to such a fine little bottom, Marcus itched to introduce it to the palm of his greedy hands.

If acquiring a position in her outrageous household were not so important, he'd match her shocking tactics, without a backward glance, and teach her a few tricks into the bargain.

As things stood, her proximity made him feel like that stallion, agitated and vigilant, as if something momentous were about to be granted. Her very scent stirred him, and though he dare not initiate an advance, neither would he disregard her slightest overture.

"Are you buying?" he asked, tongue in cheek.

The siren stiffened, all lucent cream porcelain in black leather, and when she raised her defiant chin and leveled him with her ebony gaze, Marcus became transfixed.

Her eyes gave her skewering power and that hint of a widow's peak added sorcery to the blend. Even as she held him in her sight, Marcus wondered what demons compelled so young a woman to flaunt society's rules as boldly as did this one.

Marcus smiled, cocked his head, and passed her the gauntlet, so to speak.

Jade raised her chin at the audacity of the unlikely man of affairs, examining her every bit as thoroughly as she did him, his blue eyes narrow, piercing in their cobalt intensity, as if he would draw her out and bare her soul . . . clear to the panic she kept hidden there.

She straightened her shoulders and firmed her stance. He would not see what she did not want him to see. "Please remember which of us holds the whip hand," she said, as much to remind herself.

"At your service," the bounder said, his cocked brow belying his words, his overt masculinity sounding a warning in her head.

Thick muscles. Wide shoulders. Hands, big and . . . capable of cold-hearted brutality. A thoroughly daunting scent, perilous and soothing at one and the same time—tobacco, leather, and spearmint—called to her like the dashing blade her imagination conjured late at night when she held no control over her mind and allowed, for a blink, that a good man might exist somewhere in this sorry world.

Dangerous. Seductive.

His skin shone bronze, his raven hair unshorn, a lazy lock falling over one eye. A scamp, a scoundrel . . . heartless. His lips appeared sculpted by a master, and when the slight curve of them, one side up, as now, hinted at a smile, a chin dimple appeared, dead center.

Impudent. Rude.

He stood annoyingly cocksure and secretly amused, his gaze so brazen, she'd swear he could see through her clothes to her lace chemisette and reveled in the sight. Half her girls would swoon, if they saw him, the rest would run screaming from the room.

If the scoundrel all-out grinned, Jade feared she would lose her breath.

"I am yours to command," he said with a bow.

Jade had lost her ability to blush at twelve, but when the ominous warmth threatened, she turned her back, went round her desk, and sat behind it, placing it square between them—placing herself, once more, in the position of authority. "Sit," she said, "if you please."

Fitzalan sat, as instructed.

"Not just any knave," Jade said, "but a practiced one," which only served to augment his aura of ambient potency, drat the blighter. "You won't do." She straightened. "You're too young and too . . . perfect, except that you need a shave."

His bark of laughter baffled Jade. She'd been prepared for anger; he was a man, after all, but 'twas incredulity furrowed his brow. "Perfect?" he asked.

Odd that vanity did not march beside magnificence in this one. "No, not perfect," she said. "No man is; you're all rotten."

He raised a shrewd brow. "You've met the wrong men."

"Scores of them," she said. "Since Ivy recommended you, I assume that he explained what I want in the man I hire. Did Ivy travel with you, by the way?"

"Actually, I traveled with him." Marcus grinned.

She hadn't been wrong, Jade saw now. Marcus Fitzalan's grin was deadly. But fortunately for her, breathing was still, more or less, an option.

"Ivy is setting up his puppet stage right now," Marcus said. "He plans a performance within the hour."

"Good," Jade said. "Was this the first time you traveled in his old gypsy wagon?" she asked, back in control, satisfied the man before her understood as much.

"The first as an adult," he said. " 'Twas like stepping back in time, with children running alongside, calling Ivy's puppets to come out and play. Difficult to believe I was that innocent once."

"Impossible to believe," Jade said acerbically, gaining perhaps a modicum of grudging respect, judging by the surprised approval in Fitzalan's heated gaze.

"I remember how excited I used to get," she said, "when his white wagon, trimmed in red and green, came rolling down the road, like Christmas in summer. I loved Ivy's puppets. I loved Ivy. Still do."

Marcus felt strangely relieved that the Lady Jade might not be as cold and formidable within as she appeared without. Sharing Ivy as a friend, as well as similar, though separate, childhood memories, made her seem . . . human. "My lady, I—"

"You may call me Jade. Everyone does. The title is a throwback to a bygone era. No one in Peacehaven gives a flying fig about my father's title. They care only that before he abandoned us, he gave new meaning to the word 'wastrel.' "

Not haughty, either, Marcus thought, her abandonment revealing an additional breadth of common ground between them. "Jade." Marcus sat forward. "Ivy said you need a man of affairs to put your finances in order, and I'm the man who can." Marcus wished he could tell her the true reason he wanted the job—that an inconspicuous resident of Newhaven could look into the accidents slowing local railroad construction, without raising suspicion. But to reveal his investigation at this juncture could cripple it.

"What experience do you have, Mr. Fitzalan?"

"You may call me Marcus. I've been running a sizeable estate in Seaford for the past year, and a smaller one before that, both with a great deal of success, I might add." He removed a sealed missive from his waistcoat and handed it to her, but she made certain their fingers did not touch as she accepted it. Odd, considering her reputation for courting scandal.

"Inside, you will find a letter of introduction from the Earl of Attleboro, my . . . former employer."

She read the note, raised a brow, and folded her hands on her desk, appearing for a minute to fight some deep inner battle. "Ivy said that you have personal business in the area as well," she said, and waited . . . for him to elaborate, Marcus assumed.

When he merely nodded, she made a moue of disapproval, and caught Marcus's fancy. He'd like to take his lazy time kissing those luscious lips into a smile.

"Did he tell you about The Benevolent Society for Downtrodden Women?" she asked, a bit on the loud side, snapping him back to their conversation, her chiding brow telling him she'd discerned the significance in his preoccupied gaze, if not his precise thoughts, praise be.

Marcus cleared his throat. "Ivy said you inherited Peacehaven Manor and the Downtrodden Society from your grandmother, that you run it here as she did."

"The Society is not downtrodden," she snapped. "The women are. The Society is benevolent."

Marcus swallowed his grin. "Your pardon. Pray, continue."

"The Society's very existence is threatened of a sudden by financial chaos," she said. "If it fails—if I fail—the women I rescue, house, and train to support themselves, will end in the street. With no homes or skills, they will be forced to support their children in unimaginable ways.

"Almost since my grandmother's man of affairs left my employ," she said, "my finances have been all of a muddle. I am not sure where I stand."

"Who was this man?"

"Was?" she snapped. "I didn't kill him. I discharged him. His name is Neil Kirby." She firmed her jaw and clasped her hands tight. "He sold an option on a tract of my grandmother's property to the railroad. Never mind that I refused, point-blank, to sell. Now, the income from the sale is missing as is the record of the sale."

Marcus schooled his features so as not to reveal the intensity of his interest. His railroad investigation had barely begun and already he knew that the Lady Jade Smithfield bore watching, which intrigued him as much as it disturbed him. "Surely the man needed your signature to complete the sale?"

"The papers had been signed, as it turned out, by my grandmother on her deathbed. Kirby had to have lied to accomplish it, because she would never have optioned that parcel. To get the land option back, I need the paperwork, and the money we were paid."

"Why do you want it back?"

Though Lady Jade paled, anger snapped her spine to the inflexibility of a ramrod. "Your business, in the event you are hired, Mr. Fitzalan, would be to keep my records, nothing more."

Marcus knew then, without doubt, that if Jade Smithfield found a way to keep the railroad from going through her property, she might very well be first in line as suspect. "Do I take your words to mean that you might overlook my . . . *perfection* long enough to hire me?"

Her chin went up. "Mine is not the average household. More than a dozen brittle, soul-scarred women and seventeen sad, frightened children live here. All my servants are men, from scullery maid to cook, all beyond reproach in fact, and beyond danger in years. You, I am afraid, would seem too much of a threat, as young as you are."

All male servants, Marcus thought, the final straw, the ultimate transgression that branded the Lady Jade Smithfield—young, beautiful, and unmarried—as a perfect scandal in the eyes of society as far away as London.

Ivy said that because Jade's grandmother had been ninety and considered eccentric, her outlandish behavior had been tolerated, but when her granddaughter stepped into her shoes at twenty-seven, and changed nothing, the gossips had gone on rampage. Marcus had in fact been in London when he first heard the gossip, and, therefore, he had been fascinated before having the opportunity to meet her.

She shook her head now at some disharmony Marcus could not discern. "If I were to hire someone as young as you, frankly I would be concerned about . . ."

"A scandal?"

Not the least amused, she set her jaw, firm, disapproving. "Women—" She cleared her throat, which eased the fury in her gaze. "*Some* women feel they need . . . a man . . . on occasion, and I would not want you—I would *forbid* you—to take advantage of the vulnerable among my residents."

13

"You wound me."

"I would if I had to."

With that threat on her lips, she reminded him of a swan, rising in hissing defense, a host of cygnets beneath her sheltering wings.

His respect for her grew. "I will not seduce any of the women in your care . . ." *Which is not to say that I will not seduce you,* he silently added.

"You, I can handle," Jade said, as if she heard his caveat. "My concern is my women. I fear *they* will try to seduce *you*," she said, entirely serious. "You must not let them."

Marcus grinned; he couldn't help himself. He'd be damned if he'd respond, negatively or positively, to being seduced before ever setting eyes on his seductress, unless 'twas *she* who sat before him. *This* seductress, he would never refuse.

Speaking of enigmas, Jade Smithfield was a classic. "You dress like a man to prove you are as strong and capable as one, do you not?"

"I dress like a man, Mr. Fitzalan, so men will take me seriously and stop looking at my—"

"Assets?" No sooner had the word passed his lips than Marcus knew he had jeopardized his position.

"I beg your pardon!" Jade Smithfield rose with righteous indignation, full of cold dark fury and bold striking magnificence.

Despite his remorse for insulting her, the stallion in Marcus quickened in anticipation of the challenge she presented.

"This interview is at an end," she said. "I despise you and every man like you."

Marcus stood. "It is I who must beg pardon. My impertinence is unforgivable. I can act the cretin, sometimes."

She waved away his apology. "You're a man. Crudity and stupidity are to be expected, though not accepted—not by me and not in this house."

"I assure you that foolhardiness and insensitivity are not chronic failings of mine, despite the fact that the momentary dullness of my wits seems matched only by the size of the foot in my mouth." Marcus ran a hand through his hair and considered speaking frankly. "Jade . . . you did say I could call you that?"

She nodded with all the warmth of an ice queen.

Marcus stood. "As a man who will, as it turns out, never enter your employ, but offers . . . fellowship, on the basis of a shared friend, and similar childhood memories, I beg you will allow me to advise you on one point before we part."

He received a second royal nod. Regina Victoria herself would be proud.

Placing the flat of his hands on the mahogany surface of his unlikely employer's desk, he leaned forward, to keep his advice between them, and capture her brazen, chin-up gaze with his earnest and open one. "When a man can see *exactly* how long a woman's legs are, and how perfectly her—" Marcus cleared his throat. Telling her how well her bottom would fit his palms would simply release the fury roiling in her, so he let the thought go, and straightened. "Well . . . he isn't likely to be thinking clearly, or seriously, on any level, save one."

Jade Smithfield's ebony eyes widened, and she paled slightly, before a crimson blush scuttled up her neck.

Marcus nodded, certain she'd got his point. "I apologize for my impertinence, though not for my admonition, and I am genuinely disappointed that we will not be working together."

Jade's clenched hands relaxed slightly, her composure

returning in slow determined measure. "With Ivy staying, you will be forced to catch the public coach for your return journey, but since it won't be along again until tomorrow, a room will be prepared for you."

A few minutes later, a brawny, barrel-chested older man—Jade's resident doctor cum housekeeper—introduced himself to Marcus as Beecher. With twinkling eyes and fond looks for the children scampering about, Beecher led Marcus from the bedchamber to which he'd been assigned and into a main-level ballroom. Ornate with gilded wainscoting and festooned mirrors, the stately room held an array of fussy gilt chairs facing a puppet stage in the throes of preparation.

The minute Marcus stepped into the room, the assemblage of women and children stilled and quieted, as if they knew he'd displeased their benefactress. But no, on second look, their reactions reflected nothing so simple as displeasure. Some of them had stepped back, others placed hands on hearts, touched their children or each other. Like game in a hunter's sight, all were frightened and too stunned to move.

Ivy warned him that most of Jade's cygnets had been assaulted—by husbands, fathers, strangers, males all. He knew they had been battered physically and emotionally, and still, Marcus stood stunned in the face of their terror. Judging by the children, their mothers' experiences had been, at the least, witnessed. At the worst, Marcus refused to consider.

Drawn by the silence, Ivy peeked from behind his puppet stage and grimaced. He came and made the introductions. Ivy—Yves St. Cyr, Puppeteer—reveled in his role as friend, mentor, and father-figure to half the children in Sussex . . . even to the ones who'd grown up, or should have done, at any rate, the scoundrels and scandals especially.

After the silver-haired puppet-master's introduction, most of the women relaxed. Ivy must seem as safe as Jade's retainers, though not nearly as old.

The children calmed, because their mothers did, all but one cowering blonde moppet, her wide-eyed china-doll gaze directed straight at Marcus himself. Even from across the room, he could see that his presence terrified her.

Damn it, he'd left enough damage in his wake for one lifetime, Marcus thought. He did not want to leave one woman, or child, with nightmares, especially not as a result of a swift appearance in their lives.

Since he would leave Peacehaven tomorrow, he had no choice but to counter China Doll's fear today.

Two

Marcus distributed pennies to the children farthest from the china doll, to calm her before he reached her. "Here's a penny for each of you," he said as he distributed the coveted coins, "to pay to watch the puppets. Drop it in the hat when it's passed." Marcus spoke loudly to make his intentions known to parents and children alike and calm them all.

The next child primped as he turned to her. Marcus smiled at her mama and handed the coquette-in-training her penny. "Why, your dress is the same pretty blue as your eyes," he said, making those indigo orbs bigger.

Marcus looked up, like a stallion scenting a mare, and saw that Jade now stood inside the ballroom watching. He'd considered her magnificent in black leather, but her scandalous splendor paled beside her ripe feminine allure in a full striped skirt of ebony on silver, her generous breasts snug in a short black bolero.

She appeared more seductive, if that were possible, especially with those slight ruffles at wrists and neck. Yet despite her feminine regalia, her stance left no question as to which of them retained full charge.

Marcus hoped she changed clothes because she took his warning to heart. He'd hate to see her ravished in business . . . or otherwise . . . except by him.

Mocking himself for the foolish thought, Marcus gave his overnight hostess his frank approval with a nod—sorry he'd acted the wrong end of the stallion. Then he sighed for what he'd never gained, but lost anyway, and looked about him.

Standing among so many families, however broken, made him remember his childhood yearning to be part of a family. That particular need vanished, of course, when he became a man and discovered that scoundrels had more fun than husbands. He regarded his hostess with speculation, wondered at her inscrutable gaze, shrugged inwardly, and continued passing his pennies.

A minute later, a bold little miss stroked his coarse whiskers. Marcus chuckled, gave her a penny, and caught Jade's I-told-you-so brow. Yes, he thought, around her, he would need to shave twice a day.

When Jade turned and left, Marcus moved on. One boy challenged him to a duel, another said he'd rather have a peppermint stick than a puppet show for his penny.

China Doll seemed both cowed and fascinated by him. He'd wager she worried as much that he'd try to give her a penny as he would not. She might allow herself to breathe, if she could receive her penny without him stepping near.

Challenged in a way he had not been for some time, determination compelled Marcus forward, until panic filled China Doll's eyes, and she lowered her head and hunched her shoulders, as if to make herself smaller and less visible.

Marcus stopped where he stood and regarded the woman who held her. "Good day to you," he said. "Will you tell me your little one's name? I do not think she is of a mind to tell me herself."

The woman paled. "I . . . I'm not Emily's mama. My name is Lacey Ashton, and I'm her friend," she said. "Her mama left her in our care . . . for a while."

Ah, like he and his brother . . . Emily must feel lost, abandoned, frightened, which deepened Marcus's compulsion to erase her fear, of him, at least. Who knew what had befallen her parents, but this was not the time for questions.

"I see that Emily is shy," he said. "But how will she get her penny if she'll not accept it from me?"

Lacey stroked the child's tawny curls. "I don't know. If she doesn't get her penny, how will she see the puppets?"

Marcus took half a step closer, knelt on his haunches, and waited for Emily's shoulders to relax. Then he reached over, intending to lift her chin with a finger, but the closer he got, the more she trembled.

Marcus drew his hand back. "Miss Emmy, I'm going to put this penny on the floor where you can reach it. Then I'm going to sit and watch the puppets from over there." He pointed to a spot near the wall, not too far distant.

When he straightened, Marcus saw that Jade had witnessed his failure. This time, however, when he met her gaze, she looked away, and the rigid set of her spine lessened, though not to a great degree.

Not sure what that meant and still hoping to see Emily smile, Marcus shrugged inwardly and moved away. The puppet show had started.

The room erupted in laughter as Ivy's German pup, a Dachshund named Tweenie, made her entrance with the brim of a bottoms-up top hat between her teeth.

With everyone's attention on the pup, Emily picked up her penny.

"It's a sausage doggy," a boy said. "A red one. Look, she's standing."

"She's begging," his mother said. "Your penny! Put it in her hat."

Once they understood Tweenie was collecting admissions, the process went giggling-quick, until peppermint-stick-boy refused to give up his penny.

Marcus laughed and stood calling for their attention. "After the show, I'll give you each a penny to keep. Give the one you've got now to Tweenie."

Soon Ivy's pup stood begging before Emily, who appeared as enamored of the pup as the penny. With a shy bit of hesitation, she turned to look at Marcus, her lashes coyly shadowing her eyes.

Marcus wanted to whoop, but he nodded solemnly instead. "Go ahead, Emily. I'll give you another." He lowered himself to the floor, his back against a gilded side chair.

Face pink, Emily opened her fist over the top hat, but her penny stuck to her palm, before it dropped "plink" inside.

Tweenie had finished collecting so Marcus patted his thigh, and the Dachshund waddled over to set the hat beside him. Then she climbed into his lap, circled thrice—stepping once where she ought not—and curled up to sleep.

Emily's gaze followed the pup, and now she looked up, eyes wide, at Marcus. He glanced down at his hand stroking Tweenie's sleek red back and swallowed his smile.

Ivy pitted Sergei the wolf puppet against Hector the hedgehog. "Be quiet now, I need to sleep," Hedgehog told the audience as he settled down to snore.

Sergei the Wolf wrapped himself in the cream wool pelt of a sheep and approached the sleeping hedgehog.

"Wake up. Wake up," the children shouted to hedgehog.

Emily split her attention between the stage and Tweenie. When she glanced at him, Marcus crooked his finger to call her over.

Emily looked quickly away.

A minute later, she climbed from Lacey's lap and sat beside her, as if to watch the puppet show from there. Then, at the rate of about an inch a minute, Emily began to sidle toward Marcus, until she sat closer to him than to Lacey.

"Take off one of your slippers," Marcus whispered. "If

21

you do, Tweenie will do a trick for you."

Emily began to struggle with a slipper.

Out of nowhere, Jade knelt to help her.

Emily stroked Jade's hair lovingly.

Again Marcus experienced an odd yearning to belong—different, mature, dangerous—and he pushed it aside.

"Pull Emily's stocking toe out a bit," Marcus said, then he gave Emily a conspiring grin. "Now, Emmy, reach your foot over here and wiggle your toes."

He wasn't sure who looked more puzzled, Emily or Jade, but at Jade's nod, Emily did as he bid, and a minute didn't pass before Tweenie's head popped up.

The pup crept slowly from Marcus's lap and toward Emily's foot, making Emily slide back, until Tweenie caught the sock's toe between her teeth.

Emily gasped and pulled her foot full back, but Tweenie wouldn't stop tugging on her stocking, pulling it this way and that, as she backed away.

The child caught the game and, that fast, a tug of war ensued between Emily and Tweenie.

When Emily fell back giggling helplessly, the puppet show came to a halt, and Marcus saw tears on more than one amazed face.

Jade looked soft, and . . . approachable, and Marcus knew a gut-deep ache for something he shouldn't want, didn't deserve, and couldn't have, because he owed a lifetime of responsibility to the brother he had all but destroyed.

"You can't stay," Jade said, firming his resolve with her own.

"I know," Marcus said, wishing he could leave immediately.

Whether the sudden round of cheers and applause

lauded Emily's giggles or Ivy's puppets didn't matter. Though Marcus needed to find another place to stay in Newhaven, from which to conduct his investigation, he felt damned good about the way his attempt to soothe Emily turned out.

Though sorry he'd lost Jade's good opinion, he wondered how he could lose something he'd never had, but devil-a-bit, that's the way he felt.

In one last pull, Tweenie won the tug-of-war and raced away with Emily's prize sock, then Ivy came out to present the child with a new pair from the assortment he carried to reimburse Tweenie's victims.

Marcus had lost one of his own to the pup the night they'd spent on the road. Ivy—or Tweenie, he should say—kept a number of Sussex women employed knitting socks of all sizes.

After Marcus distributed another round of pennies, Lacey Ashton approached him. "I came to thank you, Mr. Fitzalan, for your patient efforts to temper Emily's fear."

"A rewarding diversion, Miss Ashton, and my pleasure."

Then Jade stood before him, and Marcus nodded a greeting. "If Emily's father is the man who frightened her witless," he said, "no wonder your low opinion of men."

"Which are you?" Jade asked, nodding toward the puppet stage. "The wolf or the sheep?"

Marcus tugged on his ear. "I, er, believe I'm the hedgehog—like you—prickly for the most part, but soft when . . . soothed."

His nemesis stiffened once more.

Marcus nearly smiled. His skill and his need for an inconspicuous place to stay in Newhaven, coupled with Jade's need for a man of affairs, made Ivy consider them a perfect match, and Marcus thought, *sure they were, like*

23

kindling and fire, they were a match.

"In the event that I am willing to reconsider your employment," Jade said, charging the silence, and him, with a fool's hope. "Do you care to explain the other bit of business Ivy said you have in Newhaven?"

"I'm afraid I cannot," Marcus said. " 'Tis a bit of private business on behalf of the Earl of Attleboro that I am not at liberty to divulge."

"Score one for loyalty," Jade snapped as she turned to oversee the arriving teacart—this minute an elegant hostess, the last, a scandal in black leather.

Everything about the woman put him on alert, made him want to know her . . . in every sense, including the biblical, except that he'd ruined what little chance he had.

Marcus knelt and welcomed Tweenie's diverting kisses. He'd rather have Jade Smithfield's, of course, but enthusiasm won over disinterest on the best of days, and despite his regret, Marcus found himself laughing.

The small cake thrust under his nose came as a surprise.

Tweenie's tail slapped Marcus's leg, either in response to the cake, or its giver, or both.

"Is that for me?" Marcus asked Emily, who offered it with a trembling hand and raised chin.

His brave china doll nodded solemnly.

"Thank you, Emily," Marcus said, accepting it.

Biting into it, he made sounds of delightful appreciation solely to entertain her. "Eccles cakes stuffed with currants; my favorite."

Emily stood watching him, a cake of her own in her other hand, a light in her eyes, no smile on her face.

"Would you care to join us for tea?" Marcus settled himself once again on the floor, his back against the wall.

Emily nodded, more or less.

"Tweenie, as you can see, likes the center of my lap, so if you'd like to pet her, you may want to perch here on my knee. Would that be comfortable for you?"

Emily hesitated, then sat, shocking him out of countenance, her back straight and stiff, so Marcus took care not to brace her. Better for her to fall, without support, than to run because of his touch.

With Tweenie's unsolicited help, she finished her cake quickly, and began petting the pup whose eyes closed in contentment. Eventually Emily relaxed her posture as well, before she slumped exhausted against him.

Tweenie caught the movement and settled her puppy snout in Em's small lap. Before Marcus knew it, both were sound asleep, a frightful warmth filling his cold scoundrel heart for serving as their pillow.

At peace, his eyelids heavy and in danger of closing, despite the cacophony about him, Marcus saw a pair of silver satin slippers topped by the striped hem of a gown, and his heart thumped and sped to attention.

Struck anew by the scandalous beauty, all thought of sleep fled.

Emily shivered, taking his attention, and because he couldn't give her his coat without waking her, he rubbed her arm.

Jade's hand grazed his as she bent to place her shawl over Emily. Then she regarded him, an energy like heat lightning, silent and invisible, passed between them.

Jade closed her hand into a fist, and frowned down at him. "I will speak to you when she wakes. In the library."

"Does this mean you have reconsidered my position?"

"Let us say that I am wavering."

"You despise me," he said.

"In almost every way," she said. "Save one."

25

Marcus tilted his head for her to continue.

"Emily hasn't laughed or stepped within reach of a man, not even my retainers, since I've known her." Jade turned and made her way across the room.

"I adore you," Marcus said watching her, surprised and chagrined that he'd spoken the thought aloud.

Three

"You do *not* adore me," Jade said unexpectedly, a week or more later and out of context, as they stood bent over her desk perusing a stack of ledgers seeking the root of her financial problems.

Marcus straightened to regard her. "You heard that?"

"No, but others did. Your avowal has been the topic of discourse for days. I told the women this morning that you said you adored me because I had about decided to hire you. Since they believe otherwise, I decided to set the record straight, here and now."

"You knew I said it, and yet you hired me? I'm astonished." More so because the gossip had not changed her mind. "The women were right," he said. "It's not because you seemed inclined to hire me."

She waved away his comment, chin high, hard protective shell in place. "You see me as a challenge, but I will not fall at your feet as scores of women have likely done since you cracked your first smile. You'd simply like to . . . to . . ."

"I certainly would," Marcus said, accepting her unconscious invitation to spar. If verbal battle she required, then verbal battle she would receive, though he'd prefer to employ more physical tactics.

As his response left her speechless, he lifted a languishing lock of hair off her silken bodice, his fingers so close to stroking the fabric, and the body beneath it, they became warm.

She caught a delayed breath and stiffened as if poised to bolt, though she remained as if frozen, while heat emanated from her in waves.

"I most definitely would like . . . to . . ." He brought the captured lock to his lips, while her scent—lavender—and her feel—silk—skittered and rushed the blood in his veins.

The Lady Jade Smithfield, he believed, was also up for any challenge, though she might not yet admit as much. Given the fact that she equated brutality with his gender—though he worked daily to change her mind—he was likely the most challenging enigma set before her.

In the same precise way, her ice-queen facade called to him as nothing in his life ever had. That, and her rebellious nature, striking beauty and generosity of spirit, made her unique, vulnerable . . . and in dire need of a knight on a white charger, though she'd deny it, and he hadn't the time, situation, or luxury to argue the point or fulfill the role.

Being acclimated into her extraordinary household taught him that Jade rescued others; no one ever thought to rescue her, which implored him to do so.

Oh, she needed him for the time being, as much as he needed her. She just didn't know it yet. Observe that he hadn't mentioned adoring her but once, days before, but his statement had preyed on her mind ever since, as a statement of hers had preyed on his.

"You don't despise me," he said, returning that lock of hair to her bodice and smoothing it into place, her widening eyes not quite ebony, but so dark a brown as to appear black. "You're fascinated by me."

She squeaked, not quite in protest, and Marcus crossed her lips with a finger. "It's the man who hurt Lacey, and the ones who hurt Molly's mother and little Emmy, you despise," he said. "I despise them too. If I ever meet Emily's father, I might have to beat him bloody."

Jade shivered and stepped away, rubbing her arms as if

against a sudden chill. "Beating is a man's way. You're the same as the rest."

"All men have faults and weaknesses, Jade. While I admit that I'm nowhere near as good as the best of them, neither am I, in any respect, near as bad as the worst of them. You need time to get to know me."

Jade shook her head. He was wrong. "Time won't change anything. The husbands and fathers you mentioned are not the first of their ilk to touch my life." She read concern in the eyes of her man of affairs.

He reached for her. "Don't tell me your father hurt y—"

"No." She stepped back, putting a safe distance between them. Marcus Fitzalan could erase a life's worth of lessons with a look. God help her, she'd almost stepped into the protection of his embrace, rather than away from it. "No. I barely knew my father. My parents were happy wanderers, always leaving me with my grandmother. My mother died abroad of a fever when I was young and my father squandered her fortune, never to return. My grandmother who raised me; *she* was abused by her husband."

"You witnessed your grandfather's abuse?"

Jade appreciated his indignation on her behalf, and yet . . . "Would you beat my grandfather bloody as well?" she asked, frustrating him, judging by his clenched fists. "You might have come in handy at one time, but no, my grandfather died when I was a babe," she said. "No need to protect me; I'll slay my own dragons, thank you very much. What my grandfather did to my grandmother, however, yielded everlasting effects. In that way, his abuse touched me and colored who I am."

"Jade, I like who you are. You're strong and noble and it suits you." He chuckled. "Though I would have described you differently at first meeting."

"Amusement gives you such a false look of innocence," she said. "What words would you have used to describe me then?"

"Word. Singular."

"And that is?"

Marcus shook his head. "I'd like to soften it for you and say lust, but that would be wrong. Lust is what I felt, of course—and still do, by the way—but it's not the right word to describe what you radiated most."

"Well, what is?"

Jade liked his admission of lust; it gave her a new and exciting feeling of power, but she felt entirely too eager for more. After their rocky beginning, she supposed they'd fallen into a relationship somewhere between business and sparring partners.

"I'm having second thoughts about telling you," Marcus admitted. "Perhaps this conversation had best wait until I've been employed for some time and you cannot do without me."

"I won't discharge you." She stepped near enough for him to breathe lavender and for his willpower to slip a notch. "Tell me," she said, touching his arm, a bold move for her.

Though she seemed only recently to have realized her power over men—over him in particular—she knew instinctively how to wield it. "Sex," he said.

"What?" she gasped, her shock tempered by the satisfaction and curiosity she failed to hide.

"The day I met you, you radiated sex in black leather."

Like the cat who lapped the cream, the minx seemed pleased, whether she'd admit it or not. "Explain," she said, not so much annoyed as intrigued, tilting her head, asking for more.

That's all it took and his body stood at the ready. Befuddled by the innocent seductress, and searching for sanity, Marcus ran his hand through his hair, stalling for time.

She crossed her arms and tapped her foot, a lush silken handful in sleek scarlet stripes, smelling of virtue and springtime. What he wouldn't give to undo every one of the buttons marching from neck to hem of her fashionable redingote dress and reveal her every curve and swell to his leisurely perusal.

Marcus swallowed. "What's to explain? All you lacked the day I met you was a whip."

"A whip," she stated, incredulously.

Artlessness. Pure. Unadulterated. *Now* she revealed it. Marcus mocked himself with a laugh. "This conversation is at an end. I refuse to be your tutor in the perversities of attraction. Forget I said it. I can sometimes be—most often in your presence, it seems—the nether end of a horse."

"A week's experience forces me to agree."

"Why thank you, Jade." He tried to look stern, but her rare smile turned his severity to mint jelly. "Suffice it to say that I like how you've turned out, though I regret your corrupt view of the male population. Not that you haven't reason. Especially as I stand before you, lack-wit that I am."

"Lack-wit or no . . ." She sighed. "I appreciate your approval, my corrupt view notwithstanding. Hopefully, it means you'll stay long enough to unravel my finances."

Relieved that she dropped the dangerous subject, Marcus wondered if her father's desertion made her expect others to abandon her as well.

With no quick answer or remedy at hand, he returned to the desk and shut the last of the ledgers. "Do you have more ledgers that I can check? I believe this predicament

31

goes further back than you think."

"We only sold the land option to the railroad eight months ago."

"Right," Marcus said, truly sorry that her finances seemed to be in such a muddle. "It now appears that you have an old problem to go with your new one."

Jade dropped into a cordovan leather chair, forgetting for a minute to remain strong.

Marcus wanted to comfort her. His body wanted a certain comfort of its own. He quelled both urges. "How much money has gone missing from your sale to the railroad?"

"I don't know. I haven't been able to find the land option since I confronted my former man of affairs with its existence and discharged him." Agitated, she rose and went to rummage through a box Marcus had already searched. "It has to be here somewhere."

"It's not," he said.

"You barely sifted through these."

"The railroad's parchment is distinctive. It has a—" He saw her surprise. "It's not there."

"How do you know what their parchment looks like?"

Marcus shrugged, certain she could see right through him. "The South Downs Railroad has options on some of Attleboro's land. I handled it. There's a bright side, you know. You may not realize it, but when that option is exercised, you stand to make a great deal of money. It's going to happen, Jade, and soon. The railroad is the future. This is only the beginning. Where did you say the other ledgers were kept?"

Jade left Marcus sifting through another series of her grandmother's papers while she went to fetch the account books he wanted.

Beyond her remarkable reaction to his potent male presence, she felt restless, nervous . . . sick. Mention of the railroad did that, but never more so than now. The railroad is nearly here, he'd said. It *will* go through.

Oh Gram, I wish you hadn't told me your secret. Jade rubbed her arms, admitting she needed to know so she could deal with the railroad and put period to the greedy expectations of one Giles Dudley, fourth cousin twice removed. The letters from Dudley's solicitor made his threat plain. He intended to inherit in her stead by proving her grandmother insane at the time she made her will, which would destroy the lives of the women and children in her care.

Her grandmother? Insane? The world would surely think so if they knew her secret.

Unless Jade could stop the railroad, the construction crew would surely dig up the proof Dudley needed.

She'd have to take care of it tonight, Jade realized.

After her decision to move forward, she stood in the center of her storeroom and tried to remember why. She scanned the shelves for a clue. Ah, ledgers. She needed the one dating back to the year before Neil Kirby's employment. Now she remembered.

She dragged a chair across the small room. Gram used to laugh, almost with pride, at how much Jade disliked Kirby, reminding her that men were often necessary evils in doing business.

Though Jade had been aghast over the land option Kirby engineered, she wasn't surprised at his dishonesty, nor the least sorry to dispatch him when she discovered it. He knew bloody well he should have come to her, not her dying grandmother, when the railroad made the offer.

Gram had clearly been too ill to know what she was signing.

To save Peacehaven, Jade needed that land option back. The only other way to stop the railroad from cutting into her land meant she must continue to be very clever, extremely careful . . . and only a bit more destructive.

The whole thing scared her witless.

She almost wished she could tell Marcus everything, Gram's secret and all. She'd already seen evidence of his integrity, though she had no proof it would last. He was still a man, damn him, and more intoxicatingly male than any she'd come across. Though he could be playing a role, to put her at her ease.

Not to be trusted.

Dangerous.

Except that Marcus was Ivy's friend, and Ivy was an excellent judge of character. Except that Ivy was a man . . . still, when he'd come to condole with her after Gram's death, and she told him she needed a man of affairs and why, he found Marcus for her.

True, she liked Marcus on sight. Too much. She knew that right off. She fought the sizzling pull the day he arrived, certain he must be bad for her . . . until Emily trusted him enough to sleep in his arms—bless him and curse him as well.

Something about Marcus Fitzalan shivered her deep inside, paradoxically making her crave more of the selfsame restiveness. Remaining in his presence reminded her of sitting too near a blaze. You knew it could scorch you, but you moved closer and closer, fascinated, despite all sense to the contrary.

Jade cursed and stood on the chair in an attempt to reach an old account book hanging off the edge of an upper shelf, still too high to grasp.

With a bit of experimentation, she discovered she could

nudge it out—and hopefully off the shelf—by smacking its exposed edge with a ledger she *could* reach. Dust flew in her face with each blow. Jade sneezed once, twice, three quick times.

The door opened and Marcus stepped in. "I followed the thumps. Your sneezes led me the rest of the way. Need help? Damsels in distress are my specialty."

"I'd have wagered as much, but I am doing fine on my own, thank you very—Oops!"

He swung her down and into his arms before she could protest—though why she should object escaped her at the moment. She had never imagined feeling so light, so protected, so . . . feminine?

His bracing arms warmed the backs of her thighs . . . nothing compared to the heat radiating from his hand at the side of her breast. She wished she had not spread her arms for balance when he toppled her, else there'd not be a distinct pulsing link between her budding breast and the center of her womanhood.

Loathe to terminate this new and oddly pleasant sensation, inclined rather to savor it, Jade avoided getting a sore neck by resting her head on Marcus's wide, sturdy shoulder.

Safe? Secure?

Outwardly . . . perhaps. Inwardly, an eruption, or an insurrection, seemed to be taking place. She should move from his embrace, immediately, if not sooner.

Gram would accuse her of hiding. Jade decided she was procrastinating . . . wickedly. She had never felt so much a woman. Provocative. Perilous.

She should move.

Just a minute more. Another.

"Put me down," she said on a sigh, still closely nestled

against him, enjoying his spearmint scent that somehow enhanced her body's unusual reaction. "I have things to do."

"In a dithering rush, are you?"

She dare not smile outwardly at his wit.

His breath warmed her face, warmed other parts too.

She had never been held by a man. Hard and strong, but surprisingly soft and . . . gentle? An enigma that should serve as a warning.

"I *am* in a hurry. Truly. I have dinner plans."

"I'm sincerely sorry to hear it."

Jade gazed at the growth of whiskers shadowing his face, making him look both dangerous and enticing. With her index finger, she touched the indentation on his chin that dimpled when he nearly smiled.

He chuckled and her fingertip fell in.

"It's deeper than I thought."

The devil stared down at her with fire in his eyes.

"We have work to do," she said in token protest. "Put me down."

He sat on the chair still holding her. "Whatever has to be done, we can, neither of us, remember what it is at this moment; you know that as well as I." He wiggled his index finger as she had done with hers before burying it in his chin dimple. "May I claim a bit of exploration in return?"

Jade's heart and body skittered and tripped. "I don't have a dimple."

"Must I explore a dimple? Are there rules?"

She tried to speak but needed to clear her throat first. "There *should* be rules."

"Fine then," he said. "We'll invent them as we go."

Four

Marcus began to trace the air above Jade's bodice, scalloping slowly around the line of buttons marching toward her waist, while hovering less than an inch above.

Then he scalloped back up again to hover above a breast.

Smaller and smaller became his circles in the air, closer and closer to the source of her tingling anticipation, until her nipple stood as if reaching.

Jade gasped.

Marcus regarded her then, his eyes bluer and deeper, waiting for her to stop him, she sensed, but she couldn't think, couldn't speak. She could only wait as anticipation thrummed in her center.

His touch, less than a stroke, came so fast, she must have blinked because she didn't see it happen, but her body knew, and sparked, and arched an unconscious invitation for more, but Marcus was too much the gentleman to accept.

Instead, he pulled her close, crushed her achy breasts against his coat, giving her a measure of relief. "I should not have," he whispered, warming her ear, melting her. "You're bad for me, my Lady Scandal, but I will not take advantage. Neither will I succumb to your allure, until I have been specifically, verbally, invited to do so. You have my word. I will never hurt you, Jade."

"You're bad for me as well," she said, heat infusing her. "Let me go. I have things to do."

He released her, giving her the freedom to escape to ponder the shocking interlude.

* * * * *

Marcus went to splash cold water on his face, determined to avoid another intimate encounter with the siren, and then he went looking for Ivy and distraction. At Ivy's invitation, since Jade would be away for dinner, Marcus decided to eschew the society of Jade's charges for the easy fellowship in the Manor kitchen. Though the ladies may not all be afraid of him, they were downright close-mouthed in his presence, and he needed to learn as much as possible about Jade and her grandmother, and their mutual aversion to the railroad.

Ivy slapped Marcus on the back when he arrived. "Glad you decided to join us. Sometimes the hens can be noisy."

Marcus laughed. "Jade ever hear you call them that?"

Ivy winked. "Never. I'd rather live."

Beecher chuckled and poured Marcus a glass of plum wine. Jade's retainers, for all they were supposed to be men being shown their lowly places, lived well. Marcus knew the Attleboro servants did not drink wine with their dinner.

Beecher introduced the cook.

"They call me Winkin," the jolly old man said. "Because when I come here, I cooked Winkinhurst Cakes and nothin' more."

"You were not hired for your cooking skill, then?"

"Nah, but I learned."

Marcus grinned. "This house is rife with fascinating stories."

Beecher gazed at the men around the table. "Between the lot of us, we've been smugglers, wreckers, excise men and tired old salts, like me. What else would you be expecting to find on the Sussex coast?"

Marcus sipped his wine. "I suspect you've stories to tell, and I want to hear them, but at the moment, I'm wondering why something I said seemed to upset Lacey." He regarded Ivy. "She's different from the rest of Jade's downtrodden. Is she the one you said you brought here?"

Ivy nodded. "From Arundel, more or less disowned by her aristocratic family. Good woman, strong, but sad."

Marcus accepted a plate of scotch eggs, some form of meat pie, and a ladle of pease pudding. "Lacey turned snow white when I mistook her for Emily's mother. I wondered if she'd ever had a child of her own."

"You're not interested in Lace, are you, Marc?" Ivy asked. "Because I have to tell you, her heart's taken."

Marcus shook his head. "Don't worry, my friend. Your original instincts are intact. I simply want to visit Emily and I'd rather not upset Lacey further with my ignorance."

Ivy smiled. "You won't. Your instincts are as good as mine."

Ivy as good as admitted to playing matchmaker for him and Jade, and Lacey had surely borne a child. "I guessed as much," Marcus said, "which brings me to another subject that's been testing my instincts." He regarded the others at the table. "How do the villagers feel about the railroad?"

"Some are for, some against," Beecher answered, sitting straighter, his expression harder. "Why?"

"Jade was skittish when I mentioned it. Made me wonder if hers was the general local reaction."

"Can't speak for the whole village," Beecher said. "Nor my mistress for that matter. She's been good to me. To all of us." His subtle warning and candid gaze encompassed the retainers at the table.

Marcus owned Beecher's measure. Head man. Ruthlessly loyal.

Ivy coughed. "You worried about Jade, Marc?"

"I can't say, but I can't help her if I don't understand the problem."

"Jade doesn't have anything to do with the railroad," Beecher stated, then he went to get another pork and apple pie for the table.

Topic closed, his tone said, but Marcus feared Beecher wouldn't have thought to defend Jade if she didn't need defending. Bloody hell.

Ivy raised a warning brow his way. "There's a supper and ball in Lewes at the Star Inn, the old Southover Priory, in a few days. It's the last of the season. Go and get in on a card game while you're there. Sure to get local opinions on everything, including the railroad."

Marcus nodded and accepted a bowl of bread and butter pudding.

A late arrival sat at the table with them. "Jade'll be at the assembly too," the newcomer said. "She's bringing a few of the ladies who've been taking deportment lessons from Lacey. To put them in a social situation, don't you know. About ready to step back into the world, they are." The speaker gave Marcus a nod. "Name's Lester. I'm the nanny." He grinned. "Jade's grandmother hired me starvin' off the street twenty odd years ago."

"As a maid," Jock, the stableman put in. "But he never got any cleanin' done 'cause the little'uns were always crowded 'round for stories."

Beecher chuckled. "Before long, they wanted Lester tucking them in and taking them for walks and such, so Constance—" Beecher cleared his throat. "Jade's grandmother—made him the nanny."

"And you?" Marcus asked Beecher. "How long have you been here?"

Beecher scratched his white beard. "Almost fifty years

now. I was another gutter rescue. Not much call for a ship's surgeon with no ship. No, nor for a drunk doctor, either. Jade's grandmother sobered me up. I tended her more often than anybody, because the bastard she married beat her bloody once a week, at least.

"When she started taking women in, she hired me on. I get a town case now and again, but mostly, I doctor this crew. Some of Jade's women are in bad shape when they arrive. Sometimes I bring one back after a call. With all the children around here, there are always scraped knees and sniffles to tend."

"Interesting," Marcus said. A cook who'd needed to learn to cook, a man who'd been starving and a drunken doctor. Constance Smithfield had saved more than downtrodden *women*. He wondered if Jade realized it.

He could hardly wait to find out.

After dinner, he set out for a walk and saw Lacey chasing Emily, both of them laughing. Emmy held Tweenie on a lead, but when the pup saw him, she yipped, pulled free, and charged, Emily right behind.

Before Marcus knew it Tweenie stood with her paws on his legs, whining ecstatically, her tail beating a wild tattoo. When Marcus reached down to pet the pup, Emily's squeal of fear stopped him. "Emily, what's the matter?"

"She piddled on you!"

Marcus regarded his wet shoe and grinned. "She does it all the time. She gets so excited to see me that she . . . piddles on my shoes."

Emily shook her head, her little lips wobbling. "Don't hurt doggy."

Marcus knelt on his haunches before her, Tweenie jumping between them. "Listen to me, Sweetheart." He scratched the pup's ear to quiet her while he tried to calm

41

Emmy. "I would never hurt Tweenie, or any doggy, or any little boy or little girl. Do you understand?"

Emily nodded.

"Do you believe me?"

"Hurt Mummy?"

Lacey's horror mirrored his sorrow over Emily's wounded spirit. He swallowed the lump in his throat, kissed Emily's brow and brought her close. "I don't hurt Mummies either."

Emily sighed with relief and leaned into him.

Glad for the invitation, he picked her up.

She pledged her trust by wrapping her arms around his neck.

Marcus didn't think he'd ever felt so tall.

A woman rounded the corner calling for Lacey, only to stop short when she saw him. Abigail Pargeter, a new member of the household, had fled from their initial introduction. Jade said she still bore bruises from the man her father tried to force her to marry.

Emily might trust him, but he still scared the devil out of Abigail. If he left with nothing else, Marcus thought, he'd own a large measure of humility.

"I'm coming Abby," Lacey said, and made to take Emily, but the imp only clasped him tighter.

Lacey realized tugging was useless. "Come along, Dear. We need to go inside now. Abby needs our help."

Emmy shook her head. "Want Mucks."

"I'll take her. You go along," Marcus said, pride swelling his chest.

"You sure, Marcus?"

He chuckled. "I can use the company. We won't be long. Emily will give me a tour of Jade's gardens."

"Jade," Emily said pointing.

Lacey handed Marcus Tweenie's lead and tweaked Emily's nose. "You be good for Mucks now." She laughed and followed Abigail.

"Is Jade back?" Marcus asked Emily. "I've missed her. Can you show me where she went?"

Emily nodded and scrambled to the ground, taking his free hand to tug him in one direction while Tweenie tugged him in the other.

"Come," Emily said and together they coaxed Tweenie to follow.

Emily led them along a twisted path through gardens coming to life. The Peacehaven Estate—as lush and beautiful as its owner, with giant beeches, blooming cherry trees, and Scotch pines bent by the wind—all marching toward a sea-gazing cliff. In the distance, peewits called their high-pitched "see, see, sees," while specks that were gulls soared and swooped on the horizon.

Marcus's motley troupe passed a holly maze, which Tweenie must stop and sniff and mark at regular intervals, and which Marcus thought would be a splendid place to walk with Jade and perhaps go missing for a while.

"Emily," Marcus said after several unexpected turns. "If this is the way you and Lacey just came, you have quite the sense of direction. Are you sure this is right?"

Emily nodded. "Swans."

Ah, a route she took to see the swans. That made sense.

Before too much longer, they arrived at a delightful ornamental lake complete with graceful waterfowl. Emily wanted back in his arms then, and he was pleased to oblige. "Was Jade here earlier?" he asked. "Lord, I'm sorry I missed her."

"Jade." Em pointed again, and Marcus looked in that direction. In the vale, beyond a small copse, lay a fallow field, its spring-carpet of violets giving it a lavender hue. A woman astride a fine chestnut hack crossed the field at a good pace, her yellow gown flowing behind her. "Are you sure that's Jade?"

"Jade," Emily said with a nod, certain she was right.

Marcus believed the track for the railroad spur would cut diagonally across the northern quarter of the land on the opposite side of the beech wood edging that field. He wanted to follow and identify the rider, but dusk already bruised the horizon and it would be full dark before they crossed the field. "We can't catch up with her now, I'm sorry to say." He kissed Emmy's nose. "Let's go home before Tweenie actually catches one of those birds."

About four hours later, around midnight, Marcus retraced their walk and beyond, as he made his way to the railroad's current construction site. But all seemed quiet. Nothing in disorder. The sheds filled with tools were locked. Drays and railroad cars of supplies waited to be unloaded. A flatbed car, soon to be reclaimed by the train, stood empty at the termination of the track. The only item that seemed to be missing was the train itself, but perhaps it was due to arrive at first light.

As Marcus returned, both happy and frustrated to have seen nothing or no one remarkable, he caught sight of a retainer entering the house by the servants entrance, and he wondered what an old man would be doing out at this hour.

In the stable, Marcus lit a lantern and found a chestnut hack with no sign of recent exertion.

He checked his pocket-watch. Nearly one in the morning.

If the rider had come right back, the horse should have had time to cool down. Then again, surely there must be more than one chestnut hack in the Newhaven stables.

Around one the next day, annoyed that Jade hadn't yet made an appearance in the study, and no closer to unraveling her finances, Marcus walked into the dining room to hear talk of a railroad accident. His ears perked up and he schooled his features as he dug into a plate of gammon, cheddar and rye, but he learned nothing more beyond the fact that the accident happened the night before.

He wished Emily hadn't been so certain the rider was Jade. While he might have predicted that Jade rode astride, he certainly would have expected her to wear trousers to do so. Lord, he wished he knew for sure.

As expected, Marcus received a message later that afternoon detailing the accident. First and foremost, no one had been hurt. The main construction line had derailed two villages away when they braked for a body on the tracks, which turned out to be a dress stuffed to look like a body. The engineer thought he saw a stocky man scrambling into the woods just before he spotted the body, but other than that, he saw nothing.

While the "prank" had been somewhat innocuous, and undertaken when few workers rode the rail, it would take days to repair the damage and get construction back on track—weeks, if parts had to be rebuilt or repaired.

Double bloody hell. If they didn't begin laying track across Jade's property soon, they were going to miss the deadline for laying it in Tidemills, and lose the charter for good. Parliament had already confirmed that they would not renew the charter again. If the South Downs Railroad failed, the hundred or so residents of Tidemills would lose their jobs when their struggling mills failed for lack of an efficient shipping method. The Attleboro Estate, itself, stood to lose as well if the railroad failed, which would wreak havoc on a more personal level.

Marcus cursed again and told the messenger to wait while he composed a return message.

Dear Garrett, get your bags packed and come for a visit. I need a rooster to infiltrate the hen house. Dig out those rusty scoundrel skills of yours and polish them up; this is an assignment from heaven. I plan to introduce you as my brother, Garrett Fitzalan, nothing more. I'll send Ivy to get you. Yours, M.

p.s. Have Brinkley make a copy of the Smithfield land option deal and bring it with you, but wait until we're alone to give it to me.

Jade had succeeded in avoiding him all day, Marcus mused after completing his day's work, and he had no intention of letting her get away with it.

The female members of the household were in final fittings, a maid said. Third floor, west wing. No men allowed.

By God, if seeing Jade meant invading an all-female sanctum, then invade he would.

Halfway up the stairs, Marcus heard the soft tread of little feet behind him and recognized the sound of his shadow.

To make Emily giggle, he turned and scooped her into his arms, but she screamed in fright.

He sat on a stair and held the trembling little form close. "Oh, Emmy-bug, Sweetheart. I didn't mean to frighten you. Are you all right?"

"Mucks scare Emmy," she said with a scold.

"Mucks loves Emmy," he answered. "Will you forgive me?"

"Treacle toffee?"

"You need to be bribed with sweetmeats, do you?"

Gazing at him from beneath her long lashes, finger in her mouth, Emily nodded.

Marcus chuckled, kissing her nose, and stood to carry her back down. "Let's go see what kind of treats you can charm out of Winkin, and then we'll go find Lacey, shall we?"

A half hour later, Marcus boldly stepped into a world of silk and lace, curvaceous forms on pedestals and dangerous women with straight pins between their lips.

When he greeted them, they scattered those pins in shrieked surprise, flying out the door he'd entered. And there he stood in an empty room. "Well, damn."

"Sofia," came a wonderfully familiar voice. "I'm ready."

Marcus grinned. Ready like him these days, but he suspected that Jade had no idea what sexual readiness entailed. She'd been too amazed by her own reaction to his touch yesterday.

When he saw her, he stopped outside the door to give his heart and his breathing a minute to calm, for she stood in her underpinnings, on a dais before a row of mirrors, so industriously plucking wayward threads from a piece of fabric that she didn't notice him.

An assortment of scant frippery caressed Jade's form, molding it to divine perfection, making his mouth dry and his palms sweat.

A corset trimmed in pink ribbons pushed up the succulent breasts she'd offered and he'd declined—more fool him. Beneath the corset she wore nothing but a short lace chemise, its tiny pink bow tucked between her breasts. Marcus swallowed. Barely-there drawers ended high on her thighs in bands of lace. Heeled slippers made her long legs, encased in opaque white stockings, appear longer still—legs he wanted wrapped around him.

Seeing her like this, he wanted, needed, even more fiercely, to lay her down and ravish her . . . and then he needed to do it again.

And he would . . . when she "needed" him as ardently.

"You're perfect," he said stepping into the room. "Exquisite."

Like a night animal caught in lantern light, she stilled when she saw him in the mirror behind her, aborting her instinct to cover herself almost as fast as it occurred. She raised her chin instead.

Still behind her, Marcus stroked her form with his heated gaze, from slippered feet to cascading tresses, making his admiration clear.

Despite that, or because of it, she straightened her spine and stood taller, and, by damn, she stood prouder as well.

She had circumnavigated him the day he arrived; now he took his turn to appreciate her from every angle. As much to tease as to savor, he took two slow, silent, sizzling turns about the dais on which she stood so splendidly displayed.

When he stopped before her, she arched an annoyed brow, making him smile inside. "They told me men weren't allowed," he said, "but I knew that you, of all people, would understand my need to break the rules."

She cocked that brow higher. "Need?"

"More needs than you can imagine where you're concerned," he said, his voice rougher than he expected, piqueing her interest, judging by the warmth in her gaze. A lifetime of needs, he very much feared.

That he might have found his missing half brought sorrow. His responsibilities made a future for them impossible, yet, as fast as it came, he thrust away his pall of disappointment, determined to accept the gift of the moment. He could do worse, during his time with Jade, than to teach her that a man could be gentle.

Besides, destiny had a way of taking a stand. He had to hope that it would continue to work in his favor.

"You've been avoiding me," he said.

Jade made to speak and stopped, her silent stance reminding him that as her employer, she owed him no explanation.

"I'm glad you eluded me, else I'd never have come," he admitted. "I vow I'll carry a picture of you like this in my mind until my dying day." With a slow, scalding perusal, he caressed her once again, from top to toe, the way he'd like to caress her in truth.

His purpose backfired and rushed his near-arousal to blatant life. Placing his foot on the dais, he rested his arm against his raised knee to disguise the evidence.

"Did you want something special?" she asked, the gleam in her eye confirming he'd failed, that she perceived his distress and turned the tables.

"You know I do." He reached for a rosebud-topped garter, hesitated, and reached higher to stroke the lace band on her drawers.

She shivered and shifted a hairsbreadth away.

Glad he remained in the concealing position, Marcus mentally applauded her move and her instinct for self-preservation. "I heard you were going to the assembly this evening."

She nodded, a good deal less certain of herself than a moment before.

"Good. I expect to be there myself, in the card room for the most part. But I'd like the honor of partnering you for the supper set." He yearned for her company and needed to

49

hold her in his arms, by God, for longer than a minute.

He needed to ask her if she'd stuffed a dress and left it on the railroad tracks.

Disgusted with himself, Marcus tossed a ruined neck-cloth and picked up another, annoyed at being caught up with a woman in a way he swore he never would. Staying at Peacehaven this evening would be the wise decision. Heading for home now, if he had to walk all the way to Seaford, would be wiser. Running would be wisest.

He sighed. Nobody had ever accused him of being wise.

Look at him, primping like a randy stripling. If his London cronies saw him, they'd run to the betting books. He only wished the odds against him weren't so high.

Of course, if his cronies had seen Jade this afternoon, they'd line up beside him. Line up? They'd trounce him, and each other, to get to her.

Ivy stepped into his room and looked him up and down. "You're dressed more appropriately for a London ballroom than an assembly card room."

Marcus threw down a second ruined neck-cloth and ignored his friend's sarcasm, however astute. "I asked Garrett to come and stay for a while—as my brother who needs my care, though I didn't mention the care part. Will you go and fetch him?"

"I'll go tonight, if you tell me you're done with blaming yourself."

"I'm trying to be done with it, but sometimes I can't help thinking, 'What if I hadn't challenged him?' "

"You've been racing each other since you were old enough to sit on a horse. Brothers often do."

Marcus sighed. "In the logical part of my mind, I know that, but—"

50

"That'll do for now. I'll bring him in the morning."

"Thank you. I think Peacehaven will be good for him."

"I think so too." Marcus ruined another neck-cloth.

"She just left," Ivy said, getting back to his original tease. "Wait until you see her."

"I'm that transparent, am I?"

"Only to me."

"What made you suspect Jade would rattle my foundations?"

Ivy shrugged. "Same instinct that told me you'd rattle hers."

Marcus forgot his purpose. "She's not half as rattled as I am. Is she? Say yes."

Ivy laughed. "Give me that neck-cloth."

Five

Marcus couldn't stand to play one more round of cards, because he couldn't bear another minute away from Jade. He didn't give a damn if he was playing Whist or Piquet, a fact brought to his attention by his annoyed Whist partner when he unwisely led with trumps.

The conversation he instigated told Marcus that the people of Lewes, Newhaven, and the surrounding areas were split in regard to the arrival of the railroad. The shipbuilders and brewers were for it, for obvious reasons—increased profits because of the ability the railroad would give them to ship and receive more goods more quickly.

Some villagers thought the railroad could make the small port of Newhaven important enough to set it up as a link to France. Many wanted the rails because they would bring tourists whose money could turn the dreary seaside village into a prime watering hole, which would increase revenue in the surrounding villages as well. Others did not want it because it would bring tourists, who brought riff-raff, who would destroy their lovely seaside village and its surrounds.

Nothing new in that.

His card-partner prompted him to take his turn, so Marcus made his move.

There appeared no apparent or dramatic reason why anyone might sabotage construction. Oh, one man said he'd blow the dirty heaving monster up if it came any closer, but people who made such blowhard statements liked the sounds of their own voices and never acted on their lofty—

The game ended suddenly, and by his partner's black

looks, Marcus realized he must have done something to hasten its speedy demise. Just as well. "I'm done for, gentlemen," he said. "Thank you for your company." Marcus downed the rest of his whiskey and rose.

He needed to see Jade. Talk with her. Touch her. Dance with her. He'd sent a generous tip with a request to the orchestra for a supper waltz. Confirmation that his petition would be granted had arrived shortly thereafter.

He exited the card room via the upper floor terrace, so he could enter the ballroom with a full view of the assemblage. When he arrived, he did not need to look hard.

Jade shone like the sun beaming down upon a garden of fading flowers.

As he approached, his heart quickened its beat. Yellow silk perfectly complimented Jade's coloring, the effect enhanced by the peach silk rosebuds in her hair, between her breasts, and marching down an inverted "V" from waist to hem. Unlike the women about her, Jade wore a slim skirt, rather than a flared, a mode she favored. He was no more surprised that his scandal chose style over fashion than he'd been that she'd decided—at her grandmother's request—not to observe mourning. In both cases, to do otherwise would be too much like following the rules.

Like a stately goddess, she watched him approach, while his pulse raced for knowing he would soon hold her in his arms.

He bowed before her with decorous formality when he wished nothing more than to sweep her into a kiss and feast on the delicious confection she resembled.

She curtseyed like an ice queen.

"I adore you," he whispered, to start her melt, and touched his lips to her inner wrist when she presented her hand.

She fluttered her fan to conceal her reaction, but her eyes above the flare hinted at a scandal's smile.

Her girls, Marcus realized, stood beside her, and even he knew that they *should* be dancing. Were the men in New-haven blind?

"I'll start them off," he whispered to Jade.

He bowed in turn before each, repeating the ritual of hand-kissing and pleasantries. Then he partnered each wall-flower—Molly's mother, Lilly, first. Then Sofia, Millie, and Lacey last, country dances all.

Marcus paid that grand price to waltz with Jade, con-soled by the fact that she would offer her undying gratitude and he would accept.

Speaking with Lilly, Sofia and Millie had not been intel-lectually stimulating, but the three were lovely, sweet, and suitably behaved for the social situation, which said much for Lacey's lessons. Their conversations followed a similar tone, however. Jade was their savior. They'd be left in the cold, or worse, if not for her.

His discourse with Lacey turned more personal and thought-provoking. Though she remained quiet, calm, and always the lady, he judged she'd been deeply hurt in her life, perhaps at the point when she'd been sent to Peacehaven by her family.

During the course of their dance, he apologized for his error the day they met.

"Being mistaken for someone's mother was unex-pected," Lacey said, "and a blow, though unintentional, I realize, because I lost a daughter."

She mentioned neither a husband nor a lost love, and Marcus offered sympathy and thanked her for trusting him with her story.

"If there is a man you love, who isn't claiming you—"

Marcus spoke for her ears, alone, as he kissed her hand after their dance. "He's a fool."

Lacey's eyes filled as she whispered her thanks.

Once he showed Jade's fledglings off, suitors crowded round.

Assuring the men's faultless deportment, Marcus stood beside Jade, a hand at her elbow to mark his possession and discourage any and all comers inclined in her direction. One dandy who made to approach her received Marcus's darkest scowl and changed course on the instant.

The supper waltz finally began and Marcus exulted as he swept onto the floor with the scandal who stole his heart.

As they turned and dipped, his hand at her back sizzling for the contact, he drank in her elegance in greedy draughts—long lashes, dazzling eyes, high cheekbones, lush lips, inches away from his own. He wanted to kiss her there, and *there*, and *there* too.

Jade watched Marcus, for all the world as if he were nibbling her here and there in his mind. Lord and didn't she wish he'd nibble in truth?

When admonishment, bearing Gram's voice, slipped into her mind for the weak thought over a man, Jade cast it aside. Nothing would stop her tonight. At her first ball, she'd dance in the arms of her favorite gallant and damn the consequences.

Her valiant suitor. Not a man in sight matched Marcus for male splendor. He wore black tailcoat and trousers with a gold waistcoat and a shirt of snow white. A topaz winked in his lapel. His neck-cloth conveyed elegance not fuss.

"Do you like what you see?" he asked.

Jade smiled to entice. "As you did this afternoon."

"You wore the same slippers then as now," he observed. "Would I find the rest the same as well, were I to . . . unwrap . . . the very splendid package before me."

Jade lowered her lashes, as much to hide nervousness as to titillate. "I would never let you unwrap, I have to say, unless I could do the same."

He pulled her closer, and her heart and body rejoiced. "It *will* happen," he said, his voice low, his breath warming the air near her ear. "The moment is yours to name." He pulled back to gaze deeply into her eyes. "Think carefully on it, however, my sweet. Mating fire with ice will alter us both."

True fear of a man hit Jade then, for the first time, a fear greater than she'd learned at her grandmother's knee. One that could neither be touched nor named.

The power Marcus Fitzalan held over her *could* alter her in crucial ways, she feared, and that's what frightened her most. Except that he seemed so different from other men.

Pups adored him.

Fearful little girls followed in his wake.

He turned wallflowers into belles, melted ice, and fears from hearts.

Could Marcus be that rarest of creatures, a man to depend on? "I've never been so tempted," she said, because he waited, because she wanted something—everything—he offered and couldn't bear to think of saying no. Except that she feared saying yes, though she barely understood the question.

"How long have we known each other?" she asked realizing how fast this malady that passed for fascination had come upon her.

"Since eternity," he said. "We're meant to be."

"I'm not certain I believe that."

"I can wait until you do." He never gave her the answer she expected, but one that touched her in unexpected ways.

"I'm not sure *I* can wait," she admitted as the music ended and he offered his arm to take her in to supper.

When he placed a plate before her, she grasped his wrist and he leaned close.

"I *know* I can't wait," she whispered.

He dismissed his hired carriage and shared hers on the way home, sitting close of necessity, bringing her a warm satisfaction. And in the darkness, while Lacey touted their success and Molly laughed like a girl again, Marcus found Jade's hand and held it under cover of her skirt, infusing her with contentment.

When they arrived at the Manor, they bid everyone goodnight, and Marcus asked her to walk with him outside for a bit to take the air.

He removed his coat, placed it on her shoulders, and made her slip it on, then amid owls' calls and sea breezes they strolled across the lawn, her hand on his arm.

When they reached the cliff overlooking the Channel, a vast expanse of shimmering silver slashed by moonlight, he covered her hand with his and squeezed. "I have a favor to ask." He faced her. "I'd like to bring my brother, Garrett, to stay here for a while—another fledgling for your nest. He's in . . . he's been hurt. An accident; my fault, rot my soul in hell."

"Oh, Marcus. Does he blame you?"

"Of course not."

"Then I suspect you shouldn't blame yourself."

He waved away her attempt at absolution, a certain indication he needed absolving too much to acknowledge her words. "May I invite him?" he asked. "Please."

"Of course you may, but I don't understand why you'd wish to."

Annette Blair

He started them walking again, absently stroking her hand on his arm. "For several reasons, really. So I can spend time with him, help him become the old Garr again. There's so much healing going on here, Jade—emotional as well as physical. Garrett needs both. He may stay . . . as he is . . ." Marcus cleared his throat with impatience when his voice cracked, "for the rest of his life. Your ladies would be good for him. I think he might be good for them. What do you think?"

"I think I would like to be kissed, please."

Marcus didn't need a second invitation. He brought Jade hard against him, closing his mouth over hers—no gentleness, no patience. He wanted to bury the horror and guilt of Garrett's accident in her silk and scent. In her.

Deep inside her.

He wanted her.

She wanted, too, judging by her trembling. She opened to his coaxing lips, slipped a soft hand beneath his waistcoat, and caressed the hair at his nape with the other. A woman's hands in his hair always drove him wild, but never so much as now, with Jade.

He slid his seeking hands beneath her coat, *his* coat, lucky coat, wrapped around her the way he'd like to be, and he learned her with his palms, from her shoulders to the small of her back, to the bottom he'd known from the start would fit his hands just right.

She arched, meeting the evidence of his need and didn't withdraw, but rocked against him as if she'd done it a hundred times, yet he knew by the kiss that this was a first.

Instinct. The need to mate.

He moved with her, hard and eager against soft and pliant. Theirs would be a perfect mating; he'd never been so certain of anything in his life. And he was ready, so

58

ready, but a kiss was all she asked.

He stepped back, breathing hard. "I'm sorry. I was too rough. I . . . don't be afraid. I feel as if . . . you seem to have some power over me, the power to turn me into a primitive chest-pounding male. But don't worry, I won't grab your hair and drag you to my cave, I promise. Not tonight, at any rate."

She laughed, easy and free, for the first time. "I'm rather fond of my power over you, Marcus Fitzalan."

He rather liked his over her, as well.

She'd laughed. He'd melted an ice queen in a yellow gown.

The rider Emily saw was wearing a yellow gown the night before they found a stuffed "body" on the tracks, but he couldn't ask Jade about that now, not tonight. "As I said, I'm yours to command."

"What if *I* say I'm *yours* to command?"

"Then we won't be getting much sleep anytime soon."

Jade felt a pleasant ripple of shock skitter through her at his threat. *No sleep anytime soon!* If his words alone could move her, how would she feel lying naked beside him?

If not sleep, what precisely did a man and woman do behind closed doors during the long dark hours of the night? The process had always remained sketchy in her mind. Titillating, but vague.

She wasn't entirely naïve; she'd seen stallions ready to breed. This afternoon, when Marcus caught her waiting for Sofia to fit her gown, he had stroked her with his hot gaze and become as ready as any stallion. Her blood had heated and skittered her veins then. It happened again times a hundred, during their kiss just now. But this time she'd arched against that very ready part of him, the corresponding center of her pulling and pulsing to bring him in, and it all became infinitely more clear.

Jade shivered, and rather than retreat from the source of danger, she stepped nearer, and Marcus enfolded her in his warmth, holding her tighter, knowing exactly what she needed.

"I'll have to sleep on the possibility of obeying your commands," she said against his neck. "As far as my own are concerned, none come to mind that I have the courage to allow."

"I await your pleasure with bated breath," he said in a low, seductive voice as he gazed into her eyes, then he stepped back, took her arm, and directed them toward the house.

Grateful, relieved, and disappointed, anticipation simmered in Jade's breast.

"There are any number of commands available to you," he said as they stepped into the foyer. "Ask me to ravish you; I'll take you to heaven. Ask me to kiss you; I will anytime, anywhere in the world . . . on your body."

There went her blood, sparking and racing again. Anywhere on her body. Glory.

They stopped as one when they saw the sprite asleep on the bottommost step. Emily.

"I was just coming for her," Lacey said, as she rounded the bend in the stairs and came into sight. "She wanted to stay up and wait for you, Jade, though she called you 'the princess,' but I wouldn't let her, so she sneaked away on her own, the bold creature."

"I kissed her goodnight after I dressed," Jade explained to Marcus. "She called me a princess then too."

"Because you're so beautiful."

"Hah," Jade scoffed. "Spoken like any gallant worth his salt."

"Mucks? Jade?" Emily called in a sleepy voice from Lacey's arms.

"We're home, Kitten," Jade said, kissing Em's brow.

"Have a good sleep, Emmy-bug," Marcus said doing the same. "We'll see you in the morning."

Emily nodded and Lacey took her up to bed.

Strolling up that main stairway, arm in arm with Marcus made one of those perfect moments Jade knew she'd remember forever.

"You've lessons to be taught," Marcus said re-claiming her attention. "Wonderful lessons I'm more than ready to teach you, but recall my warning. Every step we take will change us. If you're not prepared for that inevitability, step back. The fire's too hot. For now."

"That's what scares me," she said as they reached his floor.

"I know." He kissed her once more, gentler, sweeter, enough to make her want to haul him up the stairs with her and . . . then what?

"Ivy will bring my brother in the morning," he said. "Thank you for allowing him to come. Now, go and dream of me." A hand at her bottom, he nudged her toward the remaining steps.

When she turned at the top to look down, aching inside for something more, he stood there, watching.

With a flourish, he bowed, her smooth-talking scoundrel of an unlikely gallant, that half smile of his fluttering her heart before he disappeared from her sight, though not from her mind.

In her room, Jade stepped from her gown and petticoats, remembering the feel of his hands grazing her back, tracing the outline of her corset through her clothes. He'd stroked the lace on her drawers as he skimmed her bottom, as if the body beneath belonged to him, not her, and he'd as soon remove the impediments he encountered on his quest.

Jade stepped to her mirror to examine the image he'd admired that afternoon—chemisette and corset, stockings and garters, and she smiled remembering his reaction.

After letting down her hair, she stripped to nothing with reasonable ease, used to doing for herself—though usually not with so many layers—to view exactly what she might allow him to see . . . perhaps . . . someday.

Her breasts, which were too big, did make her waist look small—a fair exchange she supposed. Her bottom seemed round enough, but not too round. The unholy length of her legs had always made her feel clownish, but Marcus didn't seem to mind.

During their conversations, her height placed his sculpted lips on a level with hers, both distracting and seducing her. If she ever gathered the courage to give in to the temptation he presented, she might be grateful for her stature. As a Long-Meg she would also meet that hard, seeking portion of him quite well, which must be considered a boon.

She turned down her covers and sighed. She'd never had the social experiences other girls of her station did, but tonight she'd been to a ball, courted by a princely suitor, complimented, waltzed and kissed for the first time. A perfect society launch, and not more than ten years late.

She didn't lament the tardiness of it, because Marcus seemed worth the wait.

She had but one regret. During their kiss, her breasts had prickled in restless anticipation, budding to hard points, but Marcus had not touched.

Perhaps she should have issued a command.

Chuckling at the preposterous notion, Jade dropped to

her bed, for the first time ever without her nightgown, to let the evening air cool her fevered body. She didn't even bother to pull up the covers. Aware of every new subtlety in her body, she focused deep inside, at her center, where she pulsed still.

If Marcus were looking down at her right now, as naked and ready as she—a sight she knew she'd enjoy—she'd open her arms and welcome him.

Skin against skin. Glory.

A week ago if anyone had told her she'd be ready to lie with a man, she would have told them to go to the devil.

If Gram were here, she'd warn her granddaughter to beware of Satan's lair.

Normally, that inner warning would stop her; she had always been ready to heed her grandmother's warnings . . . until Marcus. Her current unwillingness to listen made her understand how and why a woman might lose herself in a man, how she might forget to fight for her goals in the process of making *his* desires and goals her focus. She might forget to fight for her needs and rights in view of his, forget even to breathe for herself, if he would do it for her.

Yes, the consequences of surrendering herself could be staggering.

Alarm sat Jade up.

Consequences others would suffer . . . which she could not allow.

She mustn't, couldn't, relinquish herself to passion and forget all else.

She needed to keep Gram's secret.

She needed to stop the railroad and defeat Giles Dudley.

She couldn't afford to lose her purpose amid a heady flight of fancy, physical or otherwise, real or imagined. She couldn't give her heart or her hand to anyone, because in doing so—she was living proof—she would diminish her power to reason, lose her focus, her very self.

If she trusted . . . the wrong man . . . not only could she lose her self-respect, strength and determination, but she could lose the Benevolent Society for Downtrodden Women, and those in her care would lose as well.

If she trusted the *wrong* man.

If she trusted *any* man, she'd been taught from birth.

Perhaps any man was the wrong man. If mere attraction made her imagine herself as weak and in need of male protection and security, perhaps a woman must remain alone and invulnerable to the opposite sex to remain strong.

Perhaps—no, not perhaps, but most likely, she hated to admit—Gram was right.

She needed to reassert her power to think and do for herself as she'd been taught, Marcus or no.

She needed to remain strong.

Marcus entered Jade's study the next morning more tired than when he'd gone to bed, because he'd tossed half the night, erect and uncomfortable.

To remedy his condition, he'd considered the problems and intricacies of the railroad, of lost records and missing finances, until his body would cool and he'd doze.

Then his dreams took over and he was back in Jade's thrall, her touch and her fragrance arching along and against him, and he'd wake throbbing and on the brink of release.

He considered storming her door—if only he knew which door.

Now, pages of accounts sat before him and he couldn't concentrate for anticipating her step in the hall—like that stallion again, agitated, vigilant.

Marcus swore and focused on the ledger entries.

He stood and went around the desk to lean against it. This way, when she came in, she could step easily into his arms. He'd be gentle. She'd be shy, because of their kiss and his intimation that he'd like to keep her awake all night loving her. But she would be eager to learn how that could happen and he . . . would be happy to show her.

She'd wear something soft against her skin this morning, something sweet and feminine, her hair flowing down her back, a stray lock on her bodice. He'd not stroke merely the lock this morning, he decided, if she seemed willing.

It would be worth a sleepless night, if stopping had piqued her interest and she awoke eager for his lessons.

He heard her voice, sharp, quick.

His body reacted, sharp, quick.

She threw the door open.

Anticipation turned to shock.

The ice queen returneth.

The single difference between her clothing at their first encounter and this morning was the addition of a black frock coat to her trousers and waistcoat. But he feared that the declaration she made remained the same, with one subtle difference—she had him in thrall now, and it would take more than a declaration of war to stop him.

Nevertheless, her message remained clear. In charge. Untouchable. Made of ice.

"Is that my coat?" Marcus asked, annoyed, amused, beguiled.

Jade raised her chin ready to face her opponent, infinitely more handsome of a sudden. More human. Be strong, she told herself. Be firm. Leave the lock of hair on his brow exactly where it is. Step too near and get singed.

She gave him a nod. "Your tailcoat fit well last night,

and it takes care of the problem. This way I won't distract susceptible males with my . . . assets." She glanced behind her. "See, no distraction. It works."

Marcus put the ledger down, leaned against her desk, crossed his ankles, folded his arms, and disproved her words with a hot sweeping gaze. "It doesn't work."

Six

Marcus straightened. "You've been in my room? Going through my clothes?"

Jade had loved the experience, bringing his coats to her face to inhale his spicy scent.

By the look of him, she guessed at his displeasure. Strong. Be strong, she told herself.

She shrugged. "Everybody comes and goes here."

"How convenient. Where's *your* room?"

She attempted a chiding brow, refusing to answer, her heart skittering so hard it battered her rib cage. This was not going the way she wanted. His question alone heated her.

"The doors do have locks, however?" he asked. "In the event such comings and goings are to be discouraged, due to a need for . . . privacy."

Marcus began to advance.

Jade stepped back. She couldn't let him touch. "Wait a minute." She was trying to thwart him, not entice him. She needed to regain her control, her purpose. She couldn't turn over strength to him that others needed to draw from her.

She took one step back for each he took forward, until she realized the implications. "Damn it, Marcus! Stop right there."

He did, his look hot enough to melt a saint's resolve. Devil's eyes, burning her alive.

"I know that look. You're nibbling on me in your mind again, I can tell. Stop it right now!"

"Fine. I'd rather nibble in truth." He reached for her.

She extended her arm fast, slapping her palm against his chest, stopping his forward surge and holding him at bay. "This . . . familiarity between us has to stop. We can't work together and continue our . . . familiarity . . . of last night."

He gave her his cocky half-grin. "You already used that word. Try the right word—intimacy."

"Familiarity's the better word, damn it!"

When Marcus eased away from her restraining hand and went to look out the window, Jade thought she finally got through.

His silence did not make her worry that she hurt him. She did *not* wish to console him or turn him into her arms.

She *must* remain intractable to make him understand the importance of . . .

Had his shoulders just rippled?

Yes, there, it happened again. More forceful.

Now an all-out quake. He burst into laughter.

"Damn it, Marcus," Jade snapped straightening her spine, firming her resolve, trying to recall any of a thousand litanies against men.

But louder than Gram's voice, rang the joy in Marcus's laughter.

Jade would wager her missing fortune that her grandmother had never come across a man who found anything in life worth laughing about. Both their lives might have been different if Gram had.

But it didn't matter; she must remain in charge and make her own choices. "I insist on a purely business relationship between us, Marcus. No dancing, no nibbling, no kisses, and above all, no commands—other than the ones I issue to my man of affairs."

That seemed to sober him fast enough. He ran his hand

through his hair, making him look all mussed and . . . kissable, drat him.

He regarded her, trying to read her, showing concern, which annoyed her to no end.

"You seem . . . frightened," he said. "Of what you felt last night?"

She refused to answer; she hated to admit to weakness. But he had reason to be confused; she had taken him by surprise this morning, especially after last night.

"Of course," he said, understanding seeming to grow apace with concern—damn his white-knight's soul. "What's between us is powerful. And it can seem overwhelming."

He gave her a look, like Ivy's pup at her begging best, his big eyes hopeful. "But that doesn't mean—"

"No. Yes! Yes it does mean. We have to start fresh, as if we're strangers. I hired you. You work for me. If you can't follow this necessary course, you'll be discharged."

Despair washed over her. A shrew; she sounded like a shrew. Damn it, wasn't there some sane middle ground between shrew and strumpet?

"I take it you're wearing those clothes to prove you mean business." Marcus raked her with his gaze once more, but this time his look revealed scorn—which she would *not* let bother her. She needed to alter the course of their relationship. She had no choice.

"I'm wearing these clothes because they're comfortable and easy to work in, because this is who I am. I won't lose myself to you, or anyone. I won't, Marcus."

"I understand, Jade. I do. In a lot of ways, I'm as frightened by the force of this . . . familiarity . . . as you are." He flashed his cocky grin, but she fought the pull. He sobered and ran a hand through his hair. "Believe me, no other woman ever came close to rattling me the way you do. If one did, I'd have walked."

"Walk now, then," she said, missing him already, hurting physically as well as emotionally, at the very notion. "It'll be better for both of us."

Shaken by the suddenness and stubbornness of Jade's reversal, Marcus admitted to himself that he would stay, of course. He needed to, and the railroad barely entered into his rationale. He couldn't leave because something in Jade called to him, as something in him, he believed, called to her. He must be near at hand when she heeded the call.

Pray God it would happen soon.

"I agree to our relationship remaining strictly business for now," he said, going so far as to sit behind the desk and pull the ledger over to prove it, but he could tell she suspected a trap.

"Promise?"

"Look, Jade—"

Something tapped the door so softly Marcus wasn't certain he'd heard it.

"Come in?" Jade called, as unsure as him.

The door opened slowly. "Mucks?" Emily saw him and trotted in, incredibly adorable, her pink dotted muslin dress rumpled, a shoe and stocking on one foot, nothing on the other.

Marcus rolled his chair back as she approached, grinning at the small ray of sunshine in the cloudburst his morning had become. "Emily? Does Lacey know you're here?"

Emily shrugged, raised her leg high and lay her bare foot on his knee.

Marcus wiggled a tiny toe. "This little piggy went to market . . ."

Emily giggled.

"I thought you came to play piggies. No?"

She shook her head. "No!"

"Did Tweenie steal your sock?"

She shook that little head harder, swinging a profusion of yellow curls to and fro.

"No?" Marcus hauled her onto his lap. "What happened to your shoe and stocking then Emmy-bug?"

"Tweenie piddled on it."

Marcus looked up to share his amusement with Jade and caught a rather wild look in her eyes. She reminded him of a cornered animal. Panicked. As if she were being . . . tortured.

By observing him and Emily?

Tortured . . . *that's* how she'd been acting all morning. Not sure where to turn, cornered. Why hadn't he seen it?

Could she be so torn by what she felt for him that she feared something as simple as his gentleness with Emily would break her resolve?

Perhaps she didn't want a business relationship any more than he did, but ran from anything deeper.

He needed to remember that she'd been taught, and seen enough horrors to believe, that a gentle man must be an aberration. And when confronted by one . . . what?

Her life's lessons made no sense, that's what. She'd lost her grounding—trembled on unsure foundations. *That,* he could comprehend.

At least he had interacted with the opposite sex. Jade held no experience relating to men of her station, except for him. And what had he done but storm the ramparts?

Bloody hell.

He had gone too fast. Frightened her.

If he allowed it, this affinity they seemed to have for each other—almost as if they'd shared a life before—would frighten him as well. Frighten him senseless, if truth be told.

Perhaps they did need to slow down. Backtrack. Start again.

Fine. He would give her the business relationship she desired until she begged for something more. Denying his feelings would be difficult, but if he must be firm and businesslike to win a woman who needed gentling more than any other of his experience—no small amount of experience—he faced a challenge that should cool him while it warmed her. A double challenge.

"Emmy," he said, ready to make a start. "Jade is my employer, so I must request a few minutes to take you and bring you back to Lacey."

Emily nodded and regarded Jade. "Mucks *miss* Jade."

Marcus rolled his eyes. "So much for business. You see, Jade, I care for Emily and she cares for me, and people who care for each other help each other. Ours is a non-business relationship. It's called friendship."

He moved toward the door, but Emily puckered her lips to give Jade a goodbye kiss and so he brought Emily to Jade.

Marcus turned away from the love Jade revealed when she kissed Emily and fought the yearning to be the recipient of such unfettered devotion from Jade.

Business only, he reminded himself in frustration. "You can deduct from my salary an amount equal to the time it takes me to get Emmy settled. That's the best I can do business-wise at the moment," he said as he left.

The door slammed behind him.

Jade stood alone in the center of her study in pain, as if something tangible had crushed her, her arms and legs weighted down.

Friendship, she thought. There was the middle ground.

"Marcus! Marcus, wait." She went after them.

In the hall, Marcus turned, losing his smile when he saw her, making Jade think she'd hurt him. But he was a man; he couldn't be as confused and vulnerable as she. Men didn't get their feelings hurt. They had none to injure.

But she looked for signs of emotional wounds anyway; Gram might have been wrong about that. Just look at the way Marcus sensed Emily's—

"Well?" he said with impatience. "What have I got, fifteen minutes? Ten?"

"No. No, it's not that. This doesn't have to do with business."

The sardonic look he threw her conveyed a silent, *Damn it, make up your mind.*

Jade looked down, feeling foolish, and focused on Emily's cute, little, naked foot. She cupped it then raised it in her palm. "Do you believe how tiny her feet are?"

Marcus softened and became the old Marcus, ready to listen.

Jade warmed. "I . . . I just realized that—"

Lacey came rushing around the corner and nearly ran into them. "Emily Patience Warren, you naughty girl, where have you been?"

Emily hid her face in Marcus's neck.

"I wondered about that," he said.

A man shouted for Jade. A woman screamed.

Jade regarded Marcus and Lacey—both shocked—and ran.

The spectacle in her foyer reminded Jade of a village fair where the greased pig got loose. She could hardly take it in. The front door stood open, a mama cat at the threshold, a kitten by its scruff, looked to be considering the suitability of lodgings. Calm amid chaos.

Children ran in circles chasing Tweenie—or she chased them—through a crowd of conjecturing spectators.

Abigail, Lilly, oh several of the women, and Lester, Harry and Dirk were bent over something on the floor.

When Jade stepped closer, she saw the body. "Oh my God."

Whether man or woman, alive or dead, she didn't know, but her heart started pounding. "Move aside. Somebody—Lester—get Beecher."

"I think she's in labor," Lacey said paling when she saw the woman. "She . . . she has to be moved to a room." Rather than kneeling to help, Lacey backed away.

Jade saw the pain in her eyes. "Millie, take Lacey into the kitchen and make her some tea, would you? I think she's feeling faint. Marcus, I may need your help."

Marcus nodded and handed Emily to Lilly. Then he came to kneel beside the woman.

Jade felt better having him there, and damn it, hadn't she just finished telling herself that needing him had to stop.

Angry with herself for thinking of herself, Jade gave her attention to the young woman with a swollen belly, prostrate in the middle of her floor. Alive, thank God, and watching them.

Jade lifted a dirty hand to hold it, to tell the soon-to-be mother she was among friends. The poor thing looked as if she'd been starving, likely living on the street. "Can you tell me your name?"

"Eloisa," she said. "Eloisa Haw . . . Higgins."

Jade and Marcus noted her hesitation and regarded each other.

"Hello Eloisa. I'm Jade. And this is Marcus. Will you let him carry you to a room where you can rest more comfortably?"

Eloisa nodded weakly.

"How do you feel," Marcus asked, shifting Eloisa's ratty hair from her eyes.

The smile she gave him transformed her, making one forget anything about her except her beauty.

Good Lord, Jade thought, Eloisa was already half in love with Marcus. If she fell that fast, no wonder her present delicate condition.

Eloisa grimaced in discomfort. "They said to come here and the crazy lady would help me."

Marcus muffled his chuckle.

Eloisa scanned the faces around her. "I only need a warm place to have my baby. I won't be a burden. If I could sleep for a bit, I could work for my supper."

"Shh," Jade soothed. "Don't worry about that. You'll stay for as long as you need, eat three nourishing meals a day and have a fine healthy baby. We needed some excitement around here. No payment necessary."

"Are you the lady?"

Jade nodded.

"You don't seem crazy."

"That's curious, because today I feel especially so. But don't be frightened. I'm harmless."

Eloisa's torso trembled with an amusement too weak to express as her threadbare shawl slipped to the floor revealing arms riddled with bruises.

Jade gazed at Marcus who'd seen them too. "Did somebody hurt you?" Jade asked her.

"I fell," she said. "Really."

"Where the devil is Beecher?" Marcus shouted.

"This cold floor can't be doing you any good," Jade said. "Marcus will bring you to a nice room with a warm bed and I'll be right there to tend you."

Jade looked up at Marcus. "Why don't you try to move her now. But stop if she cries out."

Impressed at the way Jade took matters in hand, Marcus nodded and began to lift the pregnant woman, hesitating only when she gasped. "Are you sure you're up to this?" he asked her.

When Eloisa nodded, he pulled her fully into his arms, then he got to his feet and looked to Jade for directions as to where to take her.

Voices from another direction had him turning in time to see Ivy push Garrett's wheelchair through the door. Pleased to see his brother, Marcus was nevertheless amused by the look on Garrett's face, which was nothing short of stunned.

Garrett's gaze shifted from him to the very pregnant woman in his arms and back again. "Marcus Fitzalan," he said in his haughty aristocratic voice. "What wild scrape have you gotten yourself into this time?"

Marcus swept Jade and the members of her household with a glance. "Jade, ladies and gentlemen, I'd like you to meet my brother Garrett. He's going to be staying with us for a few weeks." He raised a brow his brother's way. "Unless I kick him out sooner."

Garrett grinned.

"My armful, by the way, Garrett, is Eloisa Higgins. She may be barely strong enough to hang on, and pardon me for saying this, Eloisa, but why your condition is referred to as delicate is beyond me. The more appropriate description that comes to mind right now is . . . weighty."

"Chivalrous as always," Garrett drawled, a gleam in his eye.

Marcus seized the gauntlet in a blink. "Show us true valor, then," he said, placing Eloisa in his astonished brother's arms.

Eloisa safely settled, Marcus stepped back and flexed his arms, appreciating the sight of his knave brother with a pregnant young woman in his lap. "Much better, and vastly amusing," Marcus said.

No sooner had he said it than Garrett's eyes widened and he gasped in surprise. "Something is warming my . . . I'm wet!"

"I couldn't help it!" the mortified woman wailed hiding her face in Garrett's coat. "Something . . . broke," she added, her voice muffled.

Marcus fell back against the wall laughing. Every time he tried to catch his breath, he'd look at Garrett's aristocratic indignation and start laughing again.

As fascinated by Marcus's unbridled laughter as by the obvious bond between him and his brother, Jade saw love, there, between them, in their banter and laughter. Even in the fact that Marcus wanted Garrett here, and Garrett came.

Marcus accepted his brother's limitations without making him seem limited. He didn't take the wheelchair as a problem. He managed to employ it by making Garrett a necessary part of their activity.

He'd initiated Garrett into the household with a vengeance, actually, but not in such a different way as when a woman like Eloisa usually arrived. The experience was always traumatic, especially to the new arrival, but she was swept quickly and naturally into the household, though never as humorously.

"Er, excuse me," Garrett said. "Jade, is it? I believe this young lady is . . . uncomfortable."

"Oh!" Jade snapped to attention.

Marcus jolted to action as well. "Does anybody know where Beecher is?"

"Town case," Lester said. "Didn't think he'd be back tonight. Old Lady Murray's got pneumonia."

"Wonderful," Jade said. "Marcus, will you take Garrett with Eloisa to . . ." She mentally considered rooms accessible to a wheel chair. "The fourth door off the east wing hall, this level." She pointed. "The hall off that one. It's the biggest bedroom down here—big enough for a cradle. And the room next to it will suit Garrett admirably, I believe. Oh and Marcus, don't leave them too soon; you'll need to lift Eloisa from Garrett's arms and put her into the bed once it's made up."

"Right."

"Sofia, do you mind seeing to linens, soap and towels enough for Garrett's and Eloisa's rooms, then see if you can find Frederick to make up their beds? Garrett will want to change into some clean and dry clothes and put his things away. I'd appreciate it if you'd also help Eloisa wash up."

Sofia nodded and left.

Jade regarded the members of her household who were milling about. "I don't suppose any of you ever delivered a baby?"

Silence.

"I have," Garrett said. "But I'd rather not do it alone."

"I can help," Marcus added, noting her surprise. "A carriage broke down near our place in a storm a few years ago. The woman, birthing her seventh, thank God, told us what to do. Garrett took charge, and saved the day."

"Marc served as my babbling-idiot apprentice."

Marcus gave a rueful half-smile. "It's true."

Jade laughed, rattled out of countenance. Of everyone, the seditious Scoundrels were the last she'd expected to come forward.

"Actually," Garrett said. "I was thinking of a woman."

"Naturally," Marcus said.

Garrett ignored him. "When the time came, Marc settled down nicely and served as a great help, so between us, we can do it. But we'd do better, and so would Eloisa, with a woman who has experience delivering a child."

Jade turned to a slight touch on her arm, surprised to see Abigail standing beside her. "I . . . I can help," Abigail said. "I have a little experience."

Jade looked from the two most virile men she'd ever beheld to the frightened woman beside her and couldn't believe Abigail had spoken in their presence.

"Are you certain, Abigail?" Jade asked.

Abigail's nod professed willingness, though it could *not* be termed a wholehearted eagerness.

Nevertheless, Jade accepted with gratitude. "Garrett, this is Abigail Pargeter."

Garrett extended his free hand toward Abigail, as Marcus had done with Emily.

Two gentlemen, Jade mused. A double paradox. Were they unique? Or were there more like them? If so, would that make her grandmother wrong?

Abigail regarded Garrett's big strong hand as if it were a snake about to strike.

Expecting her to bolt, Jade wondered who among the women could possibly—

"Abigail," Garrett said softly. "We need you. Eloisa needs you."

Abigail's breath shuddered out of her. She straightened her shoulders, stepped forward and—most surprising— placed her trembling hand in Garrett's.

He squeezed it. "Thank you. I can already see that you're a generous and brave woman."

"Lead the way, Abigail," Marcus said normalizing the

fraught moment and pushing Garrett's chair forward.

Every soul in that foyer stood still as stone watching the unlikely group depart, each face reflecting stunned amazement.

Jade released her breath. "Lester, since Beecher is away, would you mind putting some water on to boil? Kettles on every burner, I should think, and keep it coming."

People drifted back to work, or to lessons or offspring. Lester, or one of the women, must have taken the children away some time before, Jade realized.

She noticed Ivy sitting on the bottom step of the main staircase watching her. Dropping down to sit beside him, she pulled her knees up, wrapped her arms around them, and allowed the tense muscles in her shoulders to relax, the sigh that escaped her, rife with responsibility.

"You did good, little girl."

She laid her head on the shoulder of the man she rather thought of as a surrogate father. "Thanks Ivy, though I feel as if I've made fifty horrid mistakes already today, but I'm not sure what they are."

"Nothing that can't be fixed, I'd warrant. You certainly welcomed some interesting new members into this incredible household of yours today."

She chuckled.

Ivy pointed with his chin. "Look, here comes another."

Mama cat was moving in after all, her poor kitten still dangling by its scruff. "Has she been there all this time?"

Ivy chuckled. "No. That's a different kitten. Look over there."

Tweenie, not much bigger than the mother cat, curled up between an umbrella stand and a bootjack, was giving a kitten a licking-wash while Mama cat placed kitten number five into her red-puppy protection.

"I don't believe it," Jade said.

"Like doesn't always seek like," Ivy said. "It's called balance. What are you going to do now?"

Jade kissed his cheek and stood. "I'm going to go up to the attic and fetch a lovely old cradle to welcome a new baby into the household. And then I'm going to think about fixing at least one of my mistakes. Add some balance to my life."

"That's my girl."

Seven

Jade managed easily enough to locate the cradle, more dusty and cobweb-draped than lovely at the moment. She was having a devil of a time getting it down the steep, narrow stairs from the attic, however, when someone wrestled it from her grasp.

"Oh, it's you Marcus." She placed a hand to her heart. "Thank you. The cradle blocked my view and I didn't see you."

"Or the steps, I gather. When Ivy told me where you'd gone, I feared you'd break your neck. And you were close." He mumbled something about damned foolish females getting themselves into dangerous situations.

Jade didn't think he referred solely to the danger of stairs. "Your frustration is because of your need to rescue damsels in distress, is it not?" she asked.

"Business is shot for today," he said. "I'm sorry."

Disappointed he didn't react to her tease, she waved away his protest and followed him down another flight. "Work at Peacehaven Manor is different from the more conventional places of employment. We do what we're called upon to do whenever and wherever. I suppose I should have made that clear your first day, but you're adapting well enough. Emily, for instance—"

"Is not work!" Marcus threw her a thunderous scowl.

Nevertheless, a few silent minutes later, he placed the cradle gently on the floor in a quiet corner of the kitchen and picked up a rag to help her clean it.

"Thank you," Jade said after a bit. "Emily is fortunate to have you."

"She doesn't have me, except as a friend. She has a mother. What about her, by the way? I've been meaning to ask. Where is Emily's mother?"

Jade shook her head. "We don't know. Both she and Emily arrived badly bruised, Catherine, with a black eye, cut and swollen shut, her wrist broken. After a few weeks, Catherine said she needed to go and see Emily's father and make certain he would provide for his daughter."

"The fool," Marcus said.

"I reacted the same way. We all tried to stop her, but she wouldn't be swayed."

"Do you know who Emily's father is?"

"That did not count among the questions Catherine felt compelled to answer, which isn't unusual," Jade said. "I assumed 'twas Emily's father who beat them."

Marcus swore beneath his breath. "How long since she went to see him?"

"Two months."

He started as if struck. "Poor baby. Between the beatings and her missing mother, it's a wonder she trusts anyone."

"Do you think Catherine intended to leave her here . . . permanently?" Jade asked. "I began to wonder after a while."

Marcus cursed Emily's father to the devil. "I think it more likely the bast—more likely that Catherine came to a bad end."

Jade's legs turned to jelly and she lowered herself to a chair while tears filled her eyes.

Marcus wanted to take her into his arms then. He supposed he simply wanted to protect her from all life's evils, but she wouldn't appreciate it.

To counter his need, he looked away and into the fire.

He didn't imagine it'd help Jade to depend on him to protect her, especially as he would have to leave her in the end,
because of what he'd done to Garrett.

Strictly business, he told himself, running a frustrated
hand through his hair before facing her again. "We—you—
somebody will have to initiate a search into Catherine's
whereabouts."

Jade nodded, still in shock.

Marcus knelt on his haunches before her. "What will you
do if Catherine is . . . never found?"

"Keep Emily, of course."

He had never wanted to kiss her more. "Thank you."

Jade bristled and rose to finish cleaning the cradle.

It wasn't his place to be thanking her, he realized. He
stood too, aware just then how much Jade's strong and
feisty spirit called to him. He realized, too, that by protecting her, he could destroy what he loved best about her.

How did one go about fostering someone's strength
when one wanted desperately to protect them from the
horrid experiences that made them strong, in the event said
experiences did not destroy them first? Marcus sighed again
as he pondered it.

Abigail appeared at the base of the stone stairs, putting a
period to his ruminations. "Marcus, Garrett says you
should come now."

"On my way," he said taking Jade's hand. "Lester, bring
the cradle, will you?"

Abby nodded and left. Lester hoisted the cradle to his
shoulder and followed her.

Jade pulled Marcus up short trying to tug her hand from
his. "Where do you think you're taking me?"

Marcus released her hand. "The birth of a child is a
wonder. A miracle. I thought you'd want to—"

"Eloisa already has a woman and two men she doesn't know to help her through a personal and intimate ordeal. A miracle yes, but not for spectators."

Marcus grimaced. "You're right. Come and wait outside the door, then, in the event Abigail loses her nerve, or she's so busy helping that Eloisa needs you to hold her hand."

Jade nodded and preceded him up the stairs. They walked in silence until Eloisa's door came in sight. "I do think Eloisa would appreciate your presence," he said. "But I have a confession to make. I'm the one who needs you there."

Jade stilled when Eloisa called her name. This time Jade grabbed his hand to tug him along, and Marcus felt a great deal better about the whole prospect.

When they entered the room, Jade stopped at the sight of Eloisa's awkward and embarrassing position, Garrett and Abby, heads bent together in concentration between Eloisa's raised knees.

"It's natural," Marcus whispered in her ear. "Imagine how Eloisa feels."

Eloisa, a true beauty with her face and hair washed, seventeen years old at most, looked to Jade for . . . something, so Jade prepared to offer all she had, apprehensive reassurance. Nevertheless, she stepped to the bed with a smile and took the girl's hand.

When a chair nudged her legs from behind, Jade sat down. Marcus then brought in the cradle.

"Abigail tells me she's always been interested in becoming a midwife," Garrett said, "the reason she wanted to help. So Marcus, I thought you could prop Eloisa up the way Sara Littleton taught us, so Abby can assist me."

Marcus nodded with relief, told Eloisa he would be her pillow, then climbed on the bed and sat behind her.

"Jade," Garrett said. "You might want to wipe Eloisa's brow now and again, to keep the sweat from her eyes." He winked at Eloisa. "Try not to break Jade's hand."

Eloisa's laugh turned to a gasp and Jade watched mesmerized as her belly began to change shape. Garrett told her to push and Marcus raised her to a near sitting position.

Eloisa cried out in earnest as her belly arched to a great mound, and when it relaxed, she did too.

Garrett and Abby spoke in low tones afterward and Marcus told Eloisa to rest against him.

The entire process happened again, several more times, exactly the same way, but with no apparent result or relief.

"Can't we do anything to lessen her pain?" Jade asked Marcus.

"She needs to feel what the baby's doing. But don't worry, Sara told us that mothers don't remember how painful it is to give their babies life, once they hold them in their arms."

"I'll remember for you, then, Eloisa," Jade said patting her hand, watching her sheet-covered middle for further signs of movement.

"Give me your other hand, Jade," Eloisa said.

The girl placed it flat against her belly, giving Jade more than a vision of the process, allowing her to ride the crest and feel the child inside struggling for freedom.

Jade wasn't embarrassed by her tears when she squeezed Eloisa's hand after the contraction. "Thank you for allowing me to share your miracle."

Eloisa shook her head. "The miracle is that I'm not in that abandoned basement with rats for company. You're my miracle. People think you're crazy because they don't understand someone who's generous and—"

Another crest.

Another push.

Eloisa relaxed and covered Jade's hand atop her belly. "I'm grateful you're here," she said. "Grateful you're you."

"I am too," Marcus said.

Always the right words, Jade thought, a warmth spreading inside, from both his words and the accompanying look he gave her. Sweat poured off him as he remained a sturdy but gentle wall against Eloisa's back, a calm voice calling her brave and strong.

Abigail worked easy and content, her attention absorbed by the birth process and the strange man confined to a chair, in whom she amazingly placed her trust.

The only one frightened, Jade realized, was her. Eloisa's pains were coming closer and closer and seemed to hurt worse and worse.

Seeking reassurance, Jade looked to Marcus.

"This is good," he said, reading her. "Nice and quick."

"Quick! You think this is quick? Are you out of your mind? This is taking forever!"

Eloisa gave a spurt of hysterical laughter.

"This is it, Eloisa," Garrett said. "There's a tiny someone nearly here with a head of dark hair. Take a deep breath and push."

Prickles ran through Jade. She felt faint. But she couldn't let herself go; Eloisa needed her.

Then a baby screamed, furious and shrill, and Jade could barely see the squirming little thing for the tears in her eyes. She stood to hug Eloisa, to allow the child-mother to sob against her.

While she did, Jade felt Marcus stroke her hair, as touched by the wonder as she was.

Jade sat when her legs threatened to give out, terribly relieved that Eloisa and her child were fine. But no sooner did she think so than Eloisa was gasping again.

Confused, Jade placed her hand on Eloisa's arching belly, shocked to feel the struggle beginning again. How could that be?

"Another baby," Jade whispered in awe. "Garrett! I think she's having another."

At Jade's shout, Garrett wheeled his chair back from the dresser where he and Abby had been tending the babe. "Abby, I need you, again."

Abigail brought the wrapped baby to Jade and went back to work.

Jade divided her attention between Eloisa and the tiniest little being she'd ever seen. When Eloisa screamed the house down, Jade expected another child to arrive on the instant, but it took so much more pushing before Garrett held another.

Still. Grey. Lifeless.

Marcus left Eloisa to wash his hands, then he took the baby to continue what Garrett had begun, clearing its mouth and nose of mucus.

Garrett and Abby tended Eloisa, something about blood and afterbirth, but Jade's concentration remained on Marcus.

He turned the lifeless little thing on its belly, within the palm of his big hand, and slapped its back, once, twice, three times. Then finally, as if someone had been holding a pillow over its mouth, and suddenly took it away, Eloisa's second baby's scream vibrated the air around them.

Jade placed the first babe in Eloisa's arms, kissed her brow, and wept with her.

Marcus handed the screaming child over to Garrett, grasped the dresser and turned decidedly green.

Garrett and Abigail said they had everything in hand, so

Jade took Marcus by the arm and propelled him from the room and down the hall.

Shutting the door behind her, she urged him to lie on the bed in the unoccupied bedroom and take several deep breaths. She untied his neck-cloth and unbuttoned the top buttons of his shirt, surprised by the dark curling hair on his chest.

She rolled up his sleeves, chafed his arms, and wiped his brow.

When his color began to return, she placed a hand on his cold, sweaty brow. "You were wonderful in there."

Marcus mocked himself with a laugh. "I'll probably kiss the floor when you have ours."

Jade stilled. Marcus lay there trembling. Icy. In shock. He didn't know what he was saying. "You saved that baby's life. I repeat. You were wonderful in there."

"You were wonderful in here." His voice trembled still.

Jade lay down beside him. "Hold me."

"My hands are all bloody."

"P . . . please," she wailed and he pulled her so hard against him, she knew there wasn't anything either of them wanted more. She wept and felt a great shuddering in him as well.

They didn't talk, they held each other, long after they'd both calmed.

"I would have stayed away, if not for you," she said. "I can't believe I would have stayed away."

"I needed you with me. I'm sorry if that bothers you, but I needed you."

"That you needed me, makes me feel wonderful," she said. "My needing you is what frightens me witless."

He sighed and pulled her closer. "Believe me, I understand." It scared Marcus as much as it thrilled him that he needed Jade so much, when he'd gone his whole life without her and did fine. Except he knew, deep inside, that going forward without her would be less than living and more like dying. He shuddered.

Jade didn't think, she just kissed him, and he kissed her back, frenzied and in need, but no more so than she. They'd shared life as it came into being, now they needed to share it at its most basic. Lips touched, nothing more, yet her soul felt nurtured.

The kiss went on, tears salting lips.

Jade wept in earnest; she wasn't sure why.

Marcus held her until she calmed. "This is most definitely *not* sticking to business," he said. "But don't be frightened. Tomorrow I'll be a perfect employee."

She chuckled. He'd known exactly what to say. "And I'll be the perfect employer."

"You already are, you let me bring my brother to work. What do you think of him, by the way?"

"I like him. I think he's wonderful."

"I'm jealous already."

Jade rose to lean on her elbow. "Why?"

"Because *he* will have other than a business relationship with you. I repeat. I'm jealous."

She tickled the dimple in his chin. "It deepens when you pout, too."

Marcus huffed and pouted some more.

She laughed. "Don't worry. Garrett doesn't—" Jade stopped, embarrassed at what she'd nearly revealed.

"Doesn't what?"

"Oh, I don't know. He doesn't make me mad, which you did the minute we met." *And he doesn't turn me hot or cold or weak.* He doesn't stir me or make me yearn, she thought, which reminded her of what she'd wanted to say when they were interrupted by Eloisa's arrival.

"Marcus, do you remember earlier today, when I chased you and Emily from the office?"

"Lord, it seems more like days, than hours, ago."

"I didn't mean to be rude. I'm sorry."

"You were angry. With reason. And I never did have a chance to apologize or tell you what I wanted."

"Tell me now."

She lay back, took a breath, and considered where to begin. "I think . . . it's good that you and Emily care about each other, that you're friends. What I especially like about your relationship is that it carries no threat for either of you."

"Define threat."

Jade curled his wrinkled neck-cloth around her finger. "It's friendship, nothing more. You know. Neither of you is in danger of getting so caught up, you might get . . . lost in the power of it."

"I understand. Continue."

"Remember, you warned me to step back from the fire, if it got too hot. Well, that's what I'd like to do—step back, but not as far back as I first thought necessary." Jade leaned on her elbow, head in hand, to watch his response. "I think that perhaps our relationship doesn't need to be just business, except it can't be like last night, either."

"That makes sense."

She released her breath. "Good. I want us to have what you and Emily have—the caring without the . . . something . . . that makes us—me—lose my . . . self. Do you understand? Can you think about it?"

"The 'something' Jade, that makes both of us lose ourselves is passion, which we can deny ourselves, though it'll be harder to deny the lust that turns to passion."

Jade groaned. "I forgot about the lust."

"Why thank you, Jade. That's the most emasculating statement ever made to me in bed."

"Define emasculating."

He shook his head. "I was almost joking. But let's not consider lust for the moment, or one of us might cry again, and this time it won't be you."

She made to speak and Marcus crossed her lips with a finger and winked. "My one certainty, with regards to you and me, is that our relationship could never be just business. So I accept your gracious and humble offer of friendship with all my heart. It's more than I hoped for this morning." He kissed her hand. "From this moment on, it will be up to you to let me know if you want anything more than friendship."

Relieved and amazed, and more grateful than she could express, Jade nodded. He was turning a great deal of power over to her.

"You do know, though, that friends hold each other," Marcus said.

"Since you walked out of my study this morning, I've felt as if I lost my best friend. I'd like to be held by my friend now and again."

Marcus placed his arm around her shoulders and kissed the top of her head. "I'm glad we're friends. Best friends. I feel better about us now."

"Me too," Jade said on a shaky laugh, swallowing the lump in her throat.

He urged her up and sat beside her on the edge of the bed, then studied his bloody hands. "Thanks for keeping me from passing out in front of everybody. Garrett would never have let me live it down."

She grinned.

Marcus did too. "Know where we can find some baby clothes?"

Jade laughed. "I'm in trouble the day you're more practical than I am."

"It's been an unusual day." He stood and offered his hand. "Look at us, both of us covered in blood." He raised a teasing brow. "And *your* new coat is ruined."

"Oh, Marcus, your beautiful coat."

"Let's retire to our respective rooms to wash. Then you can come to mine and choose another."

"I want to change into a dress anyway. Choose a coat for me and bring it to my room—directly above yours, one floor up."

Marcus knew then that it was going to be harder, now that they were friends, to keep his hands and lips, and everything else, out of trouble.

By the time they got Eloisa and her babies washed and settled, and her attendants got washed, changed, and back to her side, the new mother's eyes kept closing. So Jade directed a late supper be served in the small salon. "We'll take the babies with us," she told Eloisa. "To give you a chance to rest and to give us a chance to get acquainted."

Eloisa closed her eyes, her smile still in place.

Amid baby passing and admiring, during an enjoyable and informal supper, Jade got to know the non-cowering Abigail better, not to mention Marcus's charmer of a brother.

"I've been meaning to compliment you, Jade," Garrett said, interrupting her reverie.

She admired him as she regarded him, the perfect gentleman, a sleeping baby in the crook of his arm. "A compliment?"

"Belated compliments on your earlier attire. Not that what you're wearing doesn't become you splendidly. You'd do any dress great justice, but I particularly enjoyed the way you enhance a pair of breeches. And Marc, your coat never looked better."

Marcus bounced a fussing baby on his shoulder as he paced the perimeter of the salon. "Jade's trousers are not meant to *attract* the male of the species," he said, rubbing the squirming little mite's back. "They're meant to *deter.*"

Garrett raised a skeptical brow. "Who are you trying to convince?"

Marcus looked affronted, making Garrett chuckle.

The babe on Marcus's shoulder fussed a bit more and Marcus sighed theatrically. "How come the one named after you is sweet and quiet, I'd like to know."

"The very same reason the one named after *you* is so much trouble."

Abigail made a strangling sound that didn't quite pass as laughter.

"Are you all right, Abby?" Jade asked.

"I'm rather . . . shocked."

"I apologize," Garrett said. "Did I offend when I teased Jade about her trousers? I meant no disrespect."

Abby waved away his apology, her face pink. "I didn't mean to imply that my sensibilities were injured. It's just that I thought all men were mean and unbending. And you and Marcus act as if you care about the people around you and each other. You're kind and understanding, and . . . amusing. I simply didn't know men like you existed."

"Neither did I," Jade said. "They are a bit of a jolt and take some getting used to."

"No doubt about it; we're special," Garrett said.

Jade about strangled, but true laughter won out. "They're regular scoundrels, Abby. Pretty words and manners. And darned if I've found a mean streak in this one, yet, though he was a bit uncivil this morning." She raised a restraining hand when Marcus made to protest. "With provocation, I'll admit. But be warned, Abby, they can be dangerous to the unsuspecting of the female persuasion."

Garrett harrumphed. "Dangerous indeed. Have you ever heard anything so preposterous, Marc?"

"I never," Marcus said.

"And on that tempting note, I must pass," Garrett drawled.

With his palm covering the tiny head nuzzled into his neck, Marcus returned his brother's grin.

God, they were an irresistible pair when they set out to charm.

"Hand me yours," Garrett said. "He seems finally to have quieted. And propel us to Eloisa's room so we can put them in their cradle."

Abigail walked beside Garrett's chair. "Are you all moved into the room on Eloisa's other side?" Garrett asked her. "You can get to her much more quickly than I, if she needs help. And . . . er, she won't want me there at feeding time, at any rate."

Garrett turned an interesting shade of pink, Jade noticed. Abby saw it too and smiled.

"Good night, Ladies," Marcus said as Abigail entered her room, Garrett echoing the sentiment.

Marcus watched Jade turn into another corridor and imagined her making her way up the stairs to a bedroom as lush and feminine as its owner. Then he pictured her unbuttoning each and every—

"Marc. She's gone. You can breathe again."

Marcus cursed and pushed Garrett's chair forward. "Killjoy."

Eight

Marcus shut Garrett's bedroom door behind them, so they were free to talk for the first time since Garrett's arrival.

Garrett began by clearing his throat. "Are you merely smitten senseless, or shot-between-the-eyes in love, Marc?"

Marcus ignored Garrett's dart and paced the room caging him in. He stopped to gaze out the window. Putting his emotions into words seemed so unguarded. He contemplated the ramifications of not confessing, but decided he didn't have much of a choice. Garrett had already seen too much.

After a ponderous silence, Marcus placed an arm on the mantle and faced his inquisitor. "Shot between the eyes, Garr. Shot dead."

"The devil you say!"

Damn, he might have gotten away with equivocation, but too late now. Marcus shrugged. "Tail over top, but I fought a good fight."

Garrett gave a good impression of a growl. "I suppose that means you haven't thought about checking further into the bloody railroad?"

"You're all heart."

"A known fact. Well, *have* you investigated further?"

Better to have something to report than not, Marcus supposed, however distasteful the news. "I have, as a matter of fact."

"And?"

"I have one suspect."

"Better than none. Who is it?"

Garrett slipped on his nightshirt and pulled himself up and into the bed.

Marcus wished he'd accept help. "Did I just see movement in your right leg?"

"Not enough to signify, so says Quack Peebles."

"I'm sorry."

Garrett waved the apology away like a pesky fly. "I repeat. Who?"

Marcus sat in Garrett's wheelchair and placed his head in his hands. "Jade."

Garrett used the precise word Marcus had been tempted frequently to use since meeting Jade.

Marcus lowered his hands and sighed. "I don't have actual evidence. I saw her from a distance and I'm not convinced it was her, but somebody who saw her from the same distance *was* certain."

"Is the witness reliable?"

"She's three years old. Did you get to see the stuffed dress the workers found on the tracks, by any chance?"

"I brought it with me. It's the only item left in that bag."

"Oh." Marcus's heart tripped. "That might give us a clue." Hands shaking, he opened Garrett's satchel and pulled it out. "Damn it to hell." He tossed the wadded item across the room. "The bloody thing is yellow."

Garrett clearly thought he'd leapt off the edge of sanity.

"But it's not Jade's," Garrett said.

"It's not?" Relief. Hope.

"Spread it out on the bed and see for yourself."

Marcus complied and stared blankly at it. "So?"

"I should think you could tell at a glance that it's several sizes larger than Jade."

Marcus sat at the foot of Garrett's bed. "Lord, I'm glad

you know women's bodies so well. I never would have real- ized it."

Garrett gave him a knowing look. "I'm of the opinion that you wouldn't be thinking with the male portion of your anatomy, Marc, and would have realized it yourself, if you knew Jade's body better."

"Stuff your opinions, Garr."

Garrett raised a brow but he remained silent, a fact which Marcus appreciated as he sat in the wheelchair and walked it in circles. Garr was probably right. If he took Jade to bed, he might be able to think straight, except she didn't want him, yet. She might not be ready for him, until he dis- covered why the railroad frightened her senseless.

Marcus steepled his hands and tapped his fingertips to- gether, as he pondered the dilemma. "Ah." He stopped the chair. "I have an idea."

"An invariable forewarning of calamity," Garrett said, brow raised.

Marcus chose to ignore the caustic comment and sat for- ward. "When's the next time something significant is due to happen concerning construction?"

"Tomorrow night. Why? We've been determined to keep it a secret."

"In my mind, I've gone over and over the events before that dress got left on the tracks. I remember telling Jade how well the railroad would do and how odd she reacted— well, odder than usual, so odd, she left to search for some- thing she inevitably needed my help to reach."

Marcus remembered their intimate interlude in that storeroom as well. He rose to pace again. "Suppose I tell Jade that the railroad's up and running again and what's supposed to take place tomorrow night. She'll be the only one who knows, other than us and the workers. I'll go to the site and keep a look out to see if she shows up."

"It's a good idea. But, Marc, consider. What are you going to do, if you're right?"

"If Jade's the person responsible for the construction accidents, then she must have a good reason for it."

"You're joking?"

"We have to help her. That's why I invited you to come here."

"I thought you invited me because of your foolish guilt over my accident. When are you going to get over it, Marc?"

"When you get over pretending the accident didn't happen."

"I can hardly forget that my legs don't work."

"But you're excellent at pretending life is wonderful."

Garrett scowled. "So you invited me to help Jade and to the devil with the railroad?"

Marcus squeezed Garrett's shoulder. "I need you, Garr, and I truly believe helping her will help us."

Garrett sighed, reached up, and squeezed Marcus's hand. "Explain what you need me to do."

Marcus ran a hand through his hair and swallowed the welling of emotion choking him—his love for Garrett and his remorse over his condition combined suddenly with a new and irrational fear for Jade. He cleared his throat. "Jade doesn't prevaricate well. She rarely has to; she's honestly sincere and trusting. But when I mention the railroad, no matter how she tries to hide her fear—which is driving me crazy—she can't."

"Given all that, what's my next step, oh master sleuth?"

"Mock me if you will, but your job is important. I want you to learn everything about Jade and her grandmother that you can. I wanted you here because Jade's downtrodden women will be more comfortable with a man who's safe."

"Ouch, damn it!"

"Because you're confined to a wheelchair, for heaven's sake. You saw the way Abigail trembled earlier. Most of Jade's charges are used to savages who beat them and throw them down stairs. They'll *assume* you're incapable of over-coming them—with brutality, I mean—because you seem weaker than they are. You're sure to inspire any number of feminine instincts. They'll want to give you their attention, protect you, see that you're comfortable, listen to you, talk to you. They'll want to give you *whatever* you need."

"Oh?"

"I threw that in to cheer you up."

Garrett tempered his frown with a near smile. "Thank you for explaining."

"I intended no insult."

"I'm less piqued, given your logic."

Marcus thought it a healthy sign that appearing weak disturbed Garrett, which might make him want to fight his way out of that wheelchair. Marcus believed that having a reason to overcome his physical impairment would matter to Garrett in the end. "I also have a good idea of how to in-troduce you to everyone tomorrow that will get you as easily accepted by the children as the women."

"Fine, tell me what you already know about Jade and her family and then tell me how you're planning to introduce me."

"Fine, start by telling me what's supposed to happen with the railroad tomorrow night. Did you bring a copy of Jade's land option, by the way?"

Having crawled into bed at two, Marcus disliked being

awakened at three by a pounding on his door. However, when he opened it to find Jade sleep-mussed and inviting in a ruffle-necked nightshift and robe, his body woke with a vengeance.

"Eloisa has childbed fever," she said, clearly distressed. "Beecher is with her, but the babies are screaming and Garrett and Abigail need help. I . . . I can't face this without you."

Marcus had already tied his dressing gown and grabbed his slippers. "Let's go."

It wasn't long before they were told by Beecher that Eloisa should recover in a day or two, though Jade continued to worry. "She's in good hands," she told Marcus, to reassure herself, as they approached Garrett's room. "Beecher's an excellent doctor."

Marcus's brother didn't look quite so dangerous sitting in bed, his hair at odd angles, and trying, uselessly, to calm two screaming babies. The grateful look he bestowed on them, when he spotted them, humanized him further.

"Where's Abby?" Jade shouted over the babies' screams.

"Finding bottles and preparing pap. I hope."

"I'll go help her."

"No!" the brothers shouted in unison, but nothing of her lingered except her honeyed scent.

Marcus swept the bedroom-turned-nursery with a skeptical eye. "Honest, Garr, if anyone ever told me I'd find you playing nursemaid, I'd snuff their lights."

"I'll snuff your lights, if you don't pick up one of these howlers and try to quiet him."

"Which one's ours?"

"We are *not* keeping one!"

Marcus chuckled at Garrett's measure of stress. "Which is the one named after me?" Marcus shouted above the din.

"The one Jade and I will care for tonight? You know," he said when Garrett just stared at him, brows furrowed. "Little Garrett will be yours and Abby's to tend, and Little Marcus will be ours. Doesn't that make sense?"

"We're not playing bloody house, you know, and I can't bloody well tell them apart!"

Jade breezed in and plugged one tiny mouth with a bottle, Abby, the other.

Silence.

Marcus and Garrett released their collective breaths.

"I met Abby on her way back. You two were screaming so loud, the whole bloody house must have heard." She raised a brow at Garrett and he had the sense to squirm.

Marcus hid his smile.

Jade examined the babies' faces. "That one's Garrett, so this one's Marcus." She lifted Marcus in her arms. "I think we should call him Mac."

Abby unplugged Garrett's bottle long enough to pick him up. "We'll call this one Garth."

"Perfect nicknames for the hatchlings. What do you think, Garr?"

"I think you've all run off your tracks. Shouldn't we ask Eloisa?"

"She'll agree," Abby said. "It'll be easier than designating which Marcus and Garrett we're talking about."

Garrett conceded with a half-shrug. "Jade, how do you tell them apart?"

"Garth has a small notch at the top of his right ear. I noticed that when you handed him to me, Abby. And later I noticed that Mac has the same notch on the opposite ear."

"You're brilliant," Marcus said, thinking that the two of them caring for Mac would be difficult enough, never mind with Garrett and Abigail looking on.

The babies finished eating and burped like a couple of Saturday-night sots, before they finally became content. Marcus thought Jade, all tousled from sleep, with Mac on her shoulder, the most beautiful sight he'd ever beheld.

He covered her hand on Mac's back. "What do you say to moving to the room we used yesterday. It's crowded in here with four adults and two babies. Separating will give us all more space, and a bed in each room might allow for at least one member of each team to catch a bit of sleep before the night passes."

With the approval of everyone concerned, Marcus collected supplies enough for a month, and he and Jade bid Abigail and Garrett goodnight.

In the vacant bedroom, Jade set Mac on the bed.

"Let's unwrap him to make certain he's got enough fingers and toes to go around," Marcus said. "I would have liked to do that earlier, and I wanted you to see his tiny feet."

Jade unwrapped the mite, her face a study in wonder. "He's perfect. Oh and you're right; his feet are precious tiny." Jade bent down to kiss the tips of five tiny little toes. "Uh, Marcus, he doesn't smell very good all of a sudden."

"Oh, I never considered that. Change him?"

"You change him. He's named after you."

"But you've done it before? Please say yes."

At her negative shrug, he sighed. "Guess we'll learn together, then." He untied the nappy and stepped away.

"Praise be, it's not as bad as I thought," Jade said.

"Looks bad to me," Marcus said, observing from a distance. "Smells bad too."

Jade grinned and washed the baby's bottom and got him all dry and sweet-smelling again, without Marcus's help, praise be. "You're such a man," she told him when she finished.

"That's why you love me?"

"Hah! But men do come in handy at times, like now."

"Oh?" He came closer and tested the mattress, remembering how she'd felt in his arms in this very bed, wishing he'd not been so lightheaded at the time.

"That's not what I meant."

"Oh. How else can I be of service, though I must warn you that my best skill—"

"Kindly name Mac's boy parts for me."

Wide awake after being washed, Mac lay there barebottomed and kicking in joyful freedom.

"You're joking."

"I'm not. My grandmother raised me. I had no brothers. I never saw a male human being naked, before Mac here. My male education consisted of observing stallions, and I'm sorry to say that Mac doesn't seem of stallion quality to me."

"Hey, give the boy a chance." Marcus lifted Mac in his arms as if to protect him from her. "He has to grow some. He'll get there. Don't go insulting his manhood his second day on earth." He turned his back on Jade and kissed Mac's little head. When the baby shivered, Marcus tucked him beneath his dressing gown and walked away, cuddling him close. "Don't you worry about her. You'll be stallion quality and chasing pert-tailed fillies before you know it."

To his champion, Mac awarded his highest honor. He piddled on him.

An hour later Marcus walked the screaming baby in nothing but his dressing gown, his nightshirt having been discarded due to rain.

Jade was in love, but determined to get over it.

She lay on the bed, as Marcus insisted, but couldn't sleep. She watched him croon and cuddle that baby boy.

She saw him wince when a tiny fist caught a handful of his chest-hair, but when he lifted the tiny fist away, he kissed it.

Jade fell deeper.

She smiled at his outrage when she'd maligned Mac's manhood, however unintentionally. He never had named those parts, drat him, but if his dressing gown came any farther apart as he paced, she might get a view to ponder.

"I have an idea," he said, turning toward her, and catching the direction of her gaze. "Damn it, wouldn't you know we'd have a baby with us when you're that interested."

Jade felt warm. Very warm. She didn't say a word. She couldn't.

Marcus sat on the edge of the bed. "You are interested, aren't you? That *is* lust in your eyes?"

"It's curiosity. You didn't name his parts."

"You want me to name mine?"

"No . . . . What's your idea?"

"Lay back."

"I said no."

"What do you take me for? This is an innocent baby, though after tonight, he's probably going to worry his whole life about the size of his . . . Do lie down, will you?"

To Jade's surprise, Marcus put the crying baby, face-down on her stomach, his little head nestled between her breasts. She put her arms around the little ball Mac made of himself and he quieted instantly.

Marcus covered them both up to Mac's tiny ears. "This is only his first night away from Eloisa, and from his twin, as well. I thought he might miss that place he's been for all these months, with Eloisa's heartbeat so close."

Jade relaxed. It felt good having Mac near her heart, but he made her yearn to carry a child of her own. She regarded Marcus watching over them, and thought, "*his* child," but she pushed the daft notion ruthlessly away. "Now you can lie down too," she told him.

He shook his head and pulled the rocker over. "I'll just sit and keep watch to make sure he doesn't slip off, or you don't roll over."

When Marcus sat, he spent a minute fighting with his dressing gown to keep all his man parts covered. After he succeeded, he caught her watching him and grinned. "All you have to do is ask . . ."

By mid-morning the following day, Eloisa's fever broke and by noon she felt well enough to have the babies back in her room. Beecher, pleased with her progress, gave everyone the news.

Marcus thought his brother and Abigail looked as if they'd had a difficult night with little Garth. It seemed Jade, who hadn't let go of baby Mac the entire three hours they slept, was the only adult who rested.

Sitting in her study waiting for her, Marcus grinned, remembering the big wet spot on her dressing gown as she made her way upstairs to wash and dress.

It had been his original intention to feed her the railroad information the first thing this morning, but frankly, the more he thought about it, the less he wanted to ruin the rest of her day. He decided he'd take her for a walk while everyone else went to tea and tell her then.

He heard her step outside the door as he studied her ledgers. "Good afternoon," he said, appreciating her in a robe-dress, green and bright as a sunlit sea. "You look splendid, as if you're dressed for a special occasion."

"Today is special. You said you wanted to introduce Garrett and show the babies off at tea."

"I do. And now we can show you off too."

Jade came around behind him to regard his figures. "I think having babies in the house is making me feel feminine," she said.

He rose from his chair and knuckled the bow at her bodice. "Maybe that's what comes of having a babe against your breast."

She colored and stepped back. "Abby said Garrett was amazing with little Garth last night."

Marcus respected her change of subject. "Garrett was?"

"According to Abby. Does he have experience?"

Marcus shook his head. "Beyond the occasional emergency delivery, and holding namesakes, no, not that I know of. How was Garr amazing?"

"She said he took complete charge but asked her to stay in case he needed legs. When I first went in, after Beecher gave us the news, I . . . ah . . . found him and Abby in bed together. They were facing each other talking, the baby sound asleep between them. Garrett said he got piddled on twice last night."

Marcus barked a laugh. "He squirted Garr? Lord, I love that boy."

How alike Garrett and Marcus were, except that Garrett lacked the half-smile-eye-twinkle thing that made Marcus such a charmer, making Garrett appear stern and serious in comparison. Garrett's lips weren't as perfectly sculpted, either.

Jade had fallen asleep last night tracing Marcus's lips with her gaze, wishing he'd been close enough for her to meet them with her lips.

"Aren't you pleased?" Marcus asked.

Jade realized she'd not been attending. "I'm sorry. What did you say?"

"This," Marcus said, tapping the paper in his hand and frowning in puzzlement. "The receipt from the South Downs Railroad for the land option." He held it out to her.

"Oh thank God. Now I'll know how much I can't find."

"Honestly, Jade, that's a frightening statement. Do you know how much money you should have, in addition to the land option amount?"

"Neil Kirby stole my money *and* my records. I kept trying to warn my grandmother, but I think she was just too sick to understand. By the time I inherited the estate and discharged him, my finances were a confused jumble."

"You know, you could apply to your banker in London for the transactions that have taken place against your account for however far back you'd like."

"I didn't know that. I'd really like to see those transactions, especially for the year *before* my grandmother hired Kirby. But how do I go about asking for them? What do I say?"

"Give me the name and address of your banker and I'll draft the letter. Then you can copy it in your own hand and sign it. We can dispatch a messenger this morning. Now that you know you received a thousand pounds for the option, you'll want to see when, or if, it was deposited."

"I love it when you talk business," she said.

Marcus stilled, alert, ready. "Jade Smithfield, are you flirting with me? Because I'm trying to be a good employee here."

"I'm sorry. Where did you say you found the paper from the railroad?"

"You were right. I didn't look hard enough the other day."

She pressed her lips to his, silk and fire, quick and wondrous, bringing instant and hard arousal. "That was a celebratory kiss," she said. "Thank you for finding—"

Marcus's body thrummed. Heat pulsed through him, settling heavy in his loins. "Did you suspend the business-only rules?"

"Only for a minute."

"The minute's not up." He pulled her into his arms, closed his mouth over hers and settled her body against the steel of his.

Nine

Marcus stood beside Garrett's chair outside the ballroom as they waited for Ivy's puppet-show to finish, so he could bring Garrett in while all the women and children were present, and introduce him to everyone at once.

The entire household rarely gathered in the same place at the same time, except during a puppet show. To draw the children, Garrett held a baby in the crook of each arm.

"You'd think Ivy would be done by now," Marcus said, less than patient.

Garrett chuckled. "Lick your paw, grumble-bear, and get it over with. Abby told me that she walked in on you and Jade and what she found."

"One kiss. One kiss in two days and we get interrupted."

Ivy gave the signal and Marcus pushed Garrett in.

The room hushed, much as it had done the first time Marcus entered. Some of the women had seen Garrett arrive, but several had not, and the children didn't know him at all. The striking absence of fear marked the difference from his own first day, Marcus noted. He'd like to think his attempt to ease their fears had something to do with it.

Jade introduced Garrett and the babies.

Marcus pushed Garrett's chair into the center of everyone and the babies drew them toward Garrett.

Marcus grabbed Jade's hand. "We're going for a walk," he told Abby. "Garrett's yours."

"Mucks?"

Marcus stopped. "Emmy-bug."

Jade chuckled at his chagrin. Then Emily raised her arms

111

and he picked her up, his look turning to love as he hugged her. "I missed you Emmy-bug."

She put her arms around his neck and lay her head on his shoulder and they both sighed in contentment.

Jade's throat tightened and she lost another piece of her heart.

He loved Emmy. He loved Mac. He certainly kissed and touched her as if . . . *Foolish woman. What is the matter with you?*

Besotted, that's what. Addled. Still reeling from the kiss that Abigail interrupted. She should be thanking her maker, Jade knew. Honestly, she might have lain right down on the carpet with Marcus, otherwise. He turned her inside out with needs and yearnings for things like babies, him as their father, Garrett as their uncle. A real life. A family.

She knew better. She did.

Her future consisted of promises to keep and people and secrets to protect. The downtrodden women she helped were her family. Their babies were the only babies she would ever hold to her breast.

God help her, when had she lost the ability to be satisfied with that?

Two hours later, with Emmy down for her nap, Jade followed Marcus, a hand firmly in his. He carried a basket in one hand, and a blanket under his arm.

"What are you hurrying to?" Jade asked, practically running beside him.

"Peace, quiet, and a minute alone—no business, babies, toddlers, brothers, ladies, or retainers to separate us."

Jade laughed, allowing herself to feel lighthearted and carefree for the moment.

At the undercliff—the sea grass beneath the cliff that edged the part of her property arrowing toward the English

Channel—Marcus dropped the basket and blanket and took her in his arms.

"A perfect beginning to a picnic," she said.

"First, we have the rest of a minute to make up for," he said, kissing her for longer than half a minute, but she didn't mind.

He stepped back with a grin. "Better. I feel better. You?"

"I do, actually," she said as she opened the blanket to spread it on the coarse grass. "Much better. And hungry."

The breeze light, the smell of the sea, fresh and invigorating, Marcus stood transfixed. "I can't decide what I want more, you or food."

Jade waved a chicken leg under his nose, perversely hoping not to tempt him. "Nobody makes picnic chicken like Winkin."

Marcus caught her off guard when he grasped her arm to pull her down and roll her beneath him. He licked her chicken-flavored fingers.

Her eyes widened.

His body swelled and hardened against her leg.

He threw the chicken back in the basket, then he tasted her mouth and she tasted his. Better than food. Or air. Or water.

The meal forgotten, they remained as close as two people could and feasted on each other. The best picnic in her memory.

"Last night, I sat in that chair on fire for you the whole time I watched you sleep," he said, his breath in her ear warming her to the farthest reaches of her body.

"Before that, when you walked Mac," she admitted, testing the texture of his ear with her lips. "I wanted to pull you down beside me on the bed."

"You wanted to open my dressing gown."

She slid her hands along his neck, to his nape, her fingers combing his hair. "Of course not! I wanted it to fall open." She swallowed his chuckle with her kiss. "I would never have the courage to open it."

"What about now?" He placed her hand against the buttons on his trousers, but her fingers fluttered up to his waistcoat, instead.

"I still don't." She buried her face in his neck. "Sorry."

Marcus groaned and pulled her closer, dying for her touch. "Tell me what you have the courage for, Jade, because I'll give you whatever you need, or take whatever you're willing to give."

"I want your weight on me."

His heart clenched and his boy parts stood at firm attention. Marcus positioned himself full atop her, unable to believe she'd asked. He kept his weight on his hands at either side of her head, more than ready to adore her in truth, however she would allow, for however long.

For eternity, if possible.

"Now kiss me," she said.

He traced her lips with his tongue, until she opened to him and he tasted her. Honey, pure and sweet. A nectar to sustain him beyond mere food.

They moved together to accommodate each other. She made a cradle for his need and he filled the void with his arousal. Like coming home. Jade moved beneath him, stroking him, firing his raging need, making him so ready, pleasure and pain grew and threatened to wreak havoc at one and the same time.

He lowered his weight, skimmed her side, learned and loved her body, his hand coming to rest by her breast, wanting, but not daring. He loved her to distraction, but had never bedded her, never cupped or kissed a full, lush

114

breast, so much her victim, it was laughable.

She moaned and arched. "Touch me there again, Marcus. Really touch me."

His body rose hard and fast like a randy stripling. Marcus feared he'd lose control.

She continued to caress him with her seeking body, her movements as painful and sweet as torture. "Touch me everywhere," she said.

Marcus stilled. "Do you mean that Jade? Can I touch you anywhere? Everywhere?"

Her eyes widened, as if his question had just now reached the functioning portion of her brain, and she faltered for a moment, likely realizing the enormity of her request, and his response, then she looked straight at him. "Yes. Please."

Jade felt Marcus's heart beat a new and rapid staccato as he lay beside her and settled her facing him. She thrilled to the look in his smoldering eyes, and saw purpose, hot and heady, reflected there. Despite giving him her blessing, the scene, so near her midnight fantasies, caused a spiraling at her center, carrying a warning she ignored as quick as she perceived it.

He took down her hair to lay it across them and filled his palm with a breast, finally, kneading and nuzzling, then he gave the same attention to the other.

He reached behind her to begin an undulating motion at the base of her spine.

Jade sighed in contentment, felt the ridge of his stallion-ready man-part rutting against her thigh and smiled. He widened the motion of his soothing hand as he worked it up her back, then down to her bottom.

The sea beckoned, the sky, the earth, primitive and pure. A gull screeched in the distance.

She reached over to undo his neck-cloth, his waistcoat and shirt buttons. Then she allowed herself the ultimate luxury of placing the flat of her hand against his chest, weaving her fingers into the silken mat of dark hair covering it.

His breath caught in his throat at her touch and his eyes closed. She parted her lips and with a groan, he fitted his mouth to the invitation of hers, slanting first this way, and then that, as if he couldn't get enough. This she understood.

His clever hand continued its soothing foray along her back and bottom with more and more purpose, pulling her closer and tighter against him—into him, if she had her way—and she molded herself seamlessly, soft to hard, concave to convex.

She kissed that dimple in his chin, testing its depth with her tongue. With kisses, she explored his face, nibbling to his cheek, his ear, his neck.

Marcus groaned a suffering sound, grasped her chin and plundered her mouth. Jade reveled in the response she had elicited and met him, thrust for thrust, tongue and body alike, until she needed him as much as she needed air.

She laid her head on his arm and closed her eyes, gasping for breath.

Touching his forehead to hers, he did the same.

His hand at her back progressed from tentative, to sure, to greedy, in the way he cupped her bottom and touched nearer her center. A range of emotions crossed his features, among them an ardor so wild, a pride at her power filled Jade. She touched a button at her bodice and loved that his eyes flared.

She unbuttoned her bodice, slowly, watching his face, feeling his response, as she moved the silken fabric aside.

Almost in reverence, he dipped his head to accept her offering.

The feel of his hand on her breast released her, as if from captivity, and allowed her to flow with the pleasure he drew from deep inside her. When his mouth lowered and opened over the budded nubbin, a roiling heat purled through her, sharp and wild.

She did not expect him to take suckle, but found herself as wildly shocked as she was greedy for his mouth. Arching for his greater access, Jade moaned and cried his name, and Marcus increased the pressure of his lips on her nipple.

In the farthest reaches of her awareness, he skimmed her legs under her gown, and along her inner thigh, his hand coming to rest at her core, only her drawers between his hand and her center.

Despite her tremor at the intimacy, she ached for more, but hesitation held her captive. When he parted her drawers and found her, she gasped, her whimper as much in desire as protest.

"Jade, Sweetheart, I just want to touch you," he said against her lips, bringing her deeper under his spell.

She faltered and he pressed his palm against her throbbing core, her body no longer hers to command, but his.

"I want to give you pleasure. Nothing more."

She touched his face. "What about your pleasure?"

"Let me love you like this and I'll be satisfied."

Jade moved her legs to give him better access, afraid she was giving him so much more.

When he touched her, he found her slick and wet and embarrassed. "I knew you'd be ready for me. Warm and ready. Oh, God, Jade, you have no idea what you do to me."

"If . . . it's anything like . . . you do to me, you . . ." She couldn't speak any longer; she could only feel.

He played her like a fine instrument, raising her higher toward perfection, but never quite allowing her to reach it before he lowered her to rest. Then he raised her up again, plying her with kisses, stopping to suckle, enhancing his mastery.

At a point where she thought she must beg him to stop or die, the crescendo built to a point almost beyond bearing and she lost herself in pleasure.

Marcus sustained her climax until he feared she'd swoon, his body nearer the edge than he'd ever been, man or boy, when not buried in a feminine sheath.

This woman possessed his heart, perhaps even his soul, but he never imagined the power her first release would have on him, on his body. Pride mixed with a love that encompassed him, held him in thrall and he was powerless against it.

When Jade arched and spun away, soaring up and over the world, Marcus rose with her and damn-near spilled his seed. Holding steady to his control, he encouraged Jade to float among the clouds before she drifted back to earth and the surety of his arms around her.

He reveled in his love's capacity for pleasure, in her acceptance of her own sensual nature, in the expressions on her face—surprise, shock, wonder, awe, and finally a blissful contentment.

He kissed the beads of moisture on her brow, her eyelids, her parted lips, grateful she trusted him to teach her the magic within her, rueful that his body had nearly betrayed him, as if she were more in control of it than he.

He lowered her gown, admiring her long, coltish legs. "Sleep for a bit," he whispered. "I'll watch over you."

Aroused still, Marcus lay back, pulling Jade against him,

amazed that the focus of his desire had changed from a need to receive . . . to a need to give.

Only Jade, no other, could inspire the like.

He held her close, loving the feel of her sleeping, content as a kitten in his arms. He dozed for a time as well, the respite welcome and sweet, until she shivered, and he felt the bite of the wind and saw the dark of the sky.

He'd not told her about the railroad, his original purpose for coming—or not coming, as the case may be. He wouldn't tell her now, except for the fact that he believed she needed his help in some mysterious way.

Sorry to spoil their afternoon, he had to do it. He plucked a blade of grass to tease her lips, then her nose, until she swatted it away and snuggled close. "It's past dinnertime, slug-a-bed."

"Hmnthngry."

Marcus chuckled and freed her nose from his shirt. "Care to repeat that?"

"I'm not hungry!"

He laughed outright. "Surly, are you? After naps? Or simply after sex?"

That snapped her eyes open and set her spine straight. "We didn't." She examined his open shirt, and hers, then checked to see if his esteemed boy part was still neatly tucked away, and she sagged with relief. "We didn't."

"Ah, my lusty love, but *you* did. Don't you remember?"

She squealed and buried her warm face against his bare chest again, and his much neglected boy part took note.

"Don't be discomfited," he whispered, stroking her hair, kissing it. "Do say, however, that I pleased you."

Another squeal.

A long silence.

"Chicken leg?" he asked. "Or ham and veal pie?"

She shifted tentatively then sat up and arranged her skirts modestly about her before she accepted a piece of chicken.

Marcus chose a slice of cold meat pie. "Garrett heard some talk back home the other morning," he said. "Something you should be interested in. Deviled egg?"

Jade took an egg and nibbled it. "Why would I be interested?"

"Because it has to do with the railroad. Do you prefer cider or stout?"

"I'm not interested in the railroad." She took the pewter tankard of stout he held poised against his lips, and drank it down.

Marcus raised his brows and waited for a reaction to set it, but nothing happened. He grinned. "You're going to be rich because of that land option you sold. Maybe you didn't intend to sell, but the income from it could support your Benevolent Society for years."

"I never thought of that."

For dessert, he handed her a Dundee cake topped with burnt cream.

She examined it as if she couldn't identify it.

"The rails are repaired and the train's running again after that accident the other night."

"That's good," she said, looking up at him, digesting his words, and, he imagined, fidgeting inside to undo the repair.

"An important shipment of lumber is expected to arrive tonight. After they finish the bridge over the River Ouse, if all goes well, they're no more than a month away from laying the rails on your property."

"It's getting chilly," she said, shivering, "don't you think. Perhaps we should go back to the house?"

"We could move into that cave for a while to sit and watch the sea," Marcus suggested.

"No!"

She caught his surprise at her tone. "I mean, no, I . . . want to go back to the house."

"Don't you think we should talk about what happened first?"

"Please, give me a chance to get used to it. It was so . . . so . . .".

"Splendid?"

"New. I never—"

He sat closer and pulled her into his arms. "I know you never, and I'm pleased to have given you your first pleasure, proud to have introduced you to the wonder of loving." He kissed her until she kissed him back.

"Oh, Marcus," she wailed pulling away. "What are you doing to me?" Her words were more a cry of frustration than love, or lust, and that troubled Marcus more than he could express.

He held her face between his hands. "Jade, Sweetheart, what's wrong? Let me help you."

She knocked his arms aside and stood. "Nothing's wrong. Everything is. You've done all you can, and I don't mean by betraying me with my own body. I despise you Marcus Fitzalan. I really do."

And she was gone, running fleet as a startled doe.

Marcus watched her go, struck by her accusation. For a minute he worried he'd taken advantage, until he remembered what she said. *I want your weight. Touch me everywhere.*

Tell me what you want, he'd said. If her reply had been, "let me go," he would have. She knew that. She knew he'd give her whatever she wanted, pleasure or freedom. If she were in temporary shock, she would recover, but she'd seemed remorseful, which about broke him.

He started cleaning away their dinner, setting plates and napkins in the basket, tossing her untouched dessert to the birds. He shook the blanket and folded it, then he tossed it down and walked to the water's edge.

There, he cupped his hands at his mouth and shouted as loud as he could above the churning sea. "Jade Smithfield I adore you!" Then he let his hands fall to his sides and hated himself, because, though he did adore her, he planned to follow her tonight to discover whether she had been the one committing crimes against the railroad.

If she had, he bloody well needed to know, and why, then he must find a way to stop her.

Marcus cursed and turned to see Jade standing high on the cliff under which they'd loved, watching him, seafoam skirts flapping about her legs, sable hair in stormy disarray. The wild scandal who owned his heart, bearing so many secrets she was bending under the weight of their burden.

He wondered if she heard his sea-tossed declaration.

"I adore you," he shouted again, certain she couldn't hear him from there, but he needed to say it anyway.

And as if she heard, but didn't care, Jade turned and walked away.

Later that night, gazing out his bedroom window, Marcus instructed himself to put Jade's turmoil of the afternoon from his mind. She needed time to come to terms with her new feelings and emotions, and he needed to find out who was keeping the railroad from moving forward.

Because of Garr's condition, Marcus needed to save the railroad, and the family home. Not that he could make up in any way for crippling his brother, but the accident *he'd* caused made seeing to Garr's future his responsibility.

Marcus ran a hand through his hair. He'd best focus on the task at hand. Other concerns would still await his attention afterward.

Searching for the best location from which to watch for anyone leaving the house, Marcus discovered that from the cliff, he could see the house without obstruction, and anyone heading toward Newhaven or the railroad construction site.

Given the fact that Jade had the same view from her bedroom window as he did from his, Marcus devised a clandestine route to the cliff so as not to be seen, especially by her. Once he mapped his route, he dressed in the dark old clothes he'd brought for a mission that once seemed exciting and now smacked of betrayal.

Be that as it may, he had no choice and left when he knew everyone would be at dinner.

Outside, he circumnavigated the house and property on his route to the jutting cliff, which also happened to be the highest point on the estate.

Evening had just turned full dark, and while he managed to depart before moonrise, he likely had a long wait. Once he arrived at his vantage point, a nightjar's cry purling and bubbling in the air, Marcus sat, knees raised, on the far side of a stone bench, a location not visible from his window.

Like a peeping tom, he looked for Jade's room, and like a lovesick pup, he watched her pass by her window as if pacing to the incessant, churning beat of the restless sea behind him.

Marcus wanted only to take away Jade's worries and keep her safe, except his stubborn siren would not allow it.

With her curtains open, the light in her room allowed him to see her in her dressing gown, unsashed and flowing

Annette Blair

behind her with each quick, agitated pass she made before her window. As she paced, she held something in one hand that she slapped against the palm of the other in a rhythm more agitated than the elements. A hairbrush, perhaps. A knife. A pistol?

Jittery, yes, but enough to carry a weapon? Enough to shoot blind, if she realized someone followed her? Was she aware of a danger that required some form of self-defense?

Bloody hell. He was so busy speculating, he nearly missed the figure dashing into the lane and heading away from the house and the railroad site, toward town.

Not that people weren't allowed to leave Peacehaven Manor, but this was the same man he'd seen slipping back into the house the night the stuffed dress got left on the tracks. His movements were too furtive to be forgotten, now or then. The man must be one of Jade's retainers, Dirk, Jack or Harry, he'd concluded after his first sighting, all long-time dependents, bar Dirk who'd been with Jade less than two years. A newcomer by Peacehaven standards, Dirk, therefore, bore watching. Whoever he was, he must have a woman friend in the village, perhaps even a married one.

Marcus imagined one of the old codgers with a wicked assignation and consigned this second sighting to the list of concerns in his mind, with a notation to research Dirk's past, just in case.

Looking up again, Marcus discovered that Jade had drawn her curtains. Now, only her shadow could be seen, and clearly.

She was undressing.

Ten

Marcus's mouth went dry, his boy part went on alert. For less than a blink, he saw the outline of Jade's nude body in silhouette, ripe and lush, and he lost his breath.

Perfect. An artist's inspiration. A lover's dream.

Everything about Jade Smithfield called to him, her laughter, her generosity of spirit, her fears, hopes, and dreams, even her temper. 'Twas mere serendipity, her nymph's body, yet seeing it outlined like this made him think of one thing, him buried hilt-deep inside her with her long splendid legs wrapped round him.

Bloody hell, she was pulling on breeches.

Marcus jumped up, realized the danger in revealing himself, and ducked back down. He had to get hold of himself. His wild emotions concerning Jade were like to get him in trouble—more important, he might endanger her.

He had expected her to leave the house tonight, so why did being proved right upset him? Lord he was in trouble.

No, damn it, *she* was in trouble.

That foolish woman needed protecting, and he'd watch over her, by damn, if she never spoke to him again as a result.

Oddly, his ability to protect her while he spied on her made him feel better about the whole sordid mess. Garrett would scoff, but who cared, as long as he got both jobs done.

Jade slipped on a coat and Marcus wondered which one she had pilfered this time.

Her curtains parted; the light in her room went out.

With the full of the moon, he ducked his head, taking no chances.

Gazing out, into the shadows, Jade remained at her window.

Marcus's legs cramped, so he stretched out behind the bench to wait her out.

He smacked his head against the bench, waking himself. Judging by the position of the moon, more than an hour had passed. Rubbing his temple, he swore in silence as he regarded Jade's window.

Blast and double blast; he'd missed her departure.

He raced in the direction she must have taken, but caught her coming from the shore, instead. Had she passed him as he slept? He dove for cover, face down in thorny barbs and horse manure. The gardeners had fertilized the rose bushes. Wonderful.

Marcus wiped his face with a hand, but stopped breathing as Jade walked by, no more than a foot away.

Keeping her ahead of him, he hid behind trees along the route as he followed in her wake.

He felt like an idiot.

He smelled like a stable.

It started to rain.

God she looked great in breeches.

When she entered open land, Marcus scurried head-down, along the far side of the unmortared stone wall enclosing the field, often moving farther away from her, rather than nearer, but keeping her in his sight. Just as she entered the beech wood, he turned his ankle in a foxhole, cursed and hobbled on.

In the woods, which opened to the construction site, having trees for cover afforded Marcus a short-lived degree of comfort.

A man, short and robust—not someone he'd seen among Jade's retainers—walked suddenly ahead of him trailing Jade, detour for detour. When Marcus spotted the intruder's pistol raised at the ready, his instincts went on full alert.

Garrett never mentioned hiring a watchman. Even so, a watchman would wield his weapon only if and when he saw proof of intent to destroy property, or worse.

Distracted of a sudden, Marcus realized that someone trailed him almost at the same instant the first man cocked and aimed his pistol at Jade. Racing forward, Marcus knocked the pistol from the man's hand from behind and kicked it away. Wrestling the gunman to the ground, Marcus got gut-punched, doubled over, and sent to his knees.

The gunman ran.

Marcus gave chase before catching his breath.

The bastard might be short, but he moved like a jackrabbit.

When Marcus saw Peacehaven Manor rear up mid-pursuit, he realized he might have kept Jade from getting shot, but he'd left her no protection from the man who had been trailing him.

Go forward? Back?

His hesitation got him knocked to the ground by a moving object. "Beecher!"

The retainer stood, hands on knees, panting. "He was gonna' shoot her!"

"Ever see him before?"

"Never."

"Someone was following me," Marcus said.

Beecher nodded. "Me. I'll go back and keep Jade safe."

Marcus released a relieved breath. "Thank God. I'll go after the shooter."

Annette Blair

Pursuing the gunman all the way into the twittens, New-haven's narrow twisting lanes, Marcus ran aground amid a gaggle of half-crown street strumpets on rampage, and lost his quarry to the brewery and shipbuilding yards beyond. Once free of the demireps—no easy task—filthy and reeking, he returned, miles and hours later, to the deserted railroad site, as empty as the lumber cars beside the unfinished railroad bridge over the River Ouse.

Marcus could hardly believe his eyes. He'd seen the fully-laden flatcars only hours before!

How the hell could one woman hide two railroad cars full of lumber by herself?

If Jade did, indeed, do it . . . he was no longer sure of that, or much of anything else.

A devil named panic nipping at his tail, Marcus ran back to Peacehaven through the pouring rain, half the time worried sick, the other half, prepared, *nay,* determined, to trounce Jade for scaring him witless.

Once there, he made straight for her room and threw open her door.

They both gasped in shock.

"Hell of a time for a bath!" Marcus said, taking in the view.

"Hell of a time for you to come calling, if you ask me," Jade said. "Where have you been? You're soaked through."

"Chasing the man who followed you out there tonight with a pistol in his hand."

Jade lifted a handful of water to rinse her face and hide her reaction. "I don't know what you're talking about. Give me a towel, will you?"

"If you didn't know, you wouldn't be so calm."

She dried her face slowly, to calm herself, and squeaked

128

when she finished and saw he'd stripped to a pair of underbreeches more form-fitting than her drawers. Shockingly form-fitting. "What are you doing?" she asked.

Marcus stepped into her tub. "At least I got a reaction out of you," he said. "You owe me a bath. I ended up on my face in horseshit, turned my ankle, fought an armed man, and got attacked by prostitutes, all to keep you safe. And where were you? Stealing a lumber shipment is my guess."

"Prostitutes?"

"Yes," Marcus sighed. "A tiresome business, but I had to let them all use me, before they would let me go. I left them all deliriously happy and sated. You don't know what you're missing."

Jade shook her head. She wanted to ask why he'd followed her, but that would be admitting too much. None of it mattered, anyway. Because she couldn't take her gaze from the sight of his muscled torso, his wide shoulders, everything, naked, as he stood in her bathtub, hands on hips, a scowl on his face, daring her to give him the argument he craved.

"Well," he said. "Are you getting out, or am I joining you?" He dangled her dressing gown just out of reach.

Jade released her breath, too tired to muster up a fight. "I'll take the dressing gown."

He held it open in front of him for her to slip into. "Stand up and turn around, I'll help."

"You're crazy."

"Maybe. I'm also cold, sore, tired and out of patience. Do it my way and I'll see and do nothing. You're way, I'll get a good look, at the least, before you're decently covered. Either way sounds fine to me. Your choice."

"Close your eyes." She didn't believe for a minute that

he would, so she stood quickly and allowed him to slip her dressing gown around her and she slipped her arms in the sleeves and tied the sash.

He smoothed the silk along her shoulders and kissed the back of her neck, then he slid his wicked hands down her back and around her waist. They stopped their foray, finally, but too soon, just below her breasts, remaining, almost unfortunately, above her dressing gown.

Denying her longing for him to touch her, skin to skin, Jade stepped from the tub before she weakened and issued a command for him to fulfill her desire.

Marcus slid down into the hot water, heaving a great sigh.

Determined not to look at him, Jade turned her back to knot her sash and pick up her brush. Then, the only garment he'd been wearing a minute before hit the wall beside her with a splash.

"Much better," he said. "Hand me the soap, will you?"

"You're a devil, Marcus Fitzalan." She turned on him, curiosity making her wish she could soap him from head to foot, herself. She threw the soap that had been within reach all along, smacking the water hard. Taking satisfaction from his grunt of surprise, she wrenched open her door, certain if she didn't leave, her weak resolve would crumble.

"Where are you going?"

"To get you some dry clothes. It'll be dawn in a couple of hours and I don't want you parading around the house naked, if you don't mind."

"You sure know how to spoil a man's fun."

Jade shut her door on his chuckle, wishing she could have slammed it, annoyed all the way down the stairs. As she gathered his clothes, she tried to stay irritated, but she couldn't get the sight of him standing above her, nearly naked, from her mind. She shuddered remembering how tempted she'd been to call his bluff.

In a way, it was a good thing that he'd come to see her. She hadn't been certain how to face him in the morning. He'd taken away that worry, at least.

After Beecher got over his fury at her for venturing to the railroad site alone in the middle of the night, he'd told her that Marcus followed her and risked his life to keep her from being shot. Then Beecher helped her dispose of the lumber.

Again, a few minutes before Marcus arrived, Beecher came to her rescue when he told her, as she paced her room, sick with worry, that he'd spotted Marcus from the turret window, limping, but looking none the worse for his stint as a knight in shining armor.

Yes, she'd worried about the man with the pistol and his reason for aiming it her way. But she'd worried about Marcus more.

She had just climbed into the tub after learning Marcus was safe, when he'd been so bold as to invade her bath.

Clean clothes gathered—including a pair of underbreeches she examined with a smile by sliding her hand through the slit at the front—Jade went back to her room, exhilarated at the prospect of sparring with her nemesis.

Perhaps she'd stay near the door and make him come and take his clothes from her hand, so he'd have to step from the tub and she could finally see . . . everything.

But her fantasy was not to be, because he lay in her bed fast asleep, his man parts completely covered by her blanket, drat him. On his side, facing the center of her bed, one knee bent, he slept as if he'd left a place just for her.

Bruises had formed on his jaw, under his eye. Another

on his chest. Almost feeling his pain, she made a sound, and he opened his eyes. "God, Scandal, I'm so bloody tired. Give me a chance to rest, will you, before you throw me out." He stroked the space beside him. "You must be as tired as me after hauling all that lumber. Come, let me hold you while we sleep. Just for an hour or so."

He'd followed her; that made her furious.

He'd risked his life for her by grappling with a gunman; that made her knees weak. She threw off her dressing gown and lay beside him.

Marcus pulled her close, threw a leg, an arm, and the blanket over her and went to sleep.

When her shock wore off and he snored softly against her hair, Jade's heart became soft and warm and content. She smiled, settled into his ready embrace, and closed her eyes.

Marcus woke with an erection and a hand full of breast.

Life was looking up.

One of Jade's legs nestled neatly between his, her face nuzzled his chest, her hand rested on his naked hip.

Some days started just plain perfect.

He nibbled her ear and she purred, arching against him like a veritable temptress. Morning-ready, the both of them, she remained in control, he discovered, as she pushed him off her and rose over him, her hair falling free on either side, shutting them away from the world.

"Do the rules remain the same?" she asked. "Have I still but to command and you will obey?"

His erection did a happy dance. "Have your wicked way with me, then . . . please."

With a lusty chuckle, she backed away and he almost wept, but then she knelt beside him and removed the blanket from the parts that interested her most.

"Glory, that's big!"

Every time Jade opened her mouth, Marcus fell deeper in love. "Stallion quality, right? And don't you *dare* say no."

She trilled a laugh, skimmed his length and circled his tip with a finger, raising him off the bed in a sizzling combination of sweet rapture and prickling surprise.

"You liked that?" She did it again.

Marcus released his breath and stopped her hand. "You're going to get more than you bargained for, if you keep that up."

"Like what? What will I get?"

He didn't know what to say, not sure how far the delightful mix of wicked siren and pure innocent's education went. To distract them both, he unbuttoned the bodice of her filmy nightgown and allowed her breasts the freedom he craved.

She watched his body's reaction with avid interest as he filled his hands with her bounty. Then she threw her head back and closed her eyes as he fondled her nipples, abrading and peaking them.

"The way you make me feel when you touch me," she said on a breathless whisper. "That's how you feel when I touch you, isn't it?"

He nodded and she fingered him again, closing her hand around him suddenly, instinct teaching her the age-old rhythm.

He rode the ecstasy of her ministrations until he could barely contain himself, then he urged her to lie beside him. "Let me touch you the way I did yesterday while you touch me like this."

She didn't say yes; she didn't say no. But her heavy-lidded, smoky eyes told him the notion aroused her as much as it did him.

To heighten and sustain her pleasure, Marcus stroked her legs from her ankles to her calf with the back of a hand, his touch as light and slow as a feather drifting on a warm breeze. The higher along her limbs climbed his caress, the deeper her breathy gasps stroked him.

When he slipped his hand between her legs, she adjusted herself to accommodate him, and he found her slick and warm, throbbing and ready.

"Kiss me," he whispered, trying to keep sane, to give her the most gratification possible while riding a fast-rising wave toward his own fulfillment.

She kissed him with greed, her tongue teasing and plundering.

Hot, untutored passion. Erotic. Mind-altering.

Keeping pace with each other, their rhythm quickened to escalating pleasure. When she gasped his name with the impact of her climax, he let himself go and pumped his seed into her hand—both of them shocked and amazed at the power of it.

He *knew* that burying himself in her tight sheath would be like nothing he'd ever experienced.

They kissed and floated, kissed some more, less frantic yet more so, desperate to milk every wild moment, to become closer than close.

He ached worse for her now. Hard again, already, he wanted inside her more than he wanted to breathe.

"There's more," Jade said. "I know there is. I want more."

A pounding at her door turned both their heads, stilled their hearts and their breathing.

"Jade? Jade, are you in there?" Lacey turned the doorknob as she called Jade's name.

Jade jumped from the bed, glorious in her nakedness,

and threw his sopping clothes into hands still warm from her body. "I'm coming, Lacey. Just a minute."

Jade pushed her dressing table aside and opened a door disguised as a wall. Grabbing his hand, she tugged him off the bed and shoved him through it, abandoning him on a landing in a dank, narrow, windowless stairwell.

"One flight down, this opens into your room," she said. "You'll have to force your wardrobe aside while you push your door open." She shut the door in his face.

Still trembling from sated exhaustion, Jade slipped into her dressing gown, and masked her frustration over the interruption before she allowed herself to open her door.

As Lacey stepped into her room, Jade noticed Marcus's clean clothes on her dresser. Lacey saw them too, and appeared to understand, only too well.

Because Lacey once knew and tasted forbidden passion, she would neither reveal what she saw, nor would she judge. She did, however, bite her lip against a smile, despite the concern in her eyes. "I'm sorry. Really. But there's a man downstairs threatening to break down doors until he finds Lilly and little Molly. Fortunately, Em had a nightmare and I went looking for warm milk, or I never would have heard him break the window."

Jade began to dress. "Does he seem dangerous?"

"Not really, one minute he's crying because he misses them, the next, he's going to tear the place down looking for them."

Jade donned her trousers, the better to deal with an irate husband. Once, she thought she appeared strong in male attire but now she knew better. Either way, she caught men off-guard when she wore pants. "Has he been drinking?"

Lacey nodded. "As usual, from what Lilly told me."

"Who's with him now?"

"I couldn't wake Beecher no matter how hard I knocked, so Lester's with him, but Lester's so frail . . ."

"Go back down," Jade said, pulling on her boots. "I'll be right behind you."

"If Marcus is hanging outside your window," Lacey said. "You'd best let him in before you leave."

Lacey touched Jade's hand. "Be careful, my dear, the elation of physical love can be buried all too quickly beneath a pall of remorse and regret. Protect at least a part of your heart, Jade, for if you do not, it will be lost forever. There is no going back."

Jade blanched at Lacey's warning.

She'd shut him in! Pitch black. Freezing. Bare ass and bare feet. Marcus gingerly made his way down the cold stone steps to his own secret door, but no matter how hard he tried, he couldn't get it open.

Not for anything.

Marcus sat down in the middle of the stairs, but he shot up when his bare ass met the icy step. After two sleepless nights, a foot chase, and this early morning's passion, this situation did not bode well for a day of rest.

Cursing, he leaned against the wall to decide his next move. He'd dropped his wet clothes while trying to get his door open and considered putting them on to cover himself, but one touch of his cold clammy shirt, and he decided against it. In this frigid place, he'd wear it, catch lung fever, and die naked and alone.

Marcus chuckled at the thought, at himself, and at his foolish predicament.

"Lust brought you to this sorry pass," he told himself as he made his way back up the stairs. Outside Jade's room, he listened for Lacey or Jade talking, or anyone moving around, but he heard nothing but his own frosty sigh. "Jade," he called in a whisper. "Jade?" A bit louder.

Any louder and the residents of Peacehaven would start looking for a ghost.

Clearly, Jade had left, and he wondered why Lacey had come for her so early. He hoped all was well at Peacehaven and that Jade could cope with the crisis without him. She'd managed quite well by her household long before he arrived, and he had confidence she would do so today. It could be as simple as someone getting sick. Anyone. The children, one of the old retainers, Eloisa, the twins, Garrett.

Garrett. Garr's room was right below his . . .

Taking the stairs at a hopeful clip, Marcus stubbed his toe and stifled his curse, making a hop-run to the next landing.

Outside Garrett's room—he hoped—Marcus searched the wall for the outline of the door that *should* be cut into it. Calling to Garrett would do no good without a door. His brother couldn't break down a wall if he wanted to. Then again, Garr could at least go looking for Jade, though she'd likely figure out he was missing sooner or later and know where to look.

When Marcus couldn't find the bloody blasted outline of a door, he cursed silently and ran his hand through his hair. Perhaps he'd searched too far left or right. Then a woman gasped, and Marcus pulled his hands away from the wall as if he'd touched fire.

This couldn't be Garrett's room. As much as he hated to listen, damn it, he had to know. He leaned against the wall to hear better, braced himself, and quite by accident found the outline of the door.

Good news and bad. Whose bloody room would he invade if he tried to force it?

He heard a woman murmur something low, now a man. Movement. A scuffle, perhaps. But that didn't make sense, because their tone—

Marcus stepped back so fast, he backed into the opposite wall. Holy bloody hell! That could have been him and Jade a short while ago. Clear as day, he heard his brother's name shouted in passion. And yes, that was Garr's return shout, then his brother's voice soothing and encouraging.

Marcus grabbed his clothes and backed up the stairs before turning and running. Then elation and frustration surged through him in one stroke as realization stopped him. Garrett had never wanted to discuss whether anything other than his ability to walk had been impaired. He'd said not to worry when Marcus broached the subject of his lack of female companionship. But Marcus *had* worried, and not a little bit. Having caused Garr's accident, he'd wanted to believe all was fine with his brother, but he'd never been certain. He didn't think he could have borne it if he'd crippled Garrett's manhood as well as his legs. Now he knew.

He grinned. Garrett the Lady Killer rides again.

He frowned as fast. Damn, but the Lady Killer's brother would find no way inside at this turn of events, however happy the discovery.

Marcus feared that he had no other choice but to explore and break through any hidden doorway he could find. He raised his gaze. "Just please, God, don't let me die of embarrassment, naked, in a roomful of women."

He climbed to the very top of the stairs first, trailing his hand along the wall as he went, in case doors existed midflight. But none did, and the stairs themselves ended abruptly at the ceiling, however weird the construction.

He found a telltale cut in the ceiling's surface, but that "door" remained as stubbornly immovable as his own.

Foiled again, he went back down. The stairs curved toward the bottom, exactly like the kitchen stairs did, so he knew where in the house he was, but there were no more doors along the wall and no landings but the bottommost, before an age-old wooden portal.

It creaked—fit to wake the dead—when Marcus pushed it, delighted out of mind that it moved at all, and looked into the darkest, coldest tavern of a . . . He examined the ceiling to confirm his suspicions and found it constructed of shored-up chalk and stone. If he guessed correctly, he stood beneath the house in a cavern of sorts, man-made by the look of it.

Ah. Perhaps, this was the cave Jade had *not* wanted to enter yesterday, which explained her firm refusal. A smuggler's cave. How very gothic: hidden stairs leading to an underground chamber, in which to hide smuggled—or stolen—goods.

Marcus reminded himself that England's coasts were riddled with caves leading to and from its older estates. Nothing unusual about a cave leading to Peacehaven. Hadn't his own fortune been enhanced considerably by the owlers in his family tree, who, like their namesakes, worked by night?

According to Fitzalan family legend, cutters had landed near Seaford Cliff daily, as many as a dozen at a time. Their holds were laden with Hyson, Chinese green tea, ankers of spirits, fine wines, perfumes, and spices from Ceylon.

Those same cutters had returned to the continent with their bellies full of English wool.

His wily ancestors had evaded revenue men and excise men. They'd thumbed their noses at coast and land guards. They'd sunk illegal tubs of spirits to hide them under the sea, then collected them at ebb-tide, after the Preventive

Water Guard had given up and returned home.

Aye, coast people were jonnick—staunch. Neither his nor Jade's forbears would have hesitated to stop a railroad or anything else in their way.

They were two of a kind, he and Jade, cut from the same sturdy cloth. Tough, resilient, durable. So evenly matched that only one of them could win the battle, but which of them would win the war?

Eleven

This cave must have served generations of nefarious brigands the way it served Jade now, surely her point of exit last night, the reason she approached from the beach, not the house.

Less relieved, and more disturbed than he cared to admit, he stepped through the thick old portal at the bottom of the stairwell . . . and it slammed shut behind him.

"Bloody bare-assed fool!" His echo mocked him even as he tried and confirmed that the blasted door had locked behind him.

Cursing fit to discompose every man jack who ever walked these chambers, Marcus set off in search of its entrance, no easy task with its wide assortment of dead ends and more legs than a nest of spiders, but he continued on. He had no choice.

When he reached the mouth, the sun shone bright, and like some Godforsaken fugitive, he peeked in both directions before he scuttled forth to wring out his clothes and lay them on the grass to dry. If Jade didn't come for him soon, he'd put them on in an hour or so, when they were at least bearable, and walk back to the house.

While they dried, he went back into the cave to explore. One of the forks had appeared to widen a great deal, though it darkened also, so he hadn't followed it at first. It might lead to a storeroom of sorts with treasure fit for a king. He mocked himself with a laugh but he sincerely feared finding a treasure in lumber.

He stopped and considered turning around and going back to sit at the mouth of the cave to wait for his clothes to dry, but he had a responsibility to Garrett and so he continued.

His chosen tunnel dead-ended in a huge chamber which, indeed, held a number of articles some would consider treasure, none of it lumber. Marcus strolled among the maze of wooden boxes, everything crated, nothing sealed, every cover addressed to the South Downs Railroad. Bloody hell.

A construction timetable and map lay atop one. Where and how the devil did she get them? A crate with railroad spikes here. Steam and water level gauges there. Pick axes, shovels, and tarpaulins further on.

She'd stolen nothing. 'Twas all addressed and crated to be sent back, but he'd wager his railroad stock that she planned to wait until after the appointed deadline passed and Parliament revoked the South Downs Charter.

Marcus went immediately back for his clothes, but couldn't reach them, because Lacey and several of the women, a number of children beside them, were playing in the sand by the water. One little boy, Bruno, he thought, dragged his trousers toward the others. "I found me a treasure," he called. "Lookee here."

Marcus made for the storage room and the crate of tarpaulins. If anyone came looking, he'd not be caught in the altogether.

Wrapped in a tarpaulin toga, he heard the occasional childish shout for an hour or more, but nothing after, for quite a while, so he finally made himself a bed of tarpaulins, covered up with another and closed his eyes. He hadn't slept in two days, and damned if this didn't feel good.

It could have been minutes or hours later when Marcus woke to Jade calling his name. His body reacted predictably to her approach, but he'd let no man-part control his thinking at this turn of events. He wiggled and shuffled into a sitting position, wrapped in a toga of rough canvas laced with sand, and leaned against the cave wall to await her.

She finally appeared, like an angel of salvation, so bloody beautiful, Marcus fought to maintain his anger. Then again, just glancing about the cavern bolstered his fury a great deal. An angel in black breeches, he should say, looking good enough to unwrap and make love to in a cave on a bed of tarpaulins.

He wanted to ask Jade what Lacey had wanted so early this morning, but he preferred to let Jade speak first, give her a chance to address the abundance of damning evidence that lay between them . . . *heavy* between them.

"I forgot," she said at last. "Your secret door was sealed a few years ago. The one in Garrett's room as well. And the attic."

He nodded, confirming he'd discovered as much. "But your door remains *unsealed?*"

"We missed you at lunch," she said, ignoring the implication, but I had my hands full. "When you missed tea too, I realized what must have happened and remembered Gram having the doors secured."

"Slipped your mind, did I? That puts me in my place. What about this?" He indicated the room with a wave of his hand. "Don't you have anything to say about this? Did all these railroad supplies slip your mind as well? How convenient. And don't tell me you don't know anything about them."

"We planned to return them."

"We?"

"I . . . I planned to return them."

Marcus scoffed. He knew better than to think she'd implicate anyone else in this. "The papers have been full of the failures of the South Downs Railroad and everybody knows their deadline. You were waiting until after June 30th to return it, weren't you? What the bloody hell do you have against progress, Jade?"

She shook her head and wrung her hands. "Some people don't think the railroad is progress."

"Most do. Did it never occur to you go to the owners of the railroad and tell them you didn't mean to sell that option? Ask for it back?"

"It's too late for that."

"If you'd done it at the beginning, they might have had the time to go around your property." *And my brother wouldn't stand to lose everything he's ever worked for.* Lord, he wanted to hit her with those words.

"They probably wouldn't have sold it back."

"At least you would have acted honestly!"

"I'm not dishonest, Marcus."

"I don't believe you are, fool that I am. I do believe you're frightened, though. Tell me why. Please let me help you."

She shook her head. "I don't know what you're talking about."

That made him mad. She didn't trust him. After everything, she didn't trust him.

"You do realize, Jade, that if you were caught with these goods, you *would* be considered a thief and could be transported or worse. But I'm not telling you anything you don't know, am I? I wonder, though, if you ever considered the people who've invested in the railroad. You could ruin them, destroy their lives."

"Investors are rich," she said, her protective shell weak at best. "No one will be hurt."

"I knew you were naïve, but I didn't think you were stupid—or is it blindness, intentional perhaps? You don't see what you don't want to."

She paled but she didn't answer.

"I repeat: what has you so frightened that you'd stoop to criminal activity just to stop the railroad from coming through? Is it revenge? Is there an investor you want to ruin?

"It can't be greed," he said. "Or can it? Do you want that option back because somebody is offering you more for that land than the railroad paid? Oh wait, I know, the old pirate who owned the estate buried his treasure on that piece of land and you haven't dug it up yet."

She blanched, quick and pure white, but she recovered fast, and furious. "The only treasure the old pirate who owned this estate ever buried there was the dog he beat to death. He might even have planted my grandmother there as well. He beat her often enough, and nearly to death, but he died before he could."

Marcus realized then that he wasn't getting through to her at all. She had changed the subject entirely. He stood, keeping decently covered. "We never sent that letter to your London bank," he said. "Get me back inside so I can pack my bags."

She looked stricken, worse than when he questioned her. "Don't leave. I . . . need you."

He scoffed. "You don't need anybody Jade. You keep proving that. Not me or anybody."

"But my finances. You promised."

"That's why I'm going to London. To get them straightened out. When they are, I'll return to explain everything and say goodbye."

"No."

"Yes." As formidable as he could be, wrapped in tarpaulin, he preceded her toward the hidden stairwell.

After she unlocked the door between the cave and the hidden stairs, he took the key from her hand. Then she picked up the glowing lantern she'd left on the landing.

He could see by its light, despite her raised chin, that her eyes were full and near to spilling over. He touched her cheek. "I'm sorry you don't feel you can trust me. More sorry than you'll ever know."

Jade wanted to step into Marcus's arms and never leave their safety. The only thing she'd ever wanted as badly was to care for the women and children who needed her. She wanted to tell him about her grandmother, how one act of hers, an absolutely necessary act, hung like a sharp blade on a weak spring over all of them. The women, little Emily, the twins; they would all suffer, if she failed to protect Gram's past to buy their future.

She wanted to tell him she couldn't have been honest with the railroad about wanting her land back, because if they'd said no, and she'd been forced to act, they would have suspected *her* of slowing construction. "Are you going to summon the magistrate?" she asked.

Marcus stepped back as if she'd struck him. "You really *don't* trust me."

"I trust that you're honest and upstanding. You discovered . . . an infraction . . . here today, and I expect you to do what any honest . . ."

Shaking his head, Marcus hauled himself and his clumsy costume up the stairs as if he couldn't bear to hear another word. In her room, not seeming to care that she watched, he stepped out of his canvas wrapper and into his trousers.

Wearing nothing else, he left her room, nodding with gentlemanly grace to Molly and Lacey, as if he weren't bare-chested and bare-footed, and as if he hadn't just bid farewell to the woman who fell in love with him.

Standing in her doorway, Jade couldn't react to the knowing smile Molly threw her. She just closed her door and gave in to tears. She who never cried, couldn't seem to stop.

She'd hurt him. How could that be? The conundrum made her weep the more.

But after a while, she remembered that someone or other always needed her, so she dried her eyes and went downstairs to make certain Marcus had everything he needed for his trip to London.

Happy to oblige Marcus, Beecher agreed to continue the search for the gunman while Marcus went to London. He would start at the brothel in the twittens where Marcus had lost the man.

Garrett showed Marcus the latest report. "What the devil do you think you're doing, walking in here to say goodbye when you didn't even have the courtesy to stop in today and tell me how last night went!" He slapped the paper in his hand. "No need to bother now, of course, it's all here in this note from Brinkley. The lumber's gone, as you must know. Where the hell were you last night? Playing house with Jade?"

Marcus laughed. "Rich, coming from you." He held up a hand. "For your information, I came by early this morning." He let the statement settle and waited until the implication sunk in. "Right. Bad timing on my part. Good timing for you, though."

"That's not the point!" Garrett snapped.

"It's not. But the fact is, while *you* were playing house, I *was* on the job." Marcus pointed to his cye, his jaw, rolled up his now impeccable sleeves to reveal more bruises. "I got thrashed and pummeled and run off my feet by a gunman. Then I was attacked by an angry mob." Garrett didn't need to know the mob was a swarm of perfumed street-tarts, Marcus thought. Garr's accusation of dereliction made him want to dispatch a jab or three of his own.

"When I got back to the site, the lumber car sat empty. No lumber anywhere. Missing. Disappeared. Like magic. Like Jade." Marcus ran his hand through his hair. "I don't know what happened, maybe the gunman was a ruse to take my attention away from her, but Garrett, I swear, he looked set to shoot her. You would have tried to stop him as well."

"Stop pacing and sit," Garrett said. "You're right. I would have. I'm sorry I lost my temper. Why London? Why now?"

Marcus sat with a sigh. "Mostly because I'm a man scorned and I'm angry, furious. But it's more than needing to get away. I need to see Jade's banker and find out where her money's gone. That information is going to lead us to her purpose—I feel it in my gut. Which should lead to solving our problem. Also, as a result of an inquiry I sent to Newhaven, I just this minute received word that Emily's mother did, indeed, travel to London. I'd like to try to find her."

"What about the railroad?"

"How long before more lumber is cut, milled and shipped?"

"Too long. A few weeks; five at the most."

"Write to me. Keep me informed. I'll open the London house. As soon as you say the lumber's on its way, I'll be back, I promise. Now," Marcus sat back. "Tell me, Garr, what happened here last night and with whom?"

"Go to hell."

★ ★ ★ ★ ★

Marcus slept little and left at dawn the following morning, missing Jade like a lovesick halfling. He traveled back to his home, Seaford Head, with Ivy, because he wanted to speak to his friend about doing him a favor, and he wanted his own carriage for the trip to London. No matter that his home sat closer to the sea, stood taller and more majestic than Peacehaven, if he had ever experienced this deep lonely ache for home before, it had not hurt half so much.

He wanted Jade beside him by day.

He dreamed about her by night.

In London, old haunts and suddenly shallow friends failed to cheer him. As a matter of fact, his old life depressed the devil out of him. The women he'd once lusted after now seemed like painted caricatures of depravity and greed.

Marcus buried himself in his purpose.

By his third day in the city he discovered that Jade's income had been directed to the account of one Giles Dudley nearly two years before. A highly insulted banker had shown Marcus the instructions to do so, signed by Jade's grandmother. The signature, as valid as the one on the land option—owed, no doubt, to the same deceitful process.

Neil Kirby must work for Giles Dudley. Marcus intended to find out for sure. He hired a Bow Street Runner to look for both men and for Catherine Warren, Emily's mother, as well.

He deposited two thousand pounds of his own money into Jade's account and wrote to Garr so he would help Jade word her instructions correctly to direct her future income properly. He did not allow Garrett to reveal anything about Dudley or the apparent theft of her money, only that pre-

149

vious to this, her income had been directed incorrectly.

By the beginning of his second week, Marcus's old friend, the Duke of Haverhill, obligingly exerted his considerable power to make Dudley's account available for Marcus's lawful perusal. He also unearthed a good deal of information about Dudley, the most interesting to Marcus being the bounder's distant connection to Jade.

Now Marcus needed to ferret out other sources of Dudley's income to determine if the worm's entire twenty-seven thousand pounds belonged to Jade. For two full days he painstakingly hand copied both accounts, Jade's and Dudley's, so he could bring the information back to Peacehaven to compare to Jade's ledgers.

By the end of the third week, Marcus learned that Dudley was trying to have Jade's grandmother declared insane, thereby nullifying her will leaving everything to Jade, and making Dudley her beneficiary instead. Marcus knew too that Dudley had left London to go on a business trip, or so his servant said.

It bothered Marcus that if Dudley succeeded in having Jade's grandmother declared insane, Jade would lose Peacehaven. More important, the people who depended on her would lose their home. That, he thought, might be enough to make someone as decent and honest as Jade turn to crime.

But why stop the railroad?

Why, why, why?

Emily couldn't sleep. She fussed and wept, and nothing Lacey did seemed to console her. Around midnight, afraid the child would make herself sick, Lacey wrapped Emily in a blanket and took her on a foray 'round Peacehaven, as it turned out, for Jade was not in her room as Lacey expected.

They found her with Eloisa, both of them in nightgowns walking two fussing babies.

When Jade heard Emily sobbing, she looked for a place to put little Mac, but Eloisa had her hands full with little Garth.

"Here," Lacey said. "Why don't we trade? I'll put Em down on the bed for a minute and you give me Mac."

Jade failed to hide her surprise.

Eloisa stopped pacing. "Thank you, Lacey. I know babies aren't your favorite form of amusement, but Mac's getting tired. I think he'll fall asleep soon, anyway."

Lacey put Emily on the bed and Jade handed Mac to her, quickly, because Emily cried harder until Jade picked her up and sat down to rock and cuddle her.

Lacey kissed Mac's small cheek, settled him on her shoulder, and as if she'd reached heaven, she began to pace and hum softly.

Emily calmed down as well, though the occasional sob escaped her heart-shaped mouth. Jade stroked the damp strands of hair from her fretful brow. "Now, my pretty little kitten, what's all this about? Why so sad?"

"Emmy w . . . want Mucks."

Having expected Em to ask for her mother, Jade sat silent and angry, for more than a beat. Damn Marcus for staying away so long. She kissed Em's tiny brow as much to show her love as to calm her ire. "He'll be back soon, Sweetheart. I'll bet he misses you every bit as much as you miss him."

Considering her words, Emily's brows furrowed slightly, as if she had difficulty believing it, drat the man. "He loves you, Emmy-bug. He wouldn't want you to cry so much you couldn't sleep, and it's time for all little girls to be asleep."

"Babies too?"

"Yes, babies too. Mac and Garth are very nearly there. Why don't you see if you can sleep first and win the race?" Emily flashed an impish grin and closed her eyes.

Jade shared a conspiratorial smile with Lacey and Eloisa when she looked up.

"I'll have to remember that one," Eloisa said.

It was not Mac but Garth losing steam in the fussing department, though Eloisa still offered Lacey first use of the baby-minder Lilly lent them—a cradle attached to a rocking chair, in which a mother could gratefully rest while rocking her baby to sleep.

Fortunately for Eloisa, who'd been pacing for hours, Lacey refused the minder, so Eloisa placed Garth in the cradle portion, sat on the chair portion, and rocked him into a peaceful sleep.

Rocking soothed Emily as well, Jade noticed, as Em changed positions, and placed her head on Jade's breast. Not long after that, her heavy little lids closed, though she'd fought a valiant fight.

"Poor baby," Eloisa whispered, watching Emily. "Everybody leaving her."

Having lost her own parents at an early age, and missing Marcus a great deal, Jade knew how Emily felt. Her heart ached for the child even as her anger at Emily's mother, and at Marcus, grew, because they left her.

Eloisa offered to take Mac, but Lace shook her head, tears forming in her eyes. "No, please. He feels so blessedly good."

"Are you all right?" Eloisa touched Lacey's arm.

"It's not that I don't care for babies, it's just that . . ." Lacey gave Emily a watery smile. "Mac is the first baby I've held since my baby daughter died."

Poor Eloisa. All the color left her face. "Oh, Lacey. I'm

so selfish. How many times have I flaunted—"

"No, I never thought that's what you were doing. You're proud of your babies, and happy to have them, as you should be. I'm the one who's sorry for staying so far away. I've been a coward, frankly, but holding Mac here is the best thing that's happened to me . . . since Ivy brought me to Jade."

"I know exactly what you mean," Eloisa said smiling at Jade. "But Mac *is* sleeping now. Would you like me to put him in the cradle?"

"Just try and take him away," Lacey said, holding Mac closer and turning aside, her smile belying her words.

Jade and Eloisa grinned and Jade felt a decided lump in her throat. "You could rock Mac for a bit, Lace," she said. "He likes that."

"I'd love to, if you don't mind, Eloisa?"

"Me? I get to do it all the time. Quite amusing with a babe in each arm, I can tell you. Go ahead. Enjoy. I'll stretch out at the foot of the bed, if you don't mind, either of you, and absorb the peace."

"Try to sleep," Jade suggested. "We won't mind, will we, Lace?"

Eloisa chuckled. "It'll take me a while to calm down," she said as she settled herself.

Peace. The room resonated silence now, with three sleeping babies, and, yes, three content adults, for the moment at least. Jade enjoyed the mutual comfort and joy of Eloisa's and Lacey's quiet company, and the warm surge of love she felt for Emily asleep in her arms.

"You know, Jade," Eloisa said. "I'm beginning to think the twins are missing Marcus as much as Emily. When is he coming back?"

Lacey seemed interested in the answer as well.

Jade sighed. "I wish I knew." She looked down to check Emily. *Out cold* was the best way to describe the deep sleep she'd fallen into. Jade regarded her friends. "Sometimes I'm so angry he stayed away so long, I don't want him to come back at all."

Eloisa looked stricken and sat up. "Don't say such a thing. You never know when someone you love will be taken away."

Also upset by the words, Lacey nodded her agreement. Both women's faces held a sadness that went deeper than simple concern. "Like the twins' father?" Jade asked softly.

Eloisa sighed and nodded.

"But how can you miss a man who beat you?"

"My husband never . . . What gave you . . . oh, the bruises. No, that wasn't Stephen. It was his heir, and he didn't so much hit me, as he helped me down the stairs . . . the quick way."

"Oh my God," Lacey said. "It's a wonder you didn't lose the babies."

"I know, and I think that might have been his intent. I did go into labor."

"And came to us, thank God," Jade said. "Tell us about Stephen. I didn't realize you'd been married."

"You knew nothing about me, yet you welcomed me like a sister." Eloisa gave her a grateful smile. "But I don't want to foist my story on Lacey, if—"

"Please, Eloisa, I'd like to hear it, if you're ready to tell it. I know that sharing your story can take time."

"I believe I am ready," she said, but her eyes clouded for a minute, as she looked into the past. "Stephen and I married about a year ago. A love match. We were happy as larks and moved into the family home, a bright future before us.

"Stephen's cousin and heir lived there as well. Stephen's

parents had raised the boys together.

"I knew right away that Arthur resented me, that he feared I'd give Stephen a son, and displace him as heir. But we were happy, anyway, Stephen and I, until Stephen was forced to go and settle urgent business concerns in the West Indies.

"I wanted to go with him, but I was too far along and . . . Stephen forbade it." Eloisa sought her handkerchief.

After she composed herself, she rose and went to the window. Jade knew she saw neither the beautifully clear night nor its bright stars.

"Stephen's ship went down," Eloisa finally said, her voice small. "All aboard were lost."

While Eloisa mourned her lost love, Jade thought about all the beautiful moments she and Marcus had shared, how she would feel if she were certain there would never be another.

Eloisa turned to regard them. "The day we got the news, I died a bit inside, and as if that were not enough, Arthur became the new . . . the heir, and he wanted me gone." Tears coursed down her cheeks. "He wouldn't let me take a single memento of Stephen. Violently angry that I wanted anything at all, he made me fear for my child's safety and I left."

She shook her head. "After several weeks in the twittens in Newhaven, living off the streets near the docks, I sneaked back to the house. All I wanted was the miniature of Stephen, to show our child someday.

"Arthur caught me and was furious I hadn't lost the babe by then. We struggled. I fell down the stairs. I don't know how, but I managed to stagger to my feet before he reached me, and I ran."

Sitting on the edge of the bed, Eloisa touched her temple

to one of the bedposts, as if neither her legs nor her mind could support the heaviness she carried. "I found you that day, Jade. All of you," she added, regarding Lacey.

Jade's anger at Marcus evaporated during Eloisa's discourse. In its place rose longing. She'd driven him away, and all she wanted now was a chance to touch him, kiss him, one last time.

"Jade, Marcus is special. He reminds me a great deal of Stephen, and when I see him with Mac, I—" Eloisa cleared her throat. "He's someone you should hold on to. I know you love him, that he loves you. It's all so obvious."

"It's all so impossible." Jade shook her head and swallowed sorrow. "Impossible."

Mac blew a bubble in his sleep. Garth made sweet suckling noises.

"It's not impossible, however," Lacey said, "for you to repay Stephen's cousin in kind."

"How?"

"Go to the magistrate. Have this Arthur blighter thrown into the streets, himself. Better still, have him arrested. Garth is Stephen's rightful heir now."

"No! No. I don't want Arthur to know about the babies. If he knew they existed, he'd hurt them. I know he would. That's why I never told anyone my story before now, why no one knows my real name. It's the reason I wrote to Arthur and told him I'd lost my child and I was going away."

Eloisa shook her head. "Listen, Jade, I know we have to leave soon, but after we—"

"You don't have to leave." Jade leaned forward, inasmuch as she could with Emily in her arms. "Stay. We love the babies. We'll fold you so seamlessly into life at Peacehaven, and keep you so busy, you won't have time to think about anything else."

"She will fit, too," Lacey said. "Don't I know and appreciate it." Lacey reached toward Jade, in the rocker beside hers, and they clasped hands for a minute.

Eloisa smiled. "I have no family, so you can't imagine how much your offer means to me, Jade. Thank you. Perhaps we will stay, for a time, until I grow wings large enough to fly from your nest with two babies in my arms."

Jade grinned at the image but Lacey sat forward as if something amazing had taken place.

"What is it Lace," Jade asked.

"Wings."

Eloisa looked as confused as Jade felt.

"Eloisa," Lacey said with wonder. "You just helped me see something it's taken me forever to understand. *My* wings are finally big enough for me to fly from Jade's nest. As a matter of fact, they're so big, I've been tripping over them and didn't realize. I do believe the next time Ivy tries to nudge me from Jade's nest, I shall let him succeed." She grinned.

Eloisa wiped away a tear. "I'm so happy for you."

"Me too," Lacey said.

"It'll be lonely without you Lace," Jade said, feeling bereft.

"Maybe *your* wings are too big, Jade," Lacey responded. "Perhaps if you clipped them just a bit, there'd be room for Marcus in your nest with you, and you wouldn't be so lonely."

Jade was shocked speechless, as it seemed were Eloisa, even Lacey, at her own words . . . until they, all three, began to laugh.

"What about the father of your child, Lacey, if you don't mind my asking?" Eloisa said. "Is there any hope for you?"

"Definitely not," Lacey said. "But he's one of the ghosts

I plan to face when I return to Arundel with Ivy." She kissed Mac's puckered little brow when he fussed, calming him again. "Because I held this little fellow in my arms, and because of your revelation, Eloisa, and your love and understanding over the past few years, Jade, I'm finally ready."

"What an extraordinary night this had been," Eloisa said. "To celebrate, Jade, do us a favor. Because we can't welcome those we've lost, do welcome Marcus with open arms when he returns. Don't waste a minute of the time you have together, no matter how short it might be."

Twelve

A letter Marcus received from Jade during week four made him miss her so much, he wanted to pack up and go back to Peacehaven, except he hadn't quite learned everything he needed to know about Dudley. And none of his leads regarding Neil Kirby bore fruit, as if the man did not exist.

While Emily's mother had definitely visited London, no one had seen her for some time now.

Marcus called in other favors on both scores.

Though Marcus remained in London, he re-read Jade's letter often:

> *My dear Marcus, I know you must think badly of me, and with good reason, we both know, but do not ever imagine that I take lightly your personal regard. Please understand that, were I free to express myself, you would know all, but I do not walk alone. Emily asks for you daily. Please come home. Yours, J.*

Home; the very notion kept Marcus focused on completing his goal. He supposed he'd known the first time he saw Jade that *she* would be his home forever after. He simply had given up hope that he would be free of his responsibility to Garr or that Jade would feel the same way.

It all seemed so impossible.

The road for the two of them might be paved with good intentions, however rutted with secrets and deeds gone bad. Some days he believed their way could be cleared. Most days, he feared it could never be.

Garrett's letters came weekly and kept Marcus informed. They always carried Abby's and Eloisa's fond regards, and sometimes Lacey's, but only one early letter had carried Jade's.

Emily asks for Mucks whenever she sees me. But she won't let me pick her up. Not even Tweenie has been able to cheer her since Ivy returned.

Jade seems to have lost her effervescence and tends to be snappish at unexpected moments. Very unlike her, so Abby says. The twins are growing by leaps, but they retain their unfortunate tendency to piddle at unexpected moments and on unsuspecting victims.

Another time, Garrett said he'd found Jade standing outside just gazing down the drive.

During week five, Garrett's letter carried good news:

I am to inform you that the gentleman you lost at the brothel has been found and is being incarcerated indefinitely due to a list of crimes "long as me arm," so says Beecher. You will tell me about this brothel when you return, will you not?

In two separate letters, Garr reported two more efforts at mischief to delay construction. Both, he said, were circumvented by the guards he'd hired, and in both cases the mischief-makers got away:

Here's news. A canal barge floundered in the middle of the River Ouse. It took sixty men four days to free her and discover the cause—a log jam, or to be more precise, a lumber jam. What boards hadn't floated downstream and into the Channel had piled up and jammed against the bracings of our railroad bridge. I don't suppose it would have taken an immeasurable amount of strength to throw them, one by one, from the lumber car and down into the river.

A portion of one letter that troubled Marcus concerned Emily:

Lacey says that Emily asks more for you than she ever asked for her mama. You'd best think about coming back to her soon. She's a sad little girl these days.

Garrett's most significant letter came during week seven:

I do believe, dear brother, that the heart I have long denied owning may be broken. Shipment of lumber and rails both due Wednesday week. Please come home. G.

Home. Marcus could see Peacehaven Manor high on the cliff from as far as the Brighton Road. Both Garrett and Jade had referred to it as the home he should return to. The skip of his heart when he caught sight of it told Marcus they were right.

Wednesday. The shipment of lumber and rails was due to arrive at midnight tonight. Until then, a reunion with so many people awaited him, he could hardly contain his anticipation.

There had only ever been him and Garr. Their parents died young of a fever. The title and estate had passed to a young boy who protected his brother. To see them to adulthood, they had a turnover of housekeepers, nursemaids and schoolmasters. And a puppeteer named Ivy.

At ages twenty-one and nineteen, the boys were set free of their keepers to run their own lives and become a family to each other. Strictly speaking, they each owned an estate, but the Attleboro Estate at Seaford Head remained home to them both. Marcus had been overseeing it, along with his own estate, for more than a year now, ever since Garr's accident. And there he would remain, for as long as his brother needed him, despite the fact that his heart would forever reside at Peacehaven Manor.

Because of Ivy, he and Garr had a bigger family now—Jade, Abby, Emily. Eloisa and the twins. Lacey, Beecher, a whole house full of family.

Marcus wanted to see them all instantly, but he wanted time with each, except he didn't want to wait a minute to see any of them. Especially Jade.

She did not walk alone, she'd written. That statement stuck in his mind. Whatever she did, she did it, not for herself, but for the people she loved.

The key to her actions lay in that optioned piece of land. Her reaction when he spoke of buried treasure teased his mind. Suppose she hadn't changed the subject but focused on it. Suppose . . .

The elusive notion that he'd nearly grasped became nothing but a vaporous joy as his carriage turned onto the Peacehaven Estate drive, and Marcus sat forward, eager, giddy with coming home. He grinned and tapped the roof with his cane, telling the driver to stop.

Ladies in pale silks sat on blankets under beech and cherry trees with fans to cool themselves. Children scampered in clusters on the sweeping lawn. A mid-afternoon romp. He wanted to run with them. But he especially wanted to run carefree with Emily giggling beside him.

He'd spotted her laying in the grass beside Jade, head to head, both of them so busy looking up at the clouds they didn't see or hear his carriage amid the children's laughter.

Marcus lifted the basket with his gift for Emily, the one Ivy had arranged for him to pick up, and he jumped from the carriage and waved his driver on.

He heard Emily and Jade talking as he got closer, about the pictures the clouds made. His throat tightened with happiness and love. He stepped nearer, until he stood within their range.

Both stared in silent shock. Then, in one move, Emily seemed to shoot up and into his arms, as if she hadn't touched ground in the interim.

She started to cry as she clutched him tight, and he thought for a minute he might join her. Her sobs were killing him.

He blinked and looked down at Jade, just sitting there watching him, unsure. Hopeful, but wary. He couldn't stand it and sat in the grass beside her, still holding Emily tight.

He leaned into Jade, until her luscious lips were a bare inch away, until they curved into a smile and she kissed him, placing her arms around both of them.

Marcus lost his balance and tumbled backward, woman and child in tow. "So good," he said on a chuckle. "So blessed good to be home."

Emily sat up on his chest and scowled down at him. He raised his knees so she could sit back. She crossed her arms. "Bad boy!"

"Who me?" he asked, trying not to laugh.

She nodded. "Emmy missed Mucks. Emmy cry," she said, less angry and more sad.

"Oh, Emmy-bug, I missed you too." He pulled her down

163

toward him and hugged her tight. "I missed you so bad. Will you forgive me for staying away so long?" He included Jade in his request.

Jade's eyes filled and she shook her head.

Emily sat up and mimicked her.

"No? You won't forgive me, then?"

Jade laced his fingers with hers. "For my part, there's nothing to forgive."

He wanted to kiss her again, pick her up and carry her upstairs to her room and not come out for a week.

"Emmy?" He lifted her stubborn little chin with a finger. "Say yes."

Emily raised her hands in the air. "Yes!" she shouted bouncing on his belly, catching him unaware and making him gasp.

His pain tickled the devil out of Jade, reducing her to giggles. Marcus would take the blow again to see such a sight.

The contents of the basket Marcus picked up on his return from London—per arrangements with Ivy—began to whimper so he pulled it nearer. "This is for you, Emmy-bug."

She climbed off his belly, allowing him to sit up as she lifted the basket by its handle, needing both hands to set it before Jade. "For Emmy," she told Jade, very much in awe.

"Open it," Jade said, the roses of her dress matching the rose in her cheeks.

Emily couldn't figure out how, so Jade lifted one of the side flaps a bit for Em to grasp. When she looked inside, Emily squealed and pulled her hand back as a tiny nose popped out.

She started to tremble and shake her hands. "A baby! A baby doggie!" She made to grasp it around its neck, but

Jade taught her how to lift and carry her baby Dachshund so she wouldn't hurt it.

Marcus kept swallowing against a ghastly display of emotions over Emily's excitement.

Holding it like a newborn, four short puppy legs in the air, a tiny puppy tongue lapping at her chin, Emily fell gently back into Marcus's lap and laid her head on his chest. "Emmy love Mucks."

"I'm home," Marcus said, the crack in his voice betraying him. "Home with my best girls."

Jade wiped away a tear with the back of her hand and cleared her throat. "What do you want to name your doggie, Emily?"

Emily sat up at that, the concept intriguing her. She looked from him to Jade and back. She scanned the yard, the other children, the look of her serious and contemplative.

"Mucks," she finally said.

Marcus chuckled with surprise. "If you want to call a girl doggie Mucks, that's fine. Except, what will you call me?"

She regarded him earnestly as silent seconds ticked by and she tilted her head. "Papa."

Marcus stilled. He took Jade's hand, squeezed it and brought Emily close. Burying his face in Emmy's blond curls, he kissed the top of her head. "I would be proud to have you call me Papa."

With a satisfied release of her breath, Emily stood up, all the while Mucks—the poor benighted girl pup—sat quietly and stoically in her arms.

"Look," Emily called out as she started walking toward the other children. "Annie! Molly! Look what I gots."

"Don't run," Jade shouted after her. "You could hurt Mucks."

Emily stopped and turned around. "Emmy knows that."

Jade chuckled. "Good." She turned back to smile at Marcus.

He drank in every nuance of her beauty and expression, so glad to be back and have her full and complete attention.

"Do you think Mucks will run if Em sets her down?" she asked.

He shook his head. "She's a calm one. She'll stay right by her. They're friends already, I think. Ivy did a great job of choosing her."

"Papa," Jade whispered touching his cheek. "What a good one you would make. But what will happen if Emily ever goes back to her real father?"

Marcus kissed Jade's hand. "The man who beat her mother wasn't her father. Her real father is a London dandy who wants nothing to do with her. He has a broken jaw for telling me so. Emily's mother went to see him, and when he refused to provide for Em and sent Catherine packing, she ran weeping into the street into the path of a moving carriage. She's gone, Jade. Catherine's gone."

Marcus got Lacey to watch Emily and propelled Jade into the house and down the hall toward Eloisa's room. But he passed it and went to the empty bedroom, *their* room, and shut them inside.

Then Jade's back met the door and Marcus closed his mouth over hers, drinking in the sounds of her weeping, and telling her with soft sweet words how sorry he was to have left her, and how much he'd missed her, that he'd help her raise Emily, if only she'd let him.

Jade forgot how angry she'd been for his desertion, despite his discovery of her hidden railroad supplies, and told him as much in the same weepy, kiss-stealing way.

She needed to be comforted.

By him.

She needed him.

She ducked unexpectedly from under his arms, aware she confused him, but when she took his hand to drag him to the bed, she did nothing more than lie down. He came to her, touching her everywhere at once, budding a nipple here, sleeking a thigh there, kissing fingers and sucking earlobes. Her bodice lay open; she didn't know how, and his tongue and his hands gentled, laved and suckled all at one time.

She was hot; she was wet. She was breaking all the rules she'd set for herself after he left. She didn't care. She tugged his earlobe with a gentle bite.

He felt as much like velvet against her lips as his length had felt in her hand that last morning.

Velvet and sin.

Delicious.

Wondrous.

The Earl of Attleboro. She slid her hand along the rutting length of the Earl of Attleboro—his title she'd deduced from the information she gleaned in the village—seducing the man who owned the railroad she wanted to destroy. A scoundrel disguised as a saint, lying to her even now.

Thirteen

Jade shoved Marcus hard. "Get off me . . . you . . . oaf!" She rolled out from under him and off the bed when he pulled back, passion dazed and confused.

Trying to regain her breath and her balance, she watched as he rose and attempted to adjust himself in his suddenly-tight trousers. His dignity returned in minuscule measure, beat by affronted beat, as he raised his head like any proud stallion. "You dragged me to the bed, Scandal, so don't go all priggish on me. It doesn't suit."

"You'd have had me against the door at any rate."

"Not if you didn't want me to. But 'no' wasn't the message you were sending."

Jade raised her chin. "You caught me off guard. I'm stronger now. What did you expect after deserting me for nearly two months?"

"You were never mine to desert, Jade."

"And I never will be."

He ran a hand through his hair, weakening her resolve, making himself look more human and less the lying aristocrat. "I'm not ready to accept that. Look, I know you're in trouble. You need to trust me. Please. Just tell me what's wrong and I'll help you. I promise. I can take care of you. No matter what's happened with the railroad so far, I can fix it. Why won't you trust me?"

Because the Earl of Attleboro owns the bloody thing, she thought, and you're him. "I don't know what you're talking about."

He growled at that and grasped her arms. "It has to stop,

Jade. I can only help you, up to a point."

"You're hurting me!"

As if she'd slapped him, he stepped back, appalled. "I'm sorry. Forgive me, please. I . . . I've never hurt a woman in my life. I'm sick for worrying about you. I've had night-mares about the danger you've put yourself in, about what might happen, I'm so bloody scared for you in this."

"You're talking foolishness."

He walked to the window to look out, his hands clasped behind him. "I'll talk sense, then. Don't go to the construc-tion site tonight." He turned back to her, his gaze skewering her with intensity. "It'll be dangerous. There'll be armed guards."

Jade felt the blood leave her head. She feared her lack of color showed. The narrowing of his eyes said it did, but she couldn't care. "What about my money? I want to go over my finances."

"As selfish as you sound, I'll try not to judge. Nothing is ever as it seems and you don't walk alone, do you?"

Jade stepped back at his venom. "I'm your employer and I would like to discuss the business you conducted on my behalf in London, if you please."

"I haven't seen my brother in two months, so I'm bloody well going to see him now, then I want to see Eloisa and the babies and a few others. After dinner, I plan to rock Emily to sleep. So, yes, I do mind, if you please." His features had lost all softness, his expression stony cold.

Jade wanted to turn the tables and throw her discovery of his identity in his face. She wanted to ask what he planned to do after he rocked Emily to sleep. But she al-ready knew he'd be waiting to catch her as she left the house, except he wouldn't succeed. Not tonight.

Jade opened the door to leave.

"I adore you," he said, but she kept walking.

Garrett wasn't in his own room, but in Eloisa's with her and the twins. A baby-minder had been brought in, Marcus noticed when he entered, an ingenious invention with three rockers, the middle one serving the chair and cradle both.

By rocking in the chair, Eloisa rocked its attached cradle, one babe within, the other in the cradle Jade brought from the attic the day of their birth.

"Separate beds, I see. Fighting already, are they?" He bent and kissed Eloisa's cheek and regarded his brother. "Like us, Garr."

Garrett smiled and extended his hand.

Marcus didn't think he'd ever wanted so badly to embrace his brother. He wasn't sure if he'd missed him so much as he'd had enough of seeing him in that wheelchair. Then again, Garr was all he had, for he'd just lost the woman he loved.

He squeezed Garr's hand, covering their clasped ones. He'd written of a broken heart, but . . . "You look well, the both of you."

Marcus regarded the babes more closely. "Don't tell me," he said. "Mac's in the minder to keep him from fretting."

"How did you guess?" Garrett drawled.

Eloisa laughed. "He's my fussbudget."

"May I," Marcus asked. At Eloisa's nod, he lifted Mac in his arms, realizing he'd missed the little tiger a good deal more than he realized. "I'm getting soft," he said to no one in particular.

"Babies do that to you," Eloisa said, shaking her head. "Look at Garrett; he spends hours with the two of them. Jade too."

"Does she now?" New and interesting information. "With both of them?"

"Well, no, actually. Garrett has an affinity for his name-sake, of course. And Jade has one for yours."

He'd best not read too much into that, Marcus thought. "The night you were ill, she slept with Mac pressed to her breast," he said to explain, as much to himself as to Eloisa.

"She held him while she slept?" Eloisa clasped a hand to her heart. "Lord, it's a wonder she didn't drop him."

"She wasn't sitting up." Marcus explained how well his notion that night had worked.

Garrett huffed. "I wish you had shared that piece of wisdom with me and Abigail. One of us might have got some sleep."

Marcus wanted to ask about Abigail when there came a scratching at the door.

"Come in," Eloisa called.

"Well, hello, stranger," Ivy said as Tweenie rushed to Marcus, paws at his knees, happy tail slapping his leg.

Ivy chuckled. "You were missed."

Marcus greeted his friend at the same time he felt a trickle of warmth on his sock. "Well, Tweenie missed me, anyway."

"No!" Emily stood in the open doorway, astonished and . . . crestfallen.

"Emmy-bug what—"

Tweenie and Mucks-the-pup met for the first time, growling, circling each other. Then as fast as it began, the skittish dance stopped. Tweenie nuzzled the half-pint and began to groom her.

Marcus grinned, but Emily didn't crack a smile. His girl *wasn't* happy. With a martial light in her eye, she marched over and pulled at his hand supporting the baby. "Play with Emmy."

"Mac is too little to play with you, Emmy. Would you like to hold him?"

"No!"

"Marc," Ivy said. "I think Emily feels Mac is . . . taking her place in your heart?"

"The devil you say."

"Green as an Irish shamrock," the puppeteer confirmed with a nod.

While Marcus would have liked to nip Emily's jealousy in its little green bud, she'd lost her mother not so long ago, and just now got him back, and she faced worse, because she would soon learn that her mother would not be returning. "Tell you what; why don't I give the baby back to his . . . back to Eloisa, and we'll take Uncle Garr to his room so I can borrow some dry socks?"

Emily nodded, hopeful, relieved. Her shuddering sigh gave her away. She feared losing him. Marcus handed Mac to his mother and lifted Emily high into his arms to kiss and jiggle her in the air. Once he'd got a giggle, he returned his attention to the company.

"Where is Abigail? I expected to find her here."

"She moved back upstairs," Garrett said.

"I didn't think she'd ever part with the twins."

"She didn't leave the twins," Garr said.

Eloisa winked. "A lover's squabble."

Garr colored and Marcus laughed.

"I'm not blind, Garrett," Eloisa said. "Nor deaf either, you should know."

"Get me out of here, Marc," Garrett said. "I haven't blushed in public since I was twelve."

With Emily's help, Marcus pushed Garrett out.

In Garr's room, Emily climbed into Marcus's lap, curled into his embrace, held on tight, and fell promptly asleep. Mucks came in and curled up at his feet.

"Tell me what happened with Abby," Marcus said.

Garrett all but trembled with despair. "One night we talked about the future, the next she ran upstairs and wouldn't come down. I've never met another woman like her, Marc. I miss her dreadfully, and I'm worried sick about her." He shook his head, disheartened. "I love her."

"Wait a minute, Garr. You're the worst scoundrel this side of London town, remember? You 'can't love only one woman and deprive the rest of your talents.' Your words."

Garrett grimaced. "I don't give a bloody fig about any of that. I want to see Abby. I need to know why she's forsaken me. I need to be certain she's all right."

Emily began stroking Marcus's whiskers as she woke from her short nap. He chuckled. "Lovesick, the both of us. And a sorrier pair of toss-aways I've never seen."

"What, you too?"

"Madder than a hornet, and I'm only just back. Hardly a kiss before she skewered me with those eyes of hers."

Garrett chuckled. "I'll talk to Jade if you talk to Abby."

"Much good it'll do you, but give it a try. I'll go find Abby. Want to go outside for a bit first? You haven't been cooped up all this time have you?" He kissed Emily's hand. "Feel better now?"

She smiled.

Garrett agreed to go outside and be properly introduced to little Mucks, which happened once Marcus coaxed Em onto Garr's lap. "If I'm Papa, Emmy-bug, then this is Uncle Garr and you need to cheer him up."

That, she understood, because she patted Garr's cheek and allowed Mucks the pup to wash his face as Marcus pushed them out to the terrace.

"Papa?" Garr said, brows raised as Marcus turned to leave them.

"Papa," Emmy confirmed with a nod as he left.

Marcus couldn't find Abigail in the sewing room, nor the playroom or the classroom. He was told she was ill. In the interest of repairing his brother's broken heart, Marcus decided he had no recourse but to intrude upon her in her bedroom.

On the same floor as Jade, Abby occupied the room three doors down and across the corridor. She replied to his knock and bid him enter, even after she heard his name. A good sign.

"Marcus I'm so glad you're back," she said, halting her forward surge, almost as if she intended to throw herself into his arms. She offered her hand instead.

Some indefinable air about her countenance seemed different. She appeared softer, more ethereal than the first time he'd seen her, yet that could be the simple result of an ease of manner due to the absence of fear from impending mistreatment. And yet, a new sadness seemed to engulf her.

He brought her hand to his lips, then he squeezed it. "I'm glad too, but my brother's worried sick about you, and since he can't climb the stairs, I'm here as his emissary."

She paled. "You can tell him I feel fine."

"That's not what Lacey said."

"Lacey's a worrier too."

"Why did you move upstairs? It looks like Eloisa still needs you."

"I didn't mean to desert her. It's just that . . . I couldn't . . ."

"Stay near Garr, I surmise. Why? He cares a great deal about you. As a matter of fact, his scoundrel heart has never been engaged, until now, with you. He wrote to me in London saying that very organ was broken."

Abby covered her quivering lips with a hand, then gave up the fight and began to weep.

Marcus went to her and enfolded her in his arms. "I think this must be how Garr feels," Marcus said, resting his cheek atop her head. "Except that he hasn't cried . . . that I'm aware of."

Abby chuckled despite herself, but she didn't move from the protection of his embrace and Marcus decided he should like Abby for a sister.

"I shouldn't have let it go so far," she said, wilted now and listless, "but he's so . . . so . . ."

"Compelling?" Marcus chuckled. "Garr *can* talk one into almost anything, can't he? When I think of the scrapes he got us into."

She wiped her eyes as she stepped from his hold. "He's wonderful. Gentle. Understanding."

"So you left him?"

She shook her head. "You don't understand what's between us."

"No, I don't. Which means that you should be speaking to him, shouldn't you?"

"I don't want to hurt him."

"You're hurting him now, Abby. He's hurting badly."

She turned her back on him to lean against the window and look out.

Marcus stepped up behind her and placed his hands on her shoulders in silent support. Down below, with Em still on his lap, Garr laughed at something she said, her pup asleep against his shoulder, a wet doggy nose in his neck.

"He's wonderful with children."

Marcus laughed. "And animals. It's the new Garr."

"Will he ever walk again?"

Marcus stepped back, disappointed. He'd thought better of her. "Does that matter to you?"

She turned. "Oh no. No, not in the way you think. It's just that . . . the way he is, somebody like me appeals to him, but I think if he were on his feet again and could have any woman he wanted—"

"He would choose you."

Abby laughed as if he told a fine joke. "The new Garr might," she said. "But not the old."

"I think you're wrong, and how do you know who the old Garr would have chosen?" He led her to a chair and sat facing her, holding her hands. "Of course Garrett's been changed by the accident, Abby. I have too. We're both more aware of how precious life is. How short it can be. We both want—need—to live it to its fullest. Instead, what do we do but come to Peacehaven and lose our hearts. Frankly, we're both scared witless we'll never recover them."

Abby's smile was sad. "If it's any consolation, I can tell you that the women you've lost your hearts to have lost theirs as well."

He grimaced. If only he could believe her. "Do me a favor?"

She tilted her head. "That depends on what it is."

"Move back downstairs. Help Eloisa. I don't mean to importune you—no that's not right; I do intend it." He unclenched her hand and kissed it. "If you do nothing else, talk to Garr. And soon."

She pulled her hands from his. "I can't talk to him. When I'm near him, I can't think straight. I end up—" She colored. "Not thinking straight. Not thinking at all, I should say."

He rose and kissed her brow. "I think Garr needs you

even more than Eloisa does. Think about talking to him."

She nodded but she looked frightened.

"Well, what did she say?"

Marcus continued to push Garr's chair along the garden path. "I couldn't get her to commit, one way or another, but I made a good case for her talking to you. Sorry."

"That's all right. Jade would barely speak to me, except to tell me that Emily has been left an orphan, which shocked me, I must say. And the child's calling you Papa, Marc. Is that wise? What's going to happen to her?"

Marcus stopped before a bench and came around to face his brother. "Jade is going to keep her. That one problem is solved at least, that is if Jade doesn't get herself injured de-railing the train or doing something else as foolish."

"Well, if Jade's keeping her, then you're all set, aren't you? You'll be her papa."

Since Marcus had never revealed his vow to Garr, that he would not leave him for as long as he sat in that chair, his brother had no notion his assumption was improbable. "No, I'm not all set. Pay attention here, Garr. Jade has no intention of keeping *me*, remember? Did you learn anything new about her grandmother, by the way, while I was gone?"

"No, but what I learned about her grandfather is inter-esting."

"What, that he abused Jade's grandmother?"

"No, that he just disappeared one day. Nobody knows, even now, if he's dead or alive."

"Jade said he died, and she should know."

"Beecher lived here when the old man did. I should think he'd know whether he died or not. Maybe Jade just takes it for granted that he died, given the fact he'd prob-ably be as old as dirt."

"Maybe," Marcus said.

"What are you going to do about her?" Garr asked.

"First I'm going to try to keep her safe." He shuddered, icy with dread, and shook the feeling off. "Once the railroad goes through, I would have . . . liked . . . to ask her to marry me." He'd still very much *like* to. But he never would.

"Don't ask," Garr said. "My proposal scared the devil out of Abby."

Marcus had to sit. "You asked Abby to marry you?"

"Of course I did. What do you take me for?"

"The scoundrel you've always been, what else?"

Garrett frowned. "Looks like we've outgrown our philandering. How will you keep Jade out of trouble tonight?"

"I have a plan."

Marcus left the house before dusk that night, certain he got away undetected. He'd unsealed the door in his bedroom wall and used the hidden stairs to the smuggler's cave. He still had Jade's key to the door leading from the stairs to the cave in his possession—having kept it the day she found him in the cave—so he could return later the way he came.

At the construction site, the train carrying the lumber and rails arrived about two hours after him, pulled by the Jenny Lind from the First Sussex Line. Marcus knew the engineer and most of the workers, including the guards who would remain on the site for the night.

The engineer used the steam engine to push the flatbed lumber cars as far as the mouth of the unfinished bridge, and the cars stacked with rails were backed up to the current termination of the temporary side spur. The unloading and stacking of supply and hardware crates took a great deal more time than Marcus expected, making him worry that Jade would arrive and find him working with men he obviously knew.

Too close to midnight to be comfortable, the train huffed and sputtered, ready to depart, and Marcus ordered the guards to get aboard and go with it—a last-minute change of plans.

The single oil lantern fitted on the engine before the stack laid a path of unwanted light. With its new parabolic reflector, the lamp cast a beam a thousand yards long, announcing the train's position to all and sundry, even to those too far away to hear it. Yes, railroading had come a long way, but tonight Marcus wished engine lighting had taken a while longer.

Keeping his eye on that beam, Marcus watched the Jenny Lind until she rounded the bend and disappeared from sight, only then breathing a sigh of relief.

The future of so many people depended on the success of the South Downs Railroad. The crew had about a mile of track to lay on Jade's land, if they ever got that far, before track finally reached Tidemills. One foot of track inside the perimeter of Tidemills by the thirtieth of the month would fulfill Parliament's requirement. Twelve miles to go, at most.

So near, yet so far.

If they reached Tidemills and kept their charter, they would be able to extend the route to Seaford next summer, and their home village would flourish—a bonus.

Tidemills, on the other hand, would die—and fast—if they failed to reach it.

Marcus sighed and put aside his anxiety, for the moment, to find himself a good spot to sit and wait on one of the flatbed lumber cars. He assumed Jade would try to dump the ties in the river again, since she could lift the short pieces of lumber, piece by piece.

The contents of the other two cars were a different story entirely. Cast-iron T-section fish-belly rails were too heavy for one *man* to carry. They also cost a great deal more than the lumber, because with railroads bisecting the world, they were in great demand in America as well as here and in Europe. Anyone with an ounce of railroad knowledge would know that destroying those rails would cripple construction much more efficiently than drowning any amount of lumber.

Good thing Jade didn't know that . . . he hoped!

Perched high above the River Ouse, Marcus took a deep relaxing breath. For the moment, at least, his world remained peaceful and quiet, except for a whisper of wind carrying the scent of wild thyme from the downs. When he settled the railroad's problems, he'd take Emmy for a walk and show her the wild orchids growing in the chalk of the downs. Little pup Mucks would enjoy such a trek as well.

Marcus remembered Emmy's delight when the pup's nose popped out of that basket. When her jealousy over baby Mac surfaced, he witnessed Emmy's insecurity and knew he needed to protect her as much as she needed him to. Amazing how fast he'd fallen in love with that little girl.

Emily looked better tonight, happier. The tiny Mucks slinking beneath her blankets to curl up behind her knees for the night delighted her and made her giggle as Marcus tucked her in.

"Night, Papa," she'd said, and as he kissed her, he wanted to promise he'd keep her safe forever . . . her and Jade, except he couldn't promise any such thing. He may never have that freedom.

Lord how he wanted them to be a family. He and Emmy and Jade. But if Garr never walked again, and Jade couldn't trust him enough to share the secret of a fear so powerful it could reduce her to breaking the law, they could never have a life together.

"I adore you," he whispered in the dark. "Please don't do anything foolish."

He heard the crack of a twig, almost as he said it, coming from the woods through which Jade must pass. Though Marcus's eyes had long-since adjusted to the dark, he could see no one as he examined the edge of the beech wood.

Then he saw her, in breeches of course, and very much alone.

He had originally intended to stay out of it by setting a trap and using the guards to catch her and lock her up to keep her safe.

But he couldn't do it. He couldn't.

He expected her to climb on the lumber car closest to the river, where he sat waiting.

Hopefully, coming face to face with him would be enough to shock her and set her on a safe path. A weak plan, he realized suddenly, yet he prayed it would work.

She hesitated, as if frightened, which meant she had more common sense than he thought. Good. But almost as if she couldn't allow him relief, she dispelled it by throwing back her shoulders and heading straight for the railcars.

Bloody hell.

A shot rang out and Jade fell to the ground.

Fourteen

Jade might be hurt, bleeding. Oh God.

A frozen second, and Marcus rolled from his perch to the far side of the car and hit the ground running, a bullet buzzing by his ear.

Jade. He needed to get to Jade without bringing attention to himself, or she *would* be done for. He circled behind the railcar. They'd caught the first gunman, damn it, and locked him up. So who the bloody devil was shooting at her now?

Another shot. A man's curse. Somebody wanted Jade dead.

"Marcus!" Jade called and relief washed over him.

From the nearer side of the lumber car, he made straight for her, standing now, the fool, and grasped her waist at a run, hauling her into the cover of the woods.

"Are you hurt?" Marcus stopped, pulled her down, and ran his hands over her.

"No." She pushed him away but he continued to hover, to protect her with his body.

Two shots in a row this time.

Marcus covered her more fully with his body. "You called my name," he said against her ear.

"I wanted you to stop shooting."

Marcus reared back, and felt the blood drain from his face. "You don't mean that."

"Of course not, dolt," she said with a shuddering sigh. "I needed your help. It's called instinct. I was scared witless."

"About time." Marcus curled her closer and tighter

under him and raised his head to peer through the trees. He heard the shot but saw the fiery flash that followed on the instant.

"The railcar," he said, and it exploded, almost in slow motion, piece by blasted piece, literally, and the sky rained splintered wood and cast-iron shards.

Marcus appreciated the thick cover of beech trees, though something warm and hard caught him on the hip. He felt a rip, flesh or clothing . . .

Flesh. The pain of it flared to fire at about the same time the pelting of debris subsided.

Considering the danger, they got off easy.

The night went quiet. "I didn't do it," Jade whispered as he allowed her to sit up, the tremble in her voice belying her calm.

"You damn near got yourself blown to hell anyway," he snapped, snatching her close, burying his face in her dusty hair. "You might have been on that car when it exploded. Oh God, Jade."

They shuddered as one.

Despite her wobbly legs, Jade pulled away and got to her feet, as if to dash from the woods to the construction site.

Marcus caught her hand and pulled her up short. "Are you out of your mind? Where the devil do you think you're going?"

"I want to find the man shooting at me."

"Why? So he can get a clear aim?"

Her struggle to free herself from his hold escalated, but he managed to overcome her, throw her over his shoulder and start walking despite the fire in his hip.

"Let me go, you bully."

"He mustn't have seen us run into the woods," Marcus said.

"Put me down."

"Be quiet and thank whoever watches over foolish women that this new gunman's eyesight equaled his marksmanship."

"Where are you taking me?"

"Back to Peacehaven."

"Let me go, damn you."

"Not until I put your foolish self in your foolish bed, safe and sound. Even then, I'm not sure I'll let go."

She kicked him and damned near ended all chance of their having children.

"Will you stop that!" He made to spank her, but ended up palming her neat bottom and enjoying the process.

Jade mocked him with her laugh. "Don't you ever stop thinking about your baser needs?"

"My baser needs have grown stronger and more persistent since the day you circled me wearing this wicked costume. Yours have rather blossomed as well. Remember that morning you—"

She smacked his back with both fists. "Go to hell, Marcus Fitzalan."

His gasp ended on a chuckle. "Only if you come with me, Jade Smithfield." He stroked her inner thigh, thinking to awaken some of her needs, heightening his own, instead, until she began to fight him in earnest.

By the time they neared her smuggler's cave, she'd become a true hellcat, biting, scratching and kicking nonstop, so Marcus walked straight into the Channel and didn't stop even when the salt water burned his cuts and blazed at his hip.

To stop Jade from kicking and screaming about the freezing water, Marcus dropped her in.

When he pulled her up, she gasped and swallowed air. "You rotten scum of a serpent's spawn," she said, before she pushed *him* under.

Above and below the water, they grappled, until Marcus's hip felt better for the salt water wash and his baser needs, however cold, stood at full alert. He wanted to put period to her fury and get them inside to a warm fire and a blazing reconciliation.

Above water once again, Marcus waylaid Jade as she lunged his way once more. "Wait!" he said. "What's that?"

Like a shot, she wrapped her arms around his neck, and her legs around his waist. "What?"

"Big and scaly," he improvised. "Swimming this way."

Jade screamed, and clung, and Marcus made for the beach, as quick as he could, though Jade somehow managed to reach land ahead of him.

Halfway to the cave, she fell to the shingle, panting. "I can't go on."

He bent to skim her long black hair back from her eyes and hook it behind her ears. "You can."

"No," she wailed. "Leave me here to die."

Marcus kissed her brow. "We were too close to death already tonight. If you don't mind, I think we should celebrate life."

She stilled and looked up at him.

He fell to his knees. "Kiss me Jade, like you mean it. As if there's no tomorrow. Kiss me like the scandal you're so proud to be."

The kiss she bestowed formed a perfect blend of the innocent and the erotic, but before she felled him with its intensity, and they ended on their backs with sand where sand should never go, Marcus broke the kiss and rose to swing her into his arms.

Jade held on and lay her head on his chest. "What kind of a celebration?"

He didn't speak, he kept walking, and once they stood in the stairwell and she grabbed the lantern from the landing, he saw her gaze, as intense as his, eyes smoky, lids heavy. They may be covered in gooseflesh, but between them they were so hot, 'twas a wonder the English Channel hadn't come to a boil.

Almost since he met Jade, he'd dreamed of making slow exquisite love to her, over and over again, of savoring her to his heart's content, of having her all to himself for time without end . . . which remained impossible and would do so until they settled the widening track between them.

But tonight, he would take every moment he could get.

He'd imagined taking her hard and fast or so slow, she'd beg for completion. He'd imagined sleeping with her in his arms for longer than a moment, longer than a lifetime.

When he got to the landing near his room, he stepped through his door. "I want you in my bed," he said in response to her questioning look.

The smoldering gaze she gave him made him stand her up and strip her in a fever, frenzied and desperate, the same way she stripped him.

When Marcus stood naked and proud before her, Jade stopped denying heart and mind and accepted Marcus Fitzalan as her destiny. Not that she would give her *self* over to him, or to any man, but *this* man she would take to her bed.

Time to live up to her name and prove what a scandal she could be.

They'd known each other for eternity, he'd said, and he'd been right. She'd been waiting for him forever, she knew. She simply hadn't known his name.

Whether berating her, or saving her, going over ledgers or walking fussy newborns, his gentleness called to her. His touch awakened her from the slumber of youth and made her crave womanhood in his arms.

He'd turned wallflowers into hot-house beauties, calmed a little girl's fears and turned them to giggles. He'd encouraged his brother to heal, championed a baby boy, and opened a heart Jade believed eternally locked—her own—tossing a life's worth of lessons over the chalk cliffs.

Marcus Fitzalan, scoundrel and friend, the love of her life.

Whatever their place in society, Earl or Lady, rich or poor, friend or foe, the secrets they harbored, and the directions their lives took—and they *must* go their separate ways—her heart would remain forever his.

Marcus wrapped his arms around her, brought her scorchingly, sinfully close, skin to skin for the first time ever. Splendid silk, cool, soft, vibrant and alive, a fast-beating heart, warm rippling muscles.

"My very own Scandal," he whispered. "It's time for learning and soaring. Time to do what I wanted the minute I saw you at the beginning of time."

He yearned as she did. Then and now. Glory.

His kiss, sweet and tender, chaste even, made her heart race and her body quicken, this coming together soared beyond the melding of bodies to a mating of spirits.

"I want you," he whispered, hoarse with passion, teasing her upper lip with his lower, coaxing and prodding, breath warm, his hands working a special magic.

"Have your wicked way with me," she whispered. "Please."

Marcus raised a brow. "My pleasure, my darling Scandal."

His husky voice purled heat through Jade in spiraling coils. She sifted her fingers through the whorls of hair on his chest, testing and abrading, pebbling a nipple, licking and kissing. She rubbed her nose against the silk as well—spearmint, freshened by the sea. "I wanted to do this, and more, when you nearly blacked out after the babies were born."

"I would have let you."

"I was afraid."

"Are you still, Jade? Are you finally ready to step into the fire?"

"I've been cold and yearning for your heat since the day we met, but I didn't know it."

After a long, tongue-stroking kiss, Marcus lifted her into his arms and nibbled her neck, her throat, the hollow beneath her collarbone, sending shafts of white-hot lightning to every hidden place in her body. Shafts of heat that shivered, and sparkled, sizzled and melted.

Jade shuddered. Her nipples pebbled. "Teach me to love you, Marcus. I want the something more you spoke about, the ultimate rise to the stars. Show me. Take me with you."

With an oath, Marcus placed her on his bed, covering her and touching her everywhere at once, and Jade absorbed each sensation with the joy of new discovery. When her breasts grazed his chest and his arousal met her pulsing center, she arched and moaned.

She never left her hearth, yet she had come home.

He hovered above her, his cobalt eyes intense, his passion hot and fit to singe, his man-part throbbing-ready and . . . huge.

Huge? "No! Wait! It's too thick, too long," she said. "It won't fit." Jade scuttled out from under him, until she leaned against his headboard, arms around her upraised knees. "You may be a stallion, Marcus Fitzalan, but I'm no mare!"

Marcus's arms gave out and he fell to the mattress, laughing so hard he rolled to his side to catch his breath.

Jade crawled down the bed to hover over him, her fear forgotten for the moment. "I love it when you laugh like that."

He touched her cheek. "I love it when you smile like that."

"Oh, look," she said with relief. "It got smaller. It'll fit better now."

"No it won't," Marcus said with another fit of laughing. "It won't fit at all now."

"I don't believe you," Jade said. "Prove it."

Catching her off guard, he tumbled her on her back, reversing their positions, him grinning above her. "Your challenge shot it with anticipation," he said. "It's big again."

"It's magic," she said.

"Tell me that when we're finished. *Please.*"

Marcus probed Jade at her center to prepare her for his invasion, giving her pleasure, he saw. Thank God! Her eyes had barely widened before they turned soft and shimmery. He entered her a bit, pulled slowly back and away. He found her sweet spot with his hand and made her moan until she wanted more of him. Then he slipped a bit further inside her, repeating the teasing process again and again, testing limits, hers and his, until she surged to take him deeper.

"I adore you," he whispered against her lips, holding himself still, with rigid discipline. "I adore you."

"I'm fascinated by you," she said.

"Are you certain, Jade?" he asked before breaching her final barrier.

"I *am* fascinated."

He released his breath in a gasp, his body tense and

pulsing as he fought to keep from burying himself in her velvet sheath. "Are you certain this is what you want? We will both be changed, not outside, but in our hearts and deep into our souls. Of this I am certain."

She stroked his lips with a finger, arched, and rolled her hips, absolutely aware and proud to torture him. "Be my lover, Marcus. Come inside me."

Jade reveled in Marcus's shout of triumph, mindful of his gentle care, his patience and love as he delved deeper and deeper, and brought her higher and higher.

In one swift move, he surged and buried himself so deep, discomfort blazed for a blink, then fire cooled and became a soothing salve, a warmth, that radiated outward and about them, pulling him with her into a cocoon of satisfaction. Alone in the universe, desire grew like stars flaming to bright scintillating life, the essence of pleasure almost too intense to bear.

Jade ascended to a plane higher than she thought possible where paradise glowed a luminous azure, burnished and pure, the clouds a cushion upon which to float. In Marcus she saw a matching glory as the gods set them gently down to marvel in wonder at where they'd been.

In the aftermath, they touched, they kissed. Jade knew Marcus as well as she knew herself, this soul mate God created for her.

"I've been sick with missing you," he said. "And tonight . . . I was so bloody scared tonight. Jade, I couldn't bear losing you." He pulled her hard against him, imprisoning her with possessive hands. "I'm so worried about you."

Because she couldn't change a thing, Jade refused to address his worry. "You broke me when you left for London," she said, addressing his former statement, instead. "Everyday you were gone was a form of torture. Why didn't you write? I was so angry and so sad that you didn't write."

"I wrote to you every night," he replied, finding her breasts in particular need of attention, and distracting her in the bargain. "In my mind as I lay awake wanting you beside me, I wrote you, and afterward, I made slow sweet love to you."

He surged to renewed life and she took him home again. Back to heaven, they went, faster and more frenzied this time, their arrival nothing short of cataclysmic.

Lazy minutes later, he rolled her over and atop him, as if content to memorize her with his hands and kiss where he could reach, and she lay her head in the hollow of his shoulder to sleep.

Sometime during the dark of night, he suckled her to completion and slipped inside her, filling her, fulfilling her, adoring her with his body, their loving slow and languorous and breathtaking, the most marvelous awakening of Jade's life.

She welcoméd his every thrust, discovering she could enhance their play with her movement. She learned to pull him in, hold him tight, and make him moan and shout her name. She would release him to withdraw, only to pull him back again. With her love, she milked him, and with his seed, he filled her.

"I adore you," he said as he all but collapsed atop her, nuzzling her ear even as he closed his eyes. "Though I think you near killed me with lust." He sighed in contentment. "I can't think of a better way to go."

Jade heard his weak chuckle as she curled into him and snuggled her nose into the hollow of his neck, settling her leg near that delicious man place, all soft and at rest now.

She drifted to sleep and dreamed of a world where no danger threatened and life's secret burdens would never tear them apart.

★ ★ ★ ★ ★

"I don't think the gunman was aiming at Jade," Garrett repeated as Marcus paced. "I believe he was trying to break one of the fine ceramic tubes of gunpowder with a bullet so it would explode on impact and ignite the rest."

Marcus turned on him. "How many tubes?"

"They found shards enough for a great deal of damage, including several unexploded tubes. We didn't have one explosion but a series of them."

"How can that be? I stayed with the railroad cars from the minute they arrived. No one could have planted gunpowder tubes while I was there."

"Then somebody planted plenty before you and the train arrived. Perhaps someone who works for us?"

"What? A disgruntled employee just happens to try and destroy us at the same time Jade is trying to do the same?" Marcus scoffed and ran a hand through his hair. "There are so many loose ends, Garr. I thought I knew who'd want Jade dead, that once we had that first gunman, we had the greedy cousin, but the locals identified the man I chased to ground. He's still locked up and he isn't Giles Dudley."

"Which doesn't rule out the cousin, Marc."

"I suppose not. Guess I'm not thinking straight."

"Look," Garrett said. "I know you're worried about Jade, but you've got to pull yourself together. And get some rest, you look like hell. What did you do, pace all night?"

Marcus actually felt heat scuttle up his neck.

Garrett's eyes narrowed in confusion for a blink then he grinned.

Marcus rolled his eyes. "Actually, I had a revelation last night."

"One usually does in such circumstances."

"I meant at the site."

Garrett cleared his throat. "Of course."

"No, really. Whoever did this knows railroading well enough to know that however scarce and expensive the wood for ties, the rails are worth thrice as much."

Garrett shrugged. "Anyone might learn of it, but I should think it most apparent to us and the owners of the foundry."

"And whoever oversees invoicing and payments there."

Fifteen

Jade appreciated the hot bath Marcus had delivered to her room after he left, and odd as it seemed after last night, she appreciated the privacy to enjoy it, her mind filled with him, his scent and texture, the feel of his lips on hers, on her breasts and elsewhere, which warmed her even now.

She needed to come to terms with this new aspect of their relationship. To examine this feeling that she would never be the same Jade Smithfield who only met Marcus Fitzalan for the first time three short months ago. The Jade who, despite her determination not to relinquish her *self* to him, felt renewed and exhilarated for the physical process that she feared had done just that.

Yet with all her doubts, she couldn't help revel in the memory of the night just passed, wanting nothing more than to soak her pleasantly aching muscles for hours of sweet contemplation.

Her door's squeal as it opened put period to that on the instant. "Jade?"

"Emily. What's the matter, Sweetheart? You look sad."

Emily approached the tub hesitantly, her tiny little Mucks waddling faithfully behind, and once she got there, Em's face fell even further, until her lips began to quiver. "Emmy wants Mummy."

"Oh, sweetheart." Jade got right out of the tub, slipped into her dressing gown and lifted Emily in her arms to cuddle her. What could she say? She couldn't pretend Catherine might still come back. Emily deserved better than false hope. But the truth felt so . . . brutal.

She kissed Em's brow. "Emmy, you know Mummy would have come back to you, if she could have, don't you?"

Emily nodded, her look so trusting, it frightened Jade as much as Marcus's gentleness did.

"Papa didn't bring her," Emmy said, shaking her head.

"Papa? Do you mean Marcus? You expected Marcus to bring your Mummy back?"

Emily nodded.

"You know him better than I do," Jade said. "He wanted very much to bring Mummy back for you." No wonder Em's sadness today, if Marcus had been her last hope of getting Catherine back.

Jade looked into Em's big cornflower blue eyes. "He loves you, you know? Papa does."

Emily nodded again. "Where's Mummy?"

Jade tucked a couple of Emily's ringlets behind her ear, remembering how Marcus doing that to her had made *her* feel cared for and protected. She carried Em to the window to look upon the rare beauty of a sunny day, and pointed toward the sky. "Remember, Emily, when we were looking up at the clouds the other day? How beautiful they looked all white and fluffy bright? Well, your Mummy is up there in heaven. She's . . . an angel now . . . watching over you from one of those beautiful clouds."

Emily's eyes slowly filled until a tear hovered and slipped off her lash. Then, as slowly, another, while she regarded Jade, as if her life depended upon Jade's every breath.

She seemed too young to understand death, or she should be, but she'd grown up where beatings and hunger were part of life, where a child likely encountered death often enough to understand the finality of it.

Jade blinked, feeling the weight of responsibility, seeking

divine guidance for Emily's sake, and wishing Marcus were here.

"Sweetheart . . ." Jade tugged on a flaxen ringlet adorning the tiny brow and had to clear her throat before she could go on. "I know you'll always love your Mummy in a very special way, deep in here, in your heart, the same way she will always love you."

Emily barely nodded, almost as if she were holding her breath.

Jade was sick inside, so afraid of doing this wrong. "Emmy, you know how Mucks had a doggie Mummy once, but you're her new Mummy now, and you love her?"

Em's nod became more certain.

"Good. You want to keep Mucks safe, don't you, and warm and happy, and give her good food and lots of hugs and kisses so she'll grow up strong and happy?"

Another affirmative nod, and a softening of that pale little face.

"Well, I want to take care of *you* the same way you take care of Mucks. I want you to be my little girl now, my very own, because, you see, Sweetheart, I love you too."

Emily released a great shuddering breath and her tears fell more quickly as she threw her arms around Jade and began to cry in earnest, until she sobbed so hard, Jade could hardly breathe for the pain in her heart.

Mucks took to howling, crying along with Em, and she pulled away and looked down, her pup's sadness of more concern than her own.

"Here, Sweetheart," Jade said. "Let me put you on my bed and bring Mucks up here with us, shall I?"

Once she had her pup, Emily curled in a ball holding Mucks close, and Jade stretched out behind them, pulling them both, pup and child, into her embrace, and Em's sobs diminished to an occasional hiccup.

"I love you, Emmy."

"Can Mummy hear me?" Emily asked without turning toward Jade.

"Yes, Darling. And when you laugh, it pleases her very much, because she loves you. So you must try to be happy, even though you miss her. If you are, she'll be very content in heaven."

"Emmy loves M . . . Mummy. Love . . . you t . . . too."

Some time passed before Jade felt Em relax, and longer still before her breathing calmed, turned peaceful, and Em slept.

Marcus's heart hit the side of his chest with a thud when he found them asleep on Jade's bed, looking like mother and child . . . and pup. A family.

His family.

His.

By the tear tracks on both faces, it looked as if something momentous had taken place.

The minute Lacey told him that Emily had asked for her mother this morning, he'd come looking for her. He could just imagine what must have transpired.

He sat on the edge of the bed and twisted one of Emily's golden curls around his finger and she opened her eyes. "Hi Emmy-bug. You all right?"

Emily peeked behind her and saw Jade still asleep. She put a finger to her lips. "Shh. Mama's sleeping."

Jade opened her eyes at that and regarded him. She must have told Emily about her mother, a task he didn't envy. Now Jade was Mama and he was Papa, except that Jade thought their becoming a family was impossible, and Lord how he prayed she was wrong.

197

Seeing Jade and Em like this filled Marcus with hope. "We can do it," he said, not imagining how, but wanting desperately to make it happen.

Jade kissed Emily's nose. "Want to take Papa and Mucks for a walk while I get dressed?" She rose from the bed, giving Marcus a tantalizing glimpse of the woman beneath the damp dressing gown.

"First, the three of us can move your things into the bedroom next door, my little Kitten," Jade said, "so I can hear you, if you need me during the night. Then perhaps we can have a picnic on the beach?"

With the resilience and trust of a child, Emily nodded and handed Mucks into Marcus's keeping, while she scrambled from the bed. "Come Papa," she said taking his hand, and filling him with pride.

Marcus cupped Jade's cheek, his love for her more consuming than the physical. It actually rose to a spiritual plane, a place he'd never been, nor aspired to be, but a gift he accepted as a blessing.

"We can do it," he repeated, before he left. *We have to,* he thought.

There must be a way.

Ten minutes later, looking fresh as springtime, Jade descended the stairs into the foyer and sat beside them on the bottom step. "Ready for—"

Mucks began barking, as ferocious as any half-pound mite on short legs, and loped for the front door.

Before Marcus reached it, the door opened and it hit the wall with a reverberating crash. Two men pushed their way inside, both older, one unkempt, in need of a wash and full of bravado, which proved some ale must actually have missed his coat and slid down his gullet.

The second man was dressed a great deal better. A

dandy. "I want my wife," he demanded. "Who's in charge here?"

Emily came for the growling Mucks, and Marcus swept them into his arms. Jade positioned herself beside them.

The disheveled man turned to his cohort. "She ain't y'wife till y'pay me for'er." He nodded at Marcus. "We come for me daughter."

Marcus handed Emily to Jade. "I'll take care of this. Take Em out of here."

Jade shook her head, refusing to budge, of course. "This is my house and these women are my responsibility," she said, frustrating, but not surprising, Marcus.

Several people apparently heard Mucks barking and the crash that followed, so a crowd had gathered. Garrett wheeled his chair around the corner and stopped ahead of the rest. "What's going on, Marc? Is everything all right?"

"This 'gentlemen,' " Marcus stressed. "Wishes to claim his daughter, who is this man's intended, I believe."

"Right'y'are guv'nr."

"Who exactly are you looking for?" Marcus asked them.

"Me girl's Abby Parg'ter."

"Abigail's your daughter," Garrett said. "Impossible."

"No, Garrett." Abigail stood trembling on the stairs watching him. "Not impossible at all. I am his daughter."

"And soon to be my wife," the dandy shouted in such a way as to order Abigail to remember it.

Abigail straightened her spine. "Now *that's* impossible." She returned her gaze to her sire. "I won't be sold."

Her father pulled a pistol from his waistcoat and aimed it at her, catching Marcus completely off guard, but not enough to keep him from stepping in front of Jade and Emily to protect them.

" 'E's payin' with coin 'a the realm, me girl," her pistol-toting father shouted, his aim steady. "You do as I say."

"I won't," Abby said, "You'll have to shoot me."

Her father cocked his pistol.

"I'll pay you more," Garrett shouted, snapping every head his way.

Abby gasped and grabbed the stair rail for support. "No," she said, but Marcus didn't think anyone heard her but him.

Her father lowered his weapon and rubbed his dirty chin, allowing Marcus to take the pistol from his hand, without protest, for the greedy blighter's gaze never left Garrett. "Well now, I was after sellin' 'er for a wife. You'll have to pay double to have 'er for y'doxy. I gots me pride."

"I doubt it," Garrett drawled. "Name your price."

Jade handed Emily to Lacey and cleared everyone from the room.

"Wait a minute, now," the rejected bridegroom groused. "A promise is a promise."

"Shut y'trap. Y'can always try'n top 'is price, if y'r that 'ot to mount'er."

The dandy turned on his heel and left the house.

Marcus climbed the stairs to Abby as her father and Garrett faced off. Abby trembled with impotent rage, and Marcus wondered who made her more furious, her father for selling her or Garrett for his willingness to purchase her.

"Garr," Marcus said. "Maybe you should consider—"

"Stay the hell out of this, Marc."

Abby's father narrowed his eyes and looked from him to his brother, disgusting Marcus. The bastard actually hoped they would try to outbid each other.

"Abby," Marcus whispered. "Let me take you upstairs."

She shook her head without taking her gaze from Garr.

"Garrett," she said, a pleading note in her voice. "Please don't—"

"You stay out of this too, Abigail," he said. "This is between me and him."

"And me, damn it!"

Garrett ignored the curse, so out of character for Abigail, he should have heeded the warning. Not his worst mistake today, but right up there at the top of a growing list.

"I'll give you a thousand pounds for her," his idiot brother said.

"Ten thousand."

"Three."

"Eight."

Tears ran down Abigail's cheeks and she seemed to become weaker and more dependent upon Marcus's support with every word they uttered. Still, she wouldn't allow him to propel her from the stairwell.

"Five," Garrett countered. "And that's twice what I was willing to pay."

Abigail's wail grew from somewhere deep inside her, revealing a grief so keen, Marcus was shaken by it.

"Sold," her father shouted with triumph, and Marcus caught Abigail as she fainted.

Furious at Abby's father, and his own brother, Marcus carried Abby up the stairs to her room, while Garr stood at the bottom shouting for him to bring her down, and while her rapacious father demanded payment in full.

Garr sent a note to Seaford Head, Jade later told Marcus, and Brinkley brought five thousands pounds sterling that night.

Early the next morning, as Marcus watched from Jade's window, Beecher helped Garr into a carriage so he could drop it personally into Barney Pargeter's oily hands.

As they drove off, Marcus wondered how a man as smart as his brother could make such a monumental error in judgment. Then he turned back toward Jade's bed, where she slept still, Emily beside her, Mucks between them. Em had awakened crying for her mother last night. They'd heard her from here, and he'd brought her in so they could comfort her. Her four-legged escort had tagged along.

Children and a dog sharing their bed with them and they hadn't even finished scaling the mountain of impediments keeping them from a future together. Marcus smiled and climbed back into the midst of them to be cuddled, and kissed, licked and kicked, and he cherished every wonderful moment.

When Garr returned, Beecher left him at the bottom of the stairs, where he remained to shout the house down for Abigail to come and talk to him.

Despite Marcus's previous night's vow never to speak to the fool again, he went running down to push Garr's chair out the front door. "Are you out of your mind? She's never going to forgive you as it is."

"Forgive me?" Garrett asked, affronted. "For what?"

"For offering to purchase her, never mind haggling to get her on the cheap!"

"Don't be stupid," Garrett said.

Marcus laughed. "Look who's calling the kettle black."

Garrett shook his stubborn head. "I never thought I'd ask this, Marc, but will you carry me up there so I can talk to her?"

Marcus took pity and squeezed his shoulder. "No, Garr. I won't. She's—"

"Why you ungrateful son of a bitch. I never wanted to strike you more than I do right now. You stuck me in this chair. You owe me."

Those words echoed loudly between them for longer than Marcus could bear. "Go ahead, hit me," he snapped. "I'd love an excuse to hit you back." After a furious minute, Marcus turned and walked away.

Three days later, Jade sat down beside Garrett's bed. He looked like he hadn't bothered to get up or shave, yesterday or today, and it was already afternoon. "You look worse than your brother," she said. "For all the time you've spent in bed, you look as if you haven't slept a wink. Marcus has circles under his eyes from lack of sleep as well. You two need to talk. He's guilt ridden."

"We both know, Jade, that it hasn't been *guilt* keeping Marc awake nights."

Jade could barely believe what the gentle Garrett implied, though she realized that powerlessness and panic lay at the root of his rage. So she stared him down silently, though her fury begged to be unleashed.

He finally had the sense to look abashed, and cleared his throat. "I haven't been sleeping. I've been trying to learn to walk. Damn near broke my neck. How's Abby?"

No wonder his frustration, if he'd been trying to walk and failed. "Abby is so upset, she hasn't been able to keep food down since . . . well, to quote her, 'Since you bought her.' "

Garrett used a word Jade had never heard and apologized immediately, for that *and* his previous insult. "I didn't see myself as buying her. I saw myself as having the where-withal to *rescue* her."

"To the rest of us, it looked and sounded like a purchase, worse that she was hardly worth the price you were forced to pay."

Garrett cursed again. "Has Beecher seen her?"

"He just returned from Newhaven. He's looking in on her now."

Garrett made to get up. "What about Marc?"

"He's taken Emily and Mucks for a walk on the downs. You don't *really* blame him for your accident, do you?"

"Most of the time, no."

"*You* never challenged *him* to a race, then?"

"Of course I did. We always—"

"Don't you realize that at any time over the years, such an accident might have happened as easily to him when *you* had issued the challenge?"

Garrett grimaced. "At some point, I suppose that did occur to me, though not in the last few days."

Jade rose, satisfied she'd given Garrett a few things to contemplate. "Talk to your brother. Release him from the guilt plaguing him. He needs your absolution more than he needs to breathe."

Garrett closed his eyes. "I know."

Jade went upstairs to Abby's room and met Beecher coming out. "How is she?"

He shook his head. "To be blunt, she's in the family way and her heart's broken on top of it. If this keeps up, she could lose the babe."

Jade stepped back. "A baby." She grasped his sleeve. "How far along is she? Was she . . . did she arrive here . . . that way?"

"Two months at most."

"But she's been here three."

"Aye, I know."

Jade kept remembering Marcus entering Abby's room the other day. How many times had he done so when she hadn't seen? "Did she tell you who the father is?"

"Absolutely refused. Mayhap she'll tell you."

Jade nodded as she turned the knob.

Abigail began to weep when Jade stepped inside.

An hour later Jade left Abigail's room in a daze, and went straight to her own room to pace.

Betrayed.

Marcus, The Earl of Attleboro, had fathered Abigail's child.

Sixteen

Jade's hand trembled as she wiped her eyes with the back of a hand. Marcus had professed to love her while sleeping in Abigail's arms. With Abby, he had shared intimacy, soft touches, kisses, and more.

He had fathered another woman's child.

Jade wished she'd never seen him slip into Abby's room.

Abigail had cried that an Earl was too good for her. Bloody hell! She was too good for him.

The bastard ran true to his sex after all. All men *were* created equal.

Lord, what to do now, Jade wondered . . . except she believed she already knew.

She would make the man she loved marry someone else, of course. They never had a future anyway, and Abigail deserved a father for her child and a husband who would care for them, and no doubt Marcus would do so, once the decision and vows were made, of that Jade was certain. Marcus Fitzalan would nurture a piglet, if 'twas given into his keeping.

Despite his betrayal, Marcus had re-defined manhood in her eyes, though he did not uphold one of her beliefs—he was not perfect, but flawed. Human. And if she didn't halt the direction in which her thoughts ran, she'd be *forgiving* the philandering Earl of Attleboro, the lying bastard.

She'd come to believe him an exception, a truly good man, and in many ways, he was still the best man she had ever met.

No, no he wasn't. Perhaps her original assessment had

been correct after all. Men were all rotten. Even Garrett had fallen from his pedestal.

Jade hated that she'd believed Marcus's sweet seductive words while he'd been going from her bed to Abigail's. How many others, she wondered, had he bedded since he arrived?

She shivered and shut her window, looking toward the downs, wondering where Marcus and Emily wandered. She'd wanted to go with them, but needed to talk to Garrett. Just as well. Now she needed time to gather her scattered wits and summon the strength to give Marcus away.

As furious as she was with him, she ached for him, even now, to take her in his arms and tell her, she'd made a mistake. Except that she couldn't have, because Marcus was the Earl of Attleboro.

Still, deep inside—more fool her—she wanted him to . . . love her . . . keep her only unto him.

Jade laughed aloud. She always knew she'd never marry, not with Gram's secret to keep and a house full of down-trodden women to keep as well. Besides, what man could live in a place as daft as this? The only one she ever wanted didn't want *her*, not exclusively, at any rate.

She marched to the wall with the hidden door cut into it and shot the bolts in place, bottom and top. She'd never sleep in Marcus's arms again, never feel him deep inside her. A sob caught in Jade's throat. She swallowed it ruthlessly. She *must* overcome her weakness for a man soon to be the husband of another.

He'd have to leave Peacehaven now, but she'd make him marry Abigail first, by God, and take Abby with him. Oh, Lord, and Emily would be heartbroken all over again, a sin Jade would never forgive.

Fortunately for Jade's peace and determination, Marcus kept Emily out all afternoon and oversaw putting her to bed, so Jade didn't have to face him until he sat across the dinner table from her.

Except for Abigail, everyone was present, even Garrett, so this presented as good a time as any to shame the Earl of Attleboro into taking responsibility for his actions. She only hoped that no one else would be hurt by her revelation.

No use putting it off. What did waiting a minute or five matter? Or a day?

But perhaps she *should* wait until tomorrow. Or the day after.

"Now," came Gram's strident voice.

Jade rose quickly to her feet—lest she change her mind—and cut the chatter like a blade.

Her family—but not—regarded her as if she'd sprouted horns. Curiosity. Speculation. Impatience. Hunger.

She almost changed her mind . . . because saying the words aloud would make them true.

Now or never. Except . . . once the accusation had been made, nothing would be the same again. Not for her. Not for Emily. Yet if she said nothing, life for Abigail and her child would be intolerable.

Jade sighed and straightened her shoulders. She cleared her tight, swollen throat. "I have an announcement to make." Her voice felt and sounded as if she'd swallowed gravel. She cleared her throat again.

Marcus must sense her nervousness, because he smiled and winked at her, swamping her with need.

Mortification, fury at his audacity, fired Jade's ire. She itched to erase his cocksure grin, caught sight of the serving bowl . . . and mushy peas flew across the table.

A horrified gasp sliced the silence.

"Abigail is with child by the Earl of Attleboro!" Jade announced, her sharp words resonating like steeple bells at a funeral.

Garrett cursed, threw down his napkin, and propelled his chair from the room.

Marcus, sitting across from her, oozed slime and fury.

Jade regarded her slathered palm.

Her nemesis pinned her with his stony regard, like a butterfly to a wax slab, until her face must be as red as his, though not as green. Her satisfaction fled on the unsteady wings of uncertainty.

She'd expected Garrett to berate the philanderer. Why had he not?

Marcus patiently raised his napkin and wiped his face. Linen rasped against whiskers. Silence reigned until Marcus, too, quit the room.

The cacophony of voices that erupted paled against the sound of Jade's heart battering her ribs. She regarded her audience as if they were speaking in tongues. Ivy gave her a sympathetic smile and indicated with a nod that she should follow Marcus.

Because her mind barely functioned and she trusted Ivy, Jade left the room.

In the foyer—trembling with rage, pride, or both—Marcus stood, his gaze trained on Garrett pulling himself from his chair to stand at the base of the stairs. Marcus's composure suffered a further battering as his brother spent long agonizing minutes attempting to raise a foot to the second step.

As if propelled by grief, Marcus moved forward.

Jade stopped him with an outstretched arm, and, oh, what a look he gave her.

She shivered, chilled to her marrow.

When Garrett finally got his foot on the next step, he crowed in triumph, but his victory was short-lived, for his weak limb failed to support his weight and he faltered.

With a curse, he grabbed the rail with both hands.

"Garr. Let me help." His veiled plea did no good. Marcus fisted his hands at his side, belying the composure he attempted to project.

"I won't be carried. Leave me be. No, wait!" Garrett turned. "Don't leave. Let me apologize first for what I said. My accident was never your fault. 'Twas fate. Meant to be. My haughty self needed bringing down a peg or ten. I needed to come to Peacehaven to heal in more ways than the obvious. That bloody chair got me here. You've always been the best brother a man could want. Accept my apology, Marc, and my thanks."

"I accept both," Marcus said, his voice thick with emotion.

Garrett nodded. "Good. Now leave me alone. I'll walk to her, if it kills me."

"If you're determined, Garrett," Jade said. "Let us help. Marcus can support your weight on one side, I'll support it on the other, but you'll be doing the walking."

He regarded them, loathe to give in, but acquiesced with a nod.

Slow as a snail going uphill, Garrett walked up the stairs between Jade and Marcus.

At the door to Abby's room, Garrett knocked and waited for permission to enter, knowing full well, she couldn't imagine who stood there.

Dressed in a turquoise dressing gown, her chestnut hair uncoiled and falling free, Abigail caught her breath and rose slowly from her window-seat when they entered . . . shocked, elated, fearful, and with so much yearning in her eyes, Jade was embarrassed to witness it.

Garrett actually growled. "You're carrying my child!"

Spoken with accusation and jubilation, the bald announcement hit Abby like a blow, while it removed a shroud from Jade's heart.

Garrett was the Earl of Attleboro?

"You can't run away from the truth of your condition," he told Abby. "And you'll not be able to run from me much longer, either. Because of your stubborn determination that I, at least, try, I have been walking. With Ivy's help," he added, almost as a caution, "in my own fashion, and very ill. I tried because you locked yourself away up here and I intended to come and talk sense into you . . . or kidnap you—and don't think I can't. Now we have a child on the way." His voice softened. "You'd best marry me, Abigail. With practice, I might be ready to walk the floor nights by the time the little scrapper arrives. Ah, love, I can't wait."

Anguish ravaging her features, Abigail turned her back to gaze out the window.

Jade wished they could leave the lovers alone, but she feared Abby would bolt if they did. And if she ran now, Jade knew that Abigail would go so far, she'd not be found.

Marcus looked as uncomfortable, but she could tell that he felt they needed to stay as well.

Abigail turned to face Garrett, her anguish replaced with fury. "Do you think that just because you're the rich and powerful Earl of Attleboro that you can buy people? Well, I'm not willing to be bought any more than I was willing to be sold. And by God I won't marry a man who haggles over me as if I were a lame racehorse!"

Garrett winced. "There are those who consider a lame man less than prime stock as well, so I guess I deserved that," he said.

Remorse etched Abigail's ashen countenance. "No." She reached out. "I didn't mean—"

"I shouldn't have haggled. You're right about that."

Her color returned in a flash while Garrett's paled. "I mean I shouldn't have tried to outbid—Damn it, I would have given anything to free you from that devil's clutches. I would have beggared myself to do it. Lacking the physical ability, all I had was the monetary power to . . . to become your knight in shining armor, if you will, however laughable *that* may sound."

Garrett raised an imploring hand, and lowered it. "All I intended, Abby mine, was your rescue, by fair means or foul."

Abby softened visibly.

"I know I bungled it, badly," Garrett admitted. "But the fact is that I had already asked you to marry me and you ran from me even then, which was before my . . . *purchase,* as you're resolved to call it. If you have reason for retreat now, you had none, then, that I know of. If you did, you never informed me. You simply disappeared up the stairs where I couldn't go. If truth be told, I've experienced a good deal of wretchedness as a result of your desertion."

Abigail sighed and turned once more to gaze outside. "I loved you too much to let you marry the daughter of a man who'll bleed you for money the rest of his life."

"Loved?" Garrett asked. "Past tense?"

Abby shook her head but she didn't answer.

"I love *you* too much," Garrett countered. "Present tense. To care how often he tries to bleed me for money, as long as I have you. Let him have the money; he'll still be poor, but we'll be rich, because we'll have each other."

"The mother of your child grew up a guttersnipe," Abby said with frustration. "*Uneducated.* Less than nothing."

"The father of your child grew up selfish and full of his own importance. And most recently, he made the biggest mistake of his life when he reduced the value of the woman he loves more than his next breath, to pounds sterling. The fact is, she's priceless.

"I can't change the past, Abigail," Garrett continued, "but I can make your future and our child's better by sharing it with you. And mine, Ab. My future will be hell without you in it. Please rescue me from hell. Please forgive the unforgivable."

Abigail turned to regard him, and Garrett took a step so strong and full of purpose, Jade and Marcus let him go.

Garrett Fitzalan, Earl of Attleboro, stood straight and proud before the woman he loved, extending his hand as he had done the day he met her. "Abigail Pargeter, would you do me the very great honor of becoming my wife?"

Abby didn't move, but Jade could practically see her resolve take flight.

"Go away, Marc," Garrett said as he regarded Abby with piercing intensity. "Take Jade with you. And change your coat. You look disgusting."

Jade's heart skipped a beat as Marcus eyed her with the steely purpose that appeared to be prevalent among the Fitzalan men as he closed his fingers around her wrist to drag her out.

Shutting Abby's door behind them, he advanced. "You thought I was the father of Abigail's child." Neither question nor accusation, he made, but a statement gravid with hidden purpose.

Jade began to retreat from Marcus's advance. "I'd suspected you were the Earl of Attleboro for some time," she admitted. "And Abby said her child's father was the Earl, so . . ."

Lord, he was making her nervous, Jade thought, smiling in her heart, because it had all been a horrid mistake and he hadn't—

"You were prepared to give me away," Marcus said, another statement rife with dubious intent.

"I thought Abigail needed you."

"More than you need me?"

Jade raised her chin. "I *don't* need you."

Marcus chuckled. "What made you think I was the Earl?"

Jade was affronted he read her so well, and laughed at her bald-faced lie about not needing him. " 'Twas said in the village that the Earl owned the railroad, and you do have an inordinate interest in the railroad, Marcus, you must admit."

"That's hardly enough to go on."

"You fit the description as well."

"Which is?"

"A rascal." A *handsome* scamp, she did not say. "A smooth talker and a rich dresser. A top-notch rider. Tall, rugged, dark hair. *Brash, cocky.*" She emphasized the last with a nod. "The day I hired you, you said you'd been employed by the Earl of Attleboro, but you stumbled over the words, so I was certain . . ."

"You never considered it could be Garr?"

She shrugged. "A smug scoundrel? That's *you.*" A wall came up against Jade's back. The end of the hall.

Her bedroom door.

Marcus reached over and opened it so she nearly fell in, him right behind, shutting them inside. "I'm furious you thought I could make love to Abby, as if making love to you wasn't the most outstanding experience of my life and . . . *destined,* damn it!"

Jade caught her breath on a sob. "I ached for you to call it a mistake, to say that you were really . . . mine."

He caught her in his arms. Their lips met like a whisper of wings, gentle, tender, a most satisfying kiss, because she'd thought never to experience it again.

"It's not a mistake; I *am* yours," he all but shouted. "But I may have to beat you for doubting it, and for ruining another of my coats." He raised a brow and flicked a dry pea off his sleeve. "How many coats is this now?"

"Beat me then," Jade said twisting from his arms, toppling him backward to her bed, and to his obvious surprise and titillation, straddling him. "Beat me senseless," she said. "But first, let me just open these . . ."

She did all the delicious things to him that he'd been doing to her, and more. She brought his sex to life under her hands and her lips, making him groan and shout and beg to reverse their positions, but she gloried in her power and refused to give up control.

She ravaged him, riding him hard and long, achieving her own climax, over and over, until he lost the fight to outlast her and cried out, giving himself, body and soul, into her keeping.

They reached heaven as one.

Then she allowed him to love her his way, every time he woke her, all night long.

Near dawn, they slept in each other's arms, sated and exhausted.

The next morning, Jade watched as Marcus roused to a tongue in his ear and called his seducer "Darling," then he raised his heavy lids and stared into the big brown eyes of a little red dog.

Jade laughed with her whole heart for the first time in years.

Still smiling about it a day later, Jade knew she'd remember the astonished look on Marcus's face long after he'd left her. Which he would do, once she destroyed his brother's railroad.

Seventeen

Since Garrett demanded to walk, unaided, down the aisle of St. Wilfred's Parish Church in Newhaven proper, the scheduled wedding of Abigail Pargeter and Garrett Alasdair Fitzalan, Earl of Attleboro, would take place on June 5, three weeks after she accepted his proposal, and three weeks before the South Downs Railroad must reach Tidemills or fail. This gave Jade time to prepare a proper wedding while she devised a plan to destroy the bridegroom's livelihood.

In the days that followed, turmoil became her alarming companion.

That the railroad was not likely to be Garrett's only means of income consoled her little. A man who had not walked in more than a year deserved no such abuse. Questioning too deeply the sources of his income would be tantamount to admitting she had not given up her fight. Yet having no notion of the ways the act she must commit could affect Garrett tested Jade sorely.

Destroying him, if losing his railroad could do so, would also destroy Abigail. While Jade's focus had always been the continuance of her downtrodden society and the care of the women who depended upon it, Jade realized that now the tables had turned. One of her very own had a stake in the opposing outcome.

Still, she supposed she must look to the well-being of the majority, but, oh, how painful her goal had become.

While Jade ruminated on the distressing situation at all hours, preparations for Garrett's wedding to Abigail took form and shape by day. By night, Jade barred Marcus from her bed, a decision he did not appreciate or understand, though he tried. He truly did. For Emily's sake.

Jade did not further explain that every time they made love, she became less and less certain of her purpose. That if she welcomed him into her bed, her body, one more time, she would falter in her determination . . . which she could never do.

For fourteen long, frustrating nights, she denied her body, and his, sustenance. For eight room-pacing hours during each of those nights, she kept herself from going to him and begging him to make her forget the pain of her own treachery.

Thankfully, during each day, Garrett's progress, Emily's kisses, Mac's warm little body, and Abby's bright future, managed to distract her.

Working on Abby's wedding finery, Jade's women seemed less downtrodden, as if they believed in happily-ever-afters and gentle men once more.

Nothing less than a miracle could have accomplished that.

The upheaval and activity offered Jade a respite from torment. Yet at times anguish dogged her and everything good seemed to vanish.

"What? What did you say, Lester?" Only a portion of her retainer's comment had penetrated Jade's fog of anxiety.

"A man in Lewes, I said, asked after the Lady of Peacehaven Manor."

Lester had just returned from an expedition to fetch the last of their yard goods order, the fabric for Abigail's gown. "One of them Frenchie dressmakers," Lester said. "The *Mam'selle* Liette said she heard a man asking for you at the apothecary. Liette's sister, Paulette, said as he was a coarse little man with beady eyes and 'thee snout of thee peeg.' "

Jade's girls laughed at Lester's imitation of the dress-maker's French accent, but Jade felt unaccountably disturbed. "That's odd," she said, tearing brown paper off a bolt of white Pekin silk. "Why would someone in Lewes ask about Peacehaven? Do the Misses Paulette and Liette know the man? Have they ever seen him before?"

"No, Ma'am, but the stranger's saying as he knows something about your grandfather you might want to hear before certain others do."

Jade's head came up with a snap, and the bolt of white silk hit the floor and rolled across the room on its ball-tipped wooden spool, causing no end of anguish to the women in the room.

When Jade recovered it, along with her equilibrium, she offered Abby her abject apologies, but Ab was not near as upset as Jade and the rest of the girls.

With trembling hands, Jade returned to opening packages of French lace trim, Spitalfields silk roses, and white sarcenet for quilling. Just a short while before, the prospect of Abby's gown had seemed exciting, but Jade's joy in the task dimmed for wondering who the stranger might be, what threat he posed, and how she would answer it.

As near to reaching her goal as to Abigail's fairytale wedding, 'twas not the time for any of grandfather's despicable deeds to come calling. No, nor for grandmother's devastating secret to rear its ugly head, either.

In the study, Marcus went over the accounts he'd copied and brought from Jade's banker detailing her cousin, Mr. Giles Dudley's theft, when Marcus received a message about Dudley, himself, from the Bow Street Runner he'd hired. It seemed Cousin Dudley had been sighted in nearby

Lewes, a village away, while former man-of-affairs Neil Kirby appeared to have disappeared from the face of the earth.

The Runner invited Marcus to the Dragon and Claw, in Lewes, for a bit of ale and perhaps a confrontation with Jade's cousin that very evening.

Marcus went to find his brother and announce his intention of going.

Garrett swore. "I wish to bloody hell I could go with you. Suppose the man's worse than a thief; you could get yourself hurt."

"I'd love to have you along, though you'd have to ride, which you haven't done in ages."

Garrett cursed. "As I've set my mind on your attending me at my wedding next week as groomsman, I think it wise someone cover your back. Fact is, I've been doing a lot of things I haven't done in ages." Garrett grinned.

Marcus chuckled, elated at the prospect of his brother's company as well as his rekindled interest in all aspects of life. "Come with me, then."

"I'm not certain I've regained enough strength in my thighs to keep my seat," Garrett admitted with disgust, until the devil entered his eyes. "Though I suppose it couldn't be much different from—"

Marcus coughed and got behind the wheelchair. "On that interesting note, let me take you to the stable to show you what I had made up for you in London. When I returned, you were so blue-deviled, I hadn't the heart to show you, or get your hopes up. But by damn, I think you're ready now."

Once Garrett agreed to use the strap-device to keep him in his saddle, Marcus brought him back to his room to change into riding clothes, and went in search of Jade. He'd just tell her he needed to go to Lewes on business with Garrett.

Because he had not wanted to get her hopes up about destroying Dudley's chance of changing her grandmother's will, he hadn't told her Dudley was stealing from her. He'd let her assume tonight's meeting had to do with the railroad.

He stopped in the middle of the stairs. She'd probably get it into her stubborn head to follow them. Better to leave without talking to her. Shaking his head, Marcus turned around and started back down.

Beecher chuckled behind him.

"Saw that did you?" Marcus said, chagrined to have been caught.

Beecher smiled good-naturedly as they went down the next flight side by side. "The lass's got you coming and going she has, but mark my words, Marcus, my boy, there's none more worth going muzzy over than our Jade."

"I know." Marcus grinned. He'd begun to think there was hope for them, real hope, now that Garrett was regaining his legs. If only he could keep the railroad on its tracks, and keep himself grounded, as well. He shook his head again. "How am I ever going to catch *her* if she's got me chasing my own tail, I'd like to know."

Beecher slapped him on the back. "If you stop and wait long enough, she'll catch you."

Marcus regarded the medical man quizzically. "Perhaps someday I'll figure that out. Meanwhile, if she or Abigail comes looking, tell them Garr and I took a ride over to Tidemills, and we won't be back until late. Tell Jade I'll see her in the morning."

Now it was Beecher's turn to shake his head, though his eyes appeared actually to twinkle.

Marcus should have known that he and Jade hadn't fooled the old codger. He was as close to a grandfather as Jade had. 'Twas a wonder the medical man hadn't aimed a pistol at him weeks ago, considering his previous sleeping arrangements.

Lord, he missed having Jade beside him at night.

Marcus shook off his melancholy and clapped the observant Beecher on the back. "Just tell her. And, thanks, old man."

As Jade slipped her arms into Marcus's bottle green frockcoat to wear with her trousers for her trip to Lewes, she was as worried about Emily as she was glad that Marcus had left for the evening. Em had been sleeping through the night lately, but that didn't mean she wouldn't wake up crying tonight. It would break her heart if Em came looking for comfort and none was to be found.

Though Jade intended to be back early, she decided to ask Lacey if she wouldn't mind sleeping in her bed until she returned, in case Emily woke.

When Lacey agreed, Jade felt better and was able to mount her Chestnut and set off toward Lewes with one less worry on her mind, which allowed her to concentrate on her current problem. What did this stranger know about her grandfather? All the way to Lewes, she pondered the worst possible scenario—that the stranger meant to blackmail her.

Jade entered Lewes proper as lavender streaked the horizon and she went directly to question the source of Lester's information.

Desmoiselles Paulette and *Liette Lague, modistes extraordinaire,* welcomed her with enthusiasm, expressing an immediate and useless desire to reproduce her *ensemble pantalons,* her trouser-costume, for their customers.

Besides being forward-thinking, they were supremely talented, honestly of French heritage, carried the choicest yard goods, and designed the best fashions this side of London and Paris. Other than their penchant for bickering over which of them was the favorite of their *Chere Maman, La Belle Jeannette,* the famous opera singer, they were beautiful and sweet, rare jewels among French modistes.

Though the dears were as welcoming as Jade expected, there was little more they could tell her, except that the apothecary had later said the stranger was staying at the Dragon and Claw.

Before Jade left, *Mademoiselle Paulette* told her that the once respectable hostelry had degenerated to more of an ale house than an inn and catered now to a very low-class clientele. Wringing her hands, Paulette begged Jade not to go there.

Liette begged her to take their stooped and aging butler for protection, else forget, *"le filthy peeg."*

Determined to find the stranger whose very purpose spoke of threat, Jade kissed their rouge-pot cheeks and tactfully declined any and all suggestions.

If finding her quarry meant stepping into the teeth of perdition, ragtag patrons and all, then step into hell she would.

Eighteen

The seventeenth-century beam and plaster building sat sandwiched between the office of a high-brow barrister and Lady Teal's Rooming House, an infamous den of wickedness hiding behind an innocuous facade.

As Jade approached the Dragon and Claw, half its departing patrons were en route to Lady Teal's, and the other half reeked and staggered, retched and belched, nearly enough to change her mind and turn her homeward.

Nearly, but not quite.

Glad she'd purloined a caped coat with matching tweed cap from Marcus's room at the last minute, Jade pulled the cap low over her forehead and stood the coat's collar up to hide as much of her face as possible before she entered.

The interior of the inn, lit solely by a pair of tallow candles in greasy wall sconces, stank of stale ale, whisky, yesterday's mutton, and the great unwashed.

This clientele meant business, most having a row of empty tankards at hand.

Jade sidled up to a deserted table in a far corner, hoping to catch the barmaid's eye. She intended to question the woman, whose breasts spilled nearly from her bodice and whose apron hadn't seen a wash since Victoria took the throne.

While Jade awaited the server's arrival, she scanned faces, ravaged by indigence and dissipation, and saw almost at once, a visage that stood the hair at her nape and sent a shudder racing through her.

What would Neil Kirby be doing in a place like this? Her

former man of affairs was as fastidious as he was dishonest, possibly more so.

By the dressmakers' earlier description—short, beady eyes, pug nose—Neil Kirby could very well be the stranger carrying information about her grandfather, but Jade doubted it.

While in her employ, Kirby had lived at Peacehaven for nearly two years. Why would he wait until now to show his hand, and why not come to her front door?

Yes, she'd discharged him, but they were both civil, though she supposed, now that she thought on it, he might have been affronted enough to seek revenge.

Or perhaps he wasn't through with cheating her.

Perhaps he'd learned something about her grandfather . . . from her grandmother? Jade shivered. It had never occurred to her before, but Gram, in her disoriented state, toward the end of her life, might have been confused enough to tell the snake her secret. But why wait until now to reveal it?

The possibility alone made Jade ill. What would she do if Kirby had uncovered the truth?

If that viper had stumbled across it, others could as well, including her greedy cousin, Giles Dudley. If *he* did, she'd lose everything her grandmother had worked so hard to attain, and the women who needed her, now and in the future, would suffer.

Jade tried to remember if Giles Dudley's threat had arrived before or after Neil Kirby left her employ, but she couldn't be certain. Either way, if Neil Kirby held such information, she would pay.

Perhaps his information concerned the railroad. Then again, in a roundabout way, Gram's secret concerned the railroad . . . and now she'd closed the circle. She'd best stop driving herself mad with speculation, and move close enough to hear what her former man of affairs had to say to the lecher ogling the barmaid.

Jade rose unobtrusively, she hoped, to change to a table near the object of her concern, while attempting to remain unnoticed by said object.

A man with forty hands, all grabbing her at once, seemed to come from nowhere. She'd been so busy watching Kirby, she'd not seen what or who stood about her.

Bald as a turnip and reeking of onions, her captor must have seen through her male disguise, for he held her in his unrelenting clutches. With a grip like iron, he steered her out of the common room and halfway up the stairs before Jade caught her breath and tried to resist, her heart drumming a wild beat.

Fighting him, however, seemed like trying to stop a steam engine with less than a stuffed dress on the tracks.

When Jade stopped caring about making a scene and gave voice to her silent scream, the man's stinking mouth swooped down on hers and she gagged.

He jumped back so fast, she might have laughed, if not for her fast tumble down the stairs, her balance having flagged with his support. Before she could stand, Onion Breath caught her by the seat of her pants and the collar of her coat, with those beefy hands of his, and shoved her back up, her collar cutting her windpipe and severing her air.

Despite the black dots dancing before her eyes, Jade caught him by surprise when she turned about and used her knee to best advantage, a move she had discovered by accident, to the detriment of Marcus's manhood, or so he'd said.

It worked. Onion Breath took the stairs the fast way now, in an unexpected rush of a howling rumble, and Jade screamed like a madwoman. The way her luck had been running, 't'would be Kirby come to her rescue, if only to save his blackmail mark.

The man who pulled her into his arms from behind did not surprise her but he did infuriate her. Pushed beyond bearing, Jade pummeled, kicked, bit and scratched the detestable man who'd sold her land and started her problems. "I will not . . ." She punctuated her words with kicks, "be touched . . . by the likes . . . of you! You thieving lout!"

Her harried rescuer evaded her every attempt to back-kick his soft man parts. "Let me go!"

He stepped back, arms raised in surrender.

Turning, viewing him through a haze of red, Jade gaped then gasped. "Marcus!" Flying into his arms, she burst into tears, and was no sooner enveloped in his blessed embrace, than her relief ended.

Without warning, Marcus, the only bulwark between her and ravishment slid to the floor in an unconscious heap.

However entertained Garrett might once have been by such a solicitous, bountifully-endowed barmaid, such overtures now disgusted him, and he wanted nothing more than to meet with Marc's Bow Street Runner and depart these squalid premises.

Where had Marc gone?

When the investigator failed to arrive well beyond the specified hour, and Marc remained absent more than half that time, Garrett called to the calf-eyed barmaid.

She came, overeager and ready to play, and he pushed her off his lap and gave her a guinea to stop her attempts to, " 'arden 'is dally-boy."

Despite his annoyance, Garrett couldn't wait to relate the tale to Abby, for his dally-boy needed no assistance with her nearby.

"I need your help," he said to the barmaid, and cursed himself for the light in her eyes. "I'm looking for my . . . cousin. We came in together. Did you see where he went? 'Twas about half an hour ago."

"Saw nobody but you, Guv." She tested her guinea's authenticity and whooped in delight to find it real. "Regular Lonnon dandy, arn'cha?"

"Can you find me a cane?"

"Wot?"

"Fact is, if I were a dandy, I would already own one. Wait, make that two."

Confusion pure and simple transformed the wench's features.

"You know, a walking stick. I'll give you five pounds if you bring me two." Garrett held up two fingers, then he opened his pocket watch. "Two canes within the next five minutes for five pounds."

She was gone like a shot. Money, she spoke fluently.

Marcus awoke in a dim hole on a hard floor, a gag in his mouth, his feet hobbled, hands tied, head aching.

Penned in. Unable to move.

Awareness came to him in slow measure until memory intruded and alarm raced his heart.

Jade.

Knowing his panic would do *her* no good, he took a deep breath and tried to think rationally. It was then he caught the scent of the pelt near his face. Lavender.

Jade. And he could hear her breathing. Safe. With him.

In a blink, his heart's rhythm calmed and he considered the hovel in which they lay. At his back, a wall—immovable. At his head, a wall—movable?—a door then. At his feet, a wooden box, or . . . the underbelly of a stair-step. A closet beneath a set of stairs, perhaps. Jade along his front, crushed against him, bound as well.

Jade. His perfect match. His heart. Safer tied and locked away with him than with the bastard who'd tried to abduct her. When he got them free, Marcus vowed, he'd not rest until he caught the brute and beat him to a pulp.

In any other circumstance, he'd ask Jade what the hell she was doing in a hovel like this, and in no soft voice, either, but his gag prevented anything more than a grunt, to which she did not respond. Bloody hell.

Jade, quiet, too quiet. The aspect frightened him, pricked his arms and legs with needles, and brought a lump of fear to lodge in his throat.

He grunted again, louder, more urgent, but received no response.

With her hair against his cheek, he couldn't tell if she faced away from him or if her hair covered her face.

With his chin, he attempted to move some of the silk aside and managed to find her ear, beside which ran a sticky substance with a metallic scent. Blood.

Injured? Oh, God how bad?

Not knowing from whence the blood flowed, or how much she'd lost, Marcus feared moving, feared causing further damage, but he had to get her out of here.

On the off chance the door at his head would give, or that someone might hear it rattle, Marcus head-butted it a good one.

Stars danced before his eyes. Awareness blurred and faded.

Garrett sat wishing he'd started walking ages ago. Damn. "Stubborn fool," he called himself as he scanned the crowd of thugs.

He caught sight of a huge bald brute with a bloody nose and vile disposition, judging by the sneer with which baldy eyed the crowd. His fresh injury worried Garrett. Perhaps Marc had been involved, and hurt. Or he got caught in a scuffle with that Dudley character, Jade's supposed cousin.

Garrett realized that the Bow Street Runner's absence should have alerted him sooner. "Damn."

Holding to a raw, dusty beam Garrett rose to scan the crowd for further signs of pugilism run amuck, but only two other fellows bore bruises and they looked to be healing.

With no other choice but to approach the bald brute, Garrett made a disjointed journey from table to table, holding to chairs, beams, the tables themselves, as he went.

When he arrived, he dropped into the chair opposite Baldy. "Buy you a draught?" he asked with feigned affability.

Baldy grunted.

Garrett took that for assent and remained silent until the giant took another long pull on his ale and appeared less hostile.

"I seem to have misplaced my cousin," Garrett began. "A real troublemaker; always in the stew. Saw your injury and thought perhaps he'd struck again."

"He alone?" the brute inquired, threateningly.

"Yes. Yes he was."

"Ain't seen him."

"He could have been with a serving girl, of course; that's a given." Though Garrett doubted it.

"Bloke who attacked me—from behind, mind you—has him a taste for prissy boys."

Garrett raised an incredulous brow. "A prissy—"

Finally, the dimwitted dally-boy champion of the Dragon and Claw, canes in hand, ambled up to halt

Garrett's response. He thanked her and handed her a five-pound note, tipped his hat to both her and Baldy, and threw down a handful of coins to pay for Baldy's drinks. "Sorry to have troubled you."

Carefully distributing his weight between the canes and his legs, Garrett made reasonable progress across the floor and in the direction of one of its several private parlors. He might be rusty, but he could *walk*, by damn.

A little man, bony and bent, palsied hands and shuffling feet, reached the first parlor at the same time he did. "Not there," the old man mumbled as he plodded toward the next, Garrett right behind him.

"Here neither," the little man muttered turning to Garrett and scratching his head. "You seen a Missy not fittin' here, Sur?"

"A Missy? No. May I ask your name?" Garrett asked, his curiosity piqued. Perhaps they could search together. He wouldn't mind company, however feeble, if truth be told. Between the two of them, they might make one able-bodied man.

"Stodges," the old man said as he tipped an invisible cap and bowed barely lower than his natural stoop. "Yur, serv'nt, Sur. Them wot makes the French frocks be wurr'd 'bout the Missy."

"Let's talk in here," Garrett said, indicating the second empty parlor, for his legs begged to stop for a bit.

Stodges sat as well, as relieved as Garrett, judging by his sigh.

"Tell me about this Miss you're looking for," Garrett said. "Does she have a name?"

His shaking head spoke of disapproval. " 'T'aint nat'ral 'ur wearin' breeches and comin' t'such a—"

"Breeches?" Garrett sat forward, afraid to inquire fur-

231

ther. "A woman wearing breeches, did you say?"

"That's so. Bold as brass."

"It can't be Jade," Garrett disallowed, more to himself than his companion.

The old man tossed him a hopeful look. "Mebbe."

"Lady Jade Smithfield?"

"That's 'ur!" The codger lit up. "You know 'ur? You seen 'ur?"

Garrett cursed, the single scurrilous word making the old man cackle, slap his knee, and throw him an expression of respect.

Garrett scoffed. Jade. 'Twas not a prissy boy his brother favored, but a woman in leather breeches. "Stodges," Garrett said, "I could use some assistance. Will you help me?"

"Help ya do wot?"

"Find the Miss, of course."

The man's poor arthritic knee got slapped again. "Blimey, guv'nr, I *gotta* find 'ur or I can't g'ome, anyroot." He shook his head. "Lead the way."

Garrett rose, decrying scandalous vixens and disappearing brothers. "My sorry legs would as soon we take turns leading the way, if you don't mind, but I *will* go first."

To Garrett's chagrin, he found Baldy's table empty, but dally-girl was happy to tell him—for free, said she with a grin and a wink—that, "Himself keeps a room up one flight, at the back of the 'ouse."

On his way, Garrett realized he'd walked farther tonight than he had since regaining his legs, and now faced with a flight of backstairs, he worried they'd give out before he found Marc and Jade.

In other circumstances, those two gone missing would make him smile, given the fact that they could barely keep their hands off each other. But Marc would never have abandoned him. And Jade was supposed to think they were in Tidemills. She must have turned the tables on his brother and become the follower for a change.

A few minutes later, Stodges beside him, Garrett gratefully knocked on Baldy's door, a portal with its corner clipped, wedged as it was beneath a set of stairs going up.

When he opened it, Baldy grunted, his disposition as sour as his breath, and made to shut it fast, but a wedged cane happened to keep it from closing.

Stodges cackled.

Baldy growled and charged like a vexed bull.

Garrett got in a jaw-cracking punch, as supremely satisfying as walking again, and Baldy fell back swearing.

"My cousin and the boy; where are they?"

Another growl, a lunge that backed Garrett against the wall, and Baldy got in a lip-splitter with an unexpectedly clean and powerful left hook.

Garrett tasted blood and wiped his mouth with the back of a hand. With the wall taking some weight off his legs, he was able to concentrate on the fight, rather than keeping upright, and got in two quick jabs, one realigning Baldy's nose, the other shutting his eye.

His glass-jawed opponent fell back and wavered on his feet just out of range.

"You come back here, you weak livered bully," Garrett taunted.

Stodges cackled and jumped behind the giant, pushing him forward for Garrett to hit again.

Garrett crowed when knuckle met bone and flashed the old man a grin as Baldy wobbled and teetered.

"This is the best fun I've had in a twelvemonth, without a woman," Garrett said as his comrade set up another shot.

Stodges appreciated his wit. Baldy was in no way amused.

Three more times the old man placed his opponent before Garrett like trout on a platter; three more times Garrett feasted on the boon.

Though Baldy's blows missed their mark more often than not, however upright Garrett remained, the tenacious giant would not give up.

Old Stodges laughed so hard, 'twas a wonder he dodged the single blow Baldy sent his way.

Garrett was fairly certain it was the old man's laughter that made their foe rear up like an avenging gargoyle, roaring and furious, to get in a hit to finish him.

The last thing Garrett saw before he hit the floor was Stodges climbing out a window.

Some battle being waged at least two floors above awakened Jade to her dark surroundings, firing both indignation and determination in her breast.

She worked at her gag like a hound at a bone, pulling with her teeth to tear it, inch by slow inch, grateful the fabric was old and threadbare, resolved not to consider its origin.

She perceived she was tied to someone else. With her wrists bound to her torso, and to the other someone's wrists, she stretched her fingers as far as they would go. Encountering the front placket on a pair of breeches, she confirmed that her partner was male, the same way Onion Breath had discovered she was not.

Nineteen

Unable to discern a spearmint scent through the high reek of spirits, she was loathe to awaken a man she could not identify. Then again, liquor covered Marcus when that bottle broke over his head, though, a man smelling of spirits at an inn did not make for conclusive evidence.

Along her length, her unconscious partner fit like Marcus, and they were of a height, also a good sign.

The fact that he remained unmoving worried her. She wished she could speak to him, at least, or he to her, but like her, he sported a gag.

When it occurred to Jade that she had no choice but to remove his gag the way she had done hers, the dual use of the word "gag" came to her quite readily, and she tried desperately not to be ill.

Ultimately, she controlled her stomach's need to spasm and attacked the foul cloth.

After several failed attempts to tear the fabric, Jade yanked so hard she managed to pull the gag down to hang about his neck.

Despite all that, the poor man did not awaken.

Jade exercised her sore jaw as she pondered the situation, hesitating to speak before she knew something more about her unwitting partner.

The only way she could determine whether the face so near her own might belong to Marcus, or not, was to discern its shape. She would look for a dimple in his chin.

Searching with the tip of her nose, she did find a very distinctive valley in the center of her partner's chin and per-

235

haps a familiar, but elusive, scent to his skin as well. She would like to check the depth of the dimple, but could think of no real way to judge it, except with her tongue, which she did not care to do, until she was certain.

This must be Marcus, common sense told her. Who else would she be tied to, but the man who attempted her rescue.

Then again, why would a dastard like Onion Breath tie her to the one man in the world she'd want to be bound to? Jade sighed in frustration.

She'd have to discern the shape of his lips as well. No one else had a mouth as perfect as Marcus.

Again nudging his face with her nose, Jade found his lips well shaped, but perhaps not perfect, then certainty came in a flash, for the man kissing her, thanking God she was alive, *was* Marcus.

Jade pulled away, loathe to do so, but a bit light-headed, a good deal grateful, and in need of air. "You were unconscious," she said, fighting for breath. "Though you seem fine now. Are you?"

"What about you?" he asked. "For a while 'twas the other way 'round."

"I do have the headache, which is not to be construed as the excuse you tell me genteel ladies offer in a certain circumstance."

Marcus chuckled, warming her and reassuring her of his well-being. "There's blood by your ear. I was worried sick."

"Likely from the gash on my head. Onion Breath dropped me down the stairs before you came to my rescue. Nothing else hurts."

"Some rescue. Onion Breath?"

Jade imagined Marcus's raised brow. "I dubbed him that for obvious reasons."

"My head hurts some as well," Marcus said. "Did he drop me down the stairs too?"

"He hit you with a bottle."

"That explains it. He didn't hurt you, did he?" Marcus asked. "I mean . . . he didn't try anything . . . you know? After he knocked me out?"

"I fought like a Bedlamite for a while, until it seemed the harder I fought, the more excited he became. I'm ashamed to admit that when I suspected he was . . . you know, eager, I began to cry." She couldn't bear to tell him that the brute had cupped her breast, looked for boy parts, and finding none, he'd gone furious and wild. "Then I saw his fist coming. After that, I don't remember a thing."

"God." Marcus buried his face in her hair. "It's a wonder he didn't . . . when I think what might have . . ."

He kissed her face wherever he could reach and she reveled in his attention, until he pulled back and growled. "What the devil are you doing here?"

Jade decided to forego defense for offense. "Me? Why are *you* here? You're supposed to be in Tidemills. Or did you have Beecher tell me that to throw me off?"

"Did you follow me, then?"

"Of course not. You're the one who's bound and determined to follow me."

"Not this time."

"Marcus Fitzalan, tell me what you're doing at the Dragon and Claw in Lewes when you're supposed to be in Tidemills."

"It's a s . . . surprise." Marcus felt the warmth of the lie climb his neck and for the first time since he woke, he praised the pall of darkness.

"Hmm. What a coincidence," Jade said. "The reason I'm here is a surprise as well."

"Lord, I'm glad you're all right. But what will Emily think if you're not in your bed? She's still tormented by her mother's desertion."

"Topped by your desertion."

Marcus groaned. "Don't remind me. I never imagined as much when I went to London."

"She fell in love with you, Papa Bear. She reminds you of it every time she follows you or goes looking for you."

"You're right, and she'll probably go looking for me tonight when she can't find you."

"Lacey's sleeping in my bed."

Marcus sighed gratefully. "Smart, but I'm glad you didn't try that until now. I'd hate to have climbed into Lacey's bed instead of yours."

Jade giggled, warming him, despite their situation.

"Shall we try calling for help?" he suggested.

She agreed and they yelled so loud, for so long, they were both hoarse, but alas, no one came. "It's no use," Marcus said. "Save your breath."

They quieted then, lost in thought.

"Have we actually agreed to keep our reasons for being here to ourselves?" Jade asked, cutting the silence.

Marcus pondered the ramifications of his explanation and shrugged. "I hate to admit it, but I think that's best for now."

"For now," she said. "In that case, I can think of a better use for our energy."

"Really?" he asked, considering several worthy possibilities. "What do you suggest?"

"I suggest we try to untie these ropes about us."

"Frankly, Jade, I expected something more original. And pleasurable."

"I'm certain you did. Here, allow your wrists to move

with mine and let me see if I can untie you. I can still move my fingers."

Sighing with disappointment, though bowing, mentally, to her greater wisdom, Marcus did as Jade bid and let her make an attempt.

"Ouch, ouch, ouch!"

"Stop squirming," Jade said. "I'm trying to get a grip on the rope."

"Our wrists are tied together here," Marcus said. "You're shoving my wrists against me and making me crack my own ballocks!"

"Oh. Sorry."

"This isn't working," he said. "Frankly, I'm afraid to let you try again."

"You don't usually have a problem with having me near your . . . softer parts."

"It's been a long time, but I do vaguely remember that. Why don't we just cut the ropes, then I'll let you near my parts as often as you—"

"Aren't you brilliant," she said, her sarcasm not lost on him. "Got a knife handy?"

"In my pocket."

"What?"

"I always carry my Sportsman's Friend in my pocket. Never know when you'll need scissors, a corkscrew or a farrier's blade for paring a hoof. The knife is quality steel. Garrett gave it to me last Christmas. It's got a pearl shell handle."

"You carry it all the . . . when was the last time you used the foolish thing?"

"Two weeks ago, to cut orchids for you on the downs. Remember the day I took Emmy and Mucks for a walk and you found out about Abby?"

"Just tell me where the bloody thing is. Honestly, I don't know why you didn't think of it sooner."

"Well, first you were unconscious, then I was unconscious, then we were kissing—"

"Where is it, damn it!"

"Don't get testy. It's in the lower pocket of my frock-coat, to the left of our bound wrists, and watch out for my—"

"Ballocks. I know."

She had trouble reaching his pocket. Her hand didn't stretch far enough, so she began to walk her fingers, pulling the fabric of his coat nearer and nearer, until . . .

"Um, Jade. That's not my knife."

"I figured as much. I didn't expect the bloody knife would swell when I touched it . . . on top of all the other handy things it does."

"It *has* been two weeks, you know. I'm more than a little—"

"Lustful. Eager. I do know. I'm feeling rather randy, myself." She sighed. "I'll try to be more careful, but I can hardly help it if—"

"Ahh. Jade. I have no self-restraint to spare, here."

"Well, it's in my way now. And it feels really nice and . . . friendly."

"This has been a long two weeks," Marcus said. "In so many ways."

"I missed you, too," she said, arching, seeking greater closeness as his hips sought hers in the same frustrating way.

Stroking him boldly now, despite the placket of his trousers between them, drat her and bless her, she was bringing him to near-painful arousal, a sweet torment after weeks of celibacy. "Oh God."

Jade managed, with tenacity, to unfasten his breeches and free him into her hands, making him ready to burst.

With like perseverance, Marcus kept from spilling his seed while clumsily shoving her clothing aside. When she didn't protest, but urged him to hurry, he slid into her sheath, supple as a leather glove, fitted, warm and welcoming. "God, it's been so long."

"Very long. Mmmm. Just the way I like it." Jade moved against him, inasmuch as she could, and took him deeper.

"I meant the duration of . . . Ahh . . . our restraint was . . . long-lived. Fourteen days."

"Fifteen."

Barely able to move, they dallied slow and torturously sweet. A splendid stroll up a steep, steep hill, each beat offering a more sensual glimpse of the blazing treasure at the peak of the climb. A celebration of life at its best to see them through a long, dark night.

When they reached the summit, glistening and exhausted, the treasure that awaited swelled and burst, showering them with stardust. Spent and serene, they drifted to sleep.

The door hit Marcus in the head.

His curse woke Jade.

Light spilled upon them in a harsh, appalling splash.

Grateful they were bound so close that nothing could be seen, Marcus stilled. "Get the hell out," he snapped to the form standing above them.

The sardonic chuckle in reply made Marcus swear. "Damn it, Garr. Shut the bloody door. We'll call you when we're ready to be rescued."

Garrett left them in silence, closed in, still bound by rope, and flesh to flesh, as well.

Marcus slipped reluctantly from Jade's enveloping

warmth, no longer afraid this might have been their final loving, but grateful, despite himself, that they'd been granted the bittersweet interlude.

"He saw us," Jade whispered. "Garrett saw us."

"He didn't see a thing, love," Marcus responded, kissing her velvet ear. "We were too close for him to see anything, and completely dressed, give or take an inch or two."

"Or ten!"

Marcus chuckled, but her comment had been a bit loud with Garr just outside the door. "Thank you, darling, but I meant an inch or two of *fabric,* not of me."

"Oh." She sighed. "He's going to want to know why we weren't ready to be rescued."

Muffled against his neck, her statement bore hope, yet if he granted it, she would face Garr unprepared. "He won't wonder, Jade, because he already knows."

"But you said he didn't see anything," she whispered furiously.

"Garr has a good imagination."

A stifled wail. "I'll never live it down."

Marcus chuckled as he kissed her nose. "I hold in reserve several humbling moments of his, with which to torture him in just such an event, and he knows it. I don't think we'll hear anything more about this."

They fumbled to put each other together.

"As usual, it was impossible for me to think straight while we were so close. I don't like being apart, Marcus. But there's no other choice for us."

"I know you think so, love, and I'll continue to respect your wishes. But I'd as soon we had no regrets."

Jade nodded; he could feel her movement, then she surprised him with a chuckle. "If you had become aroused *sooner,* I wouldn't have had to wonder who I was tied to. I would have known immediately."

"Any man you were tied to would react that way, my dear, sweet Scandal."

"Really?" She all but purred. "But I *would* have known, on the instant, whether it was you or not." She stroked him, root to tip, calling forth a half-growl-half-shout.

"That singular sound," she said. "Is the sound of a smug scoundrel admitting he can be tamed by an innocent miss from Sussex."

"A *mischievous* miss, a rare scandal from Sussex—a seductress, sometimes an ice queen, sometimes breathing fire, but at all times bearing the key to taming me." He kissed her nose. "Are we ready? Can I call Garr in, now, to untie us?"

"I suppose we can't stay here for the rest of our lives." Regret laced her words. "Emily would miss you."

"Us. She'd miss us."

"And we'd miss her."

Hope filled Marcus as he called Garr to let them out; Jade had united them, if only in words, and only for Emily's sake, yet he took that as a good sign, however fragile his hope.

They rode home in a coach, the three of them, their horses tied behind, because not a one of them had the strength to mount or keep their seats . . . for various and sundry black and blue reasons.

"God's teeth, I had a rousing good time," Garrett said. "Damned if I've fought like that in a devil's age." He flexed a bruised fist and beamed with pride.

"Garr the Scapegrace wins the day," Marcus said.

Garrett bowed his head graciously, duly lauded. "Stodges was a right one. Did you hear? He went straight for the magistrate and got Baldy locked up."

"Baldy?"

"Onion Breath," Jade explained.

They grinned, all three, sporting sore heads, every one. Among them they could boast of half a dozen gashes, more bruises than could be counted, two split lips and three and a half black eyes.

Jade was grateful that the eyes, turning a vivid blue-black as she watched, belonged to the scoundrels Fitzalan.

She ached in every part of her body, save one, and smiled remembering.

Garrett caught her satisfaction and winked.

Warmth stole up her neck.

"Where did you hire this hack?" Marcus groaned, unaware of the undercurrents passing between Jade and his brother. "That floor was softer than the jostling we're getting in this rickety heap."

"No doubt your comfort on that floor had to do with the . . . er . . . position you were in," Garrett drawled.

Jade sunk deeper into the squabs.

"He's jealous," Marcus said near her ear, loud enough for him to hear. Then he nipped her lobe and kissed her quick but hard, almost wishing they didn't have to step back into a world where she believed he didn't belong.

It had come home to him, with Garrett walking and about to marry, that the only thing left keeping him and Jade apart was Jade's aversion to the railroad. In other words, Jade, herself.

A steep and challenging mountain.

He couldn't even see the top, but Jade was worth the climb.

They arrived at Peacehaven near three in the morning, every window in the house ablaze, every member of the household, it appeared, waiting at the door, all speaking at once.

Emily had gone missing.

They'd been searching for hours.

"Damn!" Marcus said. "She must have seen one of us leave."

He held up his hands when everyone began, again, to talk at once. "Lacey first."

It seemed Lacey had gone up for the night barely twenty minutes after Jade departed, only to discover Emily's bed empty.

"But I kissed her, sound asleep she was before I left," Jade said.

"Then she must have awakened and saw you leave," Marcus said, unthinking.

Jade cried out as if he'd slapped her.

He took her hand. "You didn't . . . I didn't mean to imply . . ." But, no use. Jade shook her head, refusing absolution, guilt swamping her, as it would him in the same circumstance.

Damn me for a loud mouth, Marcus thought. Nothing he could say would help, so he held her hand and attempted to sort through the mess of information to find the answers they needed in order to find Emily. "Lacey, what did you do when you found her bed empty?"

"I checked Jade's room, then I went to check yours." Lacey placed her hand on his arm. "She's not alone, Marcus. Mucks is missing too."

Astounded by her *naiveté*, Marcus hated to point out that a half-pint pup could hardly be considered ample protection for a child wandering alone in the middle of the night. "Where else did you look?"

"The whole bloomin' house, attics to cellars," Beecher said. "Even checked the nursery and woke the children to see if any of them knew where Emily went."

Lacey swallowed a sob. "We walked the water's edge with torches, as well. The Channel, not the river."

Jade's knees seemed to give out. Marcus lifted her in his arms and carried her to the salon to lay her on the settee, but he'd no sooner done so than she stood to pace.

Everyone followed them, chattering and conjecturing.

Beecher called for quiet this time. "Jade, darlin', Marcus, that little girl's been following the two of you about since her mother left. Where were you, tonight? She might be lost on the road even now."

"We might have passed her by," Jade whispered.

"Re-light the torches," Marcus ordered. "We'll trek the Lewes Road together and spread out into the underbrush along the way, giving it a wide sweep. That way, we'll know all the ground has been covered."

"The road leading to the Lewes Road parallels the river," Jade said, but her words were no more than a wobbling rasp.

"You're beaten," Beecher said, regarding the travelers. "Literally. Let *us* walk to Lewes. Why don't the three of you wait here, in case Emily returns? Rest for a bit."

"No," they said as one.

"We won't stop as long as she's missing," Marcus said, and Jade and Garrett agreed.

Everyone else departed as Garrett kissed Abby's brow. "Stay here and take care of our little one." He caressed her middle as if he were caressing their child. "I love you both. Get some rest."

"Be careful," Abigail said, not masking her worry.

Garrett nodded, bracing himself on his canes, and made his way outside, well behind everyone else. By the time he cleared the house, he saw their torchlights bobbing in the darkness far down the drive.

With no way to catch up, he decided he might be smart to search nearby. Aware of his own limited ability, he wondered how far Emily's little legs could take her. She would tire quickly, and when she did, she'd seek shelter to rest, hopefully.

A place that would appear safe to a child.

Garrett made his plodding way to high ground, the cliff he could see from his window.

From there he surveyed Jade's property, starting at the western edge across to the valley between her land and the mouth of the River Ouse to the east, Newhaven Harbor at its base.

Scanning the area, he saw a building, familiar in these parts, a round structure made of quarry-stone blocks—dungeons some called them because each had only two windows. The one in the distance seemed like a child's toy from here, yet it had once been all too real to the Sussex smuggling trade and the smugglers' families who went hungry.

Fifty years before, the Preventive Water Guard had set up a Coast Blockade, constructing the round towers as stations guarding the coast. A few were built inland as well at Newhaven Harbor and up the River Ouse. Several officers' families had lived in each station, while the officers, themselves, used them for bases of operation.

Most of the towers had fallen prey to coastal storms over the years, like the one near his home in Seaford, nothing but rubble marking their earlier existence. The rare few left standing were deserted.

The one Garrett could see remained intact. He started in its direction, an unexplained logic urging him on.

With his lagging gait, amid dew-drenched high grass in the dark of night, he faced quite the walk. Nevertheless, he would do whatever he could to find the little girl that he hoped for all their sakes might one day become his niece.

He lost sight of the odd round barracks as he went down one small hill and up the next, but he plodded on. When he feared he might have to stop and wait to be rescued himself, his reward came.

A dog barking. A tiny sound for a tiny dog.

"Mucks?" Garrett shouted. "Emily? Are you there?"

The pup met him, whipped to excitement, running in circles, toward him and back toward the tower in a frenzy, barking madly.

"I'm hurrying," Garrett said. "Fast as I'm deucedly able."

It seemed an eternity since he'd seen the guard tower from the cliff, but it came into sight again, as he topped another rise.

But Emily wasn't there. At least not anymore.

While Garrett hesitated at the threshold, Mucks ran farther afield, toward the river.

With the closest he could get to haste, Garrett forged on.

He approached the riverbank as dawn broke, and he saw her . . . floundering, fighting to stay above water, losing the fight. Though she was not too far distant, it might have been miles for all the use his blasted legs would be.

The river flowed with the tide and if she drifted further south, she'd be lost to the Channel.

Another test for his legs, an impossible one. "Emily, It's Uncle Garr! I'm coming!"

Saying goodbye to Abigail, vowing his love, Garrett dove into the River Ouse.

Twenty

Shock arrested Garrett by small prickling inches, numbing him, yet bringing him vitally to life. His legs worked better in the water. He'd never been so grateful for anything.

He'd expected to sink like a stone, but had to try, even if he died doing it.

Emily had the sense—and likely a last spurt of strength and energy because she saw him—to try and meet him halfway. Hope could be a powerful ally—no one knew that better than he.

His swim to the point where they met seemed to take an eternity.

When he reached her, Emily clung too tight to his neck, cutting his air, and he feared they were done for after all. But when her panic diminished, she responded to his plea to loosen her hold. And once they headed toward shore, she aided their watery sojourn by moving her legs against the pull of the tide.

Her natural instinct to swim likely accounted for her ability to stay above water, though her strength would have run out soon enough. Clearly, she was tired.

The fact that ebb tide was at its lowest and weakest point worked in their favor and Garrett thanked the deity. When he got Emily to the bank, they held each other so tightly, he could feel their hearts, like battering rams against their chests.

The water on Emily's face ran with tears, as did his. "You're not lost any more, Emmy-bug." He squeezed her, catching his breath. "I found you. Uncle Garr found you."

"No!" She pushed away from him in a fever, and began to slip and slide her dripping, determined way up the muddy bank.

Bloody hell.

Garrett's legs, made suddenly of India rubber, gave out when he tried to stand. "Where are you going?" he shouted in desperation. "Mama and Papa will want to know."

His words stopped her. She turned, fired with longing for less than a blink, then fell to the ground weeping.

Garrett all but crawled over to her, and once he got there, she gave up the fight and allowed him, again, to hold her. Eventually, her hysterical gibberish conveyed her sobbing certainty that Marcus and Jade had gone to join her mother in heaven.

She didn't want an uncle, or anyone she might lose, again. She wanted to go to heaven too.

Heart heavy, Garrett rose, standing the child with him— a colossal effort forged of the same rigid tenacity and inflexible pride that, at one time, all and sundry predicted would be his doom. He reassured Emily, as he managed it, that she was wrong. Mama and Papa were fine and looking for her.

She didn't quite believe him, though she quieted somewhat.

"You tried to follow, didn't you? Was it Mama you saw leaving?"

She nodded and began to weep more quietly, hiding her face against his leg.

"Mama and Papa are out looking for you right now, Emmy-bug, and they're very worried. They were going to look as far away as they must to find you, but because I can't go very far with these sorry legs of mine, I had to search nearby. Thank God."

Another reason, Garrett thought, for his accident and the wheelchair. He'd never before considered that God ordained any part of his life, or any life, for that matter. But now, after Abigail and Emily, he believed, and was grateful.

Emily looked around. "Chair?"

"No more wheelchair for me," Garrett said. "Not even if someone brought it here right now, though I'd be tempted well enough."

She seemed to understand.

He hugged her. "Ah, Sweetheart. Your Mama and Papa are going to be so happy to see you."

Hope grew just a bit brighter in those small, sad, world-weary eyes of hers.

Garrett's heart hitched, an inner ache spreading to every part of him, for all she'd endured, her pain becoming his. "Let's go find them."

Emily regarded him doubtfully for so long, Garrett almost wanted to fidget, then she must have decided she could trust him, because she grinned and his heart grew light and young again.

"The problem is," he said earnestly. "Despite the fact that I'm standing at the moment, I can't take a single step alone. Will you walk beside me, Emily, and help me?"

She nodded, just as earnest, and scrambled to fetch his canes as he directed. And once he had them in hand, he asked her to please hold his cane so he wouldn't fall.

She shivered as they walked, dripping wet, and he felt the cold for the first time, but Emily didn't seem the least bothered, she put so much concentration into helping him.

Garrett felt a hot, tight sting behind his eyes. This little mite who'd suffered so much was caring for him, her own discomfort be damned.

He was humbled.

251

When they arrived at Peacehaven, they found the house deserted, so Garrett guided Emily toward Eloisa's room. Because of the babies, she would have stayed, and could dry Emily, wrap her in something warm and tuck her into her bed for a bit.

He'd take Em to find Jade and Marcus after he changed into dry clothes, if he had to harness the horses to a carriage himself.

Abigail was with Eloisa; Garrett had never been so grateful for anything, except how well his legs worked underwater, which gave him an idea of how to strengthen them further, and more quickly—perhaps in time for their wedding.

Eloisa clucked and took Emily in hand, carrying out the task he'd imagined she would, without him needing to ask.

Abigail kissed and welcomed Emily, then did the same for him, escorting him to his room to change, but not before he promised to take Em to find her parents.

"They're not her parents," Abigail whispered as he leaned against her, on his last legs, so to speak.

"They will be, if we can get Jade to admit it."

"And Marcus."

"Marc wants nothing more. He's sick with wanting it. Having a family's always been a dream of his. And here, the family he wants . . . well, it's Jade who doesn't seem able to accept him, or the railroad, though we don't know why."

He gave her a sidelong glance. "Women can be a stubborn lot."

Abigail cuffed him. "Did you ever think to ask Jade why?"

"I haven't, but Marc has and he says it's hopeless."

"What about asking Ivy? I swear he knows everything about both of them."

Garrett gazed at his bride-to-be with new respect. "You're brilliant. I'll speak to Ivy as soon as Emily is reunited with Marc and Jade."

Abigail and Garrett learned from Emily, during their carriage ride to find Jade and Marcus, that the fearless child covered more distance than Garrett imagined she could. But having walked down the drive, and possibly a quarter mile down the road, if her indications were correct, she had circled round, ending near the guard tower.

There, she sought shelter, and when she woke and started out again, she seemed to have fallen in the river, north of where he found her.

"I might have been too late," Garrett whispered, smoothing her blonde curls as she sat on Abigail's lap looking eagerly out the window. "A few minutes more and I would have been too late. God."

"No," Abigail said, touching his arm. "You were meant to find her."

Garrett smiled and regarded his love. "Like I was meant to find you."

Then Emily screamed, "Papa!" and old Lester stopped the carriage.

Through the open door, they watched Emily run and fly into Marcus's arms, Jade right behind him, enough tears among them to sink a ship.

Abigail choked on a sob. Garrett's lodged in his throat. He soothed it with his lover's kiss, celebrating every gift that had come to them, and a future he thought never to have. He even took a moment, holding Abigail close, to send a prayer heavenward for the future of the embracing trio in the middle of the road.

The day of Garrett and Abigail's wedding dawned gray

and cloudy, but in all hearts, the sun shone bright.

Jade rode with Abby in the carriage.

Marcus waited beside Garrett at the altar.

St. Wilfred's was a charming country church, without ninth, sixth or even second nave. Not the resting place of a monarch, but of souls who never traveled beyond the Sussex coast. Neither its spire nor its foundations were of monastic origin, nor had it ever been the seat of a bishop.

Yet it remained one of Jade's favorite churches for its small size and simple elegance. As she entered beside the bride, she saw it looked more beautiful filled with wedding guests and a multitude of yellow roses.

Abigail stopped beneath the gothic entrance, a most beautiful, radiant bride, her perfection enhanced by the love in her eyes.

As cherubs gazed from above and doves cooed in the eaves, Jade walked first up the aisle to the spot from whence she would stand witness beside the man she could never take for husband. Deep inside, she might feel like weeping because of it, but watching Abigail continue on to the handsome scamp who gave her his hand and heart, Jade couldn't help but rejoice.

High in Ivy's arms, Emily kept her gaze trained on them throughout the ceremony. They dared not promise never to leave her, for one of them eventually must—though they had not yet determined which of them would—so it had been impossible to set her fears to rest.

Jade looked into Marcus's rich, cobalt eyes shimmering with yearning, and prayed for the strength to resist him, especially here before a sacred alter, a minister at hand.

Marcus wanted to fight the unyielding determination he could see working against him even now, but Jade wore her resolve like armor, reinforcing its strength with every beat of her heart.

More than he wanted his next breath, he wanted to win this woman, as radiant in breeches on the first day he saw her as now in silk and lace. He wanted to walk her up this very aisle and stand before the selfsame prelate, taking her only unto him for as long as they both should live. He wanted that little girl in the front pew to be theirs as well, and to give her sisters and brothers to love and protect.

Marcus tried to believe himself stronger than Jade and nearly laughed in self-derision. The Lady Jade Elizabeth Smithfield had turned out to be the worthiest adversary—man or woman—Marcus Gordon Fitzalan had faced in his thirty years of life.

He was, truth to tell, frightened witless that Jade would win, that her skewed view of their situation would prevail, in which case, they would both lose, as would Emily and the children who would never be born to them.

Marcus took a minute to beg for help, due to the environ, and added his heartfelt thanks, in the event he'd been heard.

The drone of the minister stopped and his brother and Abigail spoke their vows with certitude.

Marcus turned to Jade then, holding her gaze, in hopes she'd listened as intently to the words as he and might feel his yearning to pledge her his troth. She gazed back as relentlessly. She understood, yearned as well, yet turned aside his plea, without uttering a word.

He may be wounded, but not broken.

When Garrett escorted Abigail down the aisle, nary a cane or wheelchair in sight, the eaves echoed with the spontaneous burst of applause.

After the ceremony, everyone traveled back to

Peacehaven for a wedding breakfast—even the Fitzalan retainers from Seaford who'd held the bridegroom's leading strings.

A table ran the length of the ballroom, its chairs occupied equally, adult beside child, Earl beside stable-hand beside maid beside Lady, as requested by the bridal couple.

Abigail's sober father sat flanked by Beecher and Ivy. Eloisa sat at one end, baby-minder and cradle beside her. Children were tended by parents, all served by a staff hired for the occasion.

After the meal, the room turned into a puppet theatre, another request of the bride and groom, though a surprise to their attendants.

Emily, tugging Jade by the hand, came to sit in Marcus's lap, patting the chair beside them.

When Jade sat down, Emily put Jade's hand in Marcus's, and he met her ebony eyes above that little blonde head as he clasped her hand tight. Emily placed a hand over theirs. If ever there'd been a sign Emily wanted them to be a family, this was it. Marcus kissed Em's head. "Thanks, Emmy-bug," he whispered to the insightful child.

"Welcome ladies and gentlemen, boys and girls, bride and groom," said Ivy. "To a special wedding presentation entitled, 'The Wedding that Could Never Be,' also known as, 'The Stubborn Bride.' "

Jade's gaze whipped to Marcus.

He shrugged and leaned close. "Garrett was closeted with Ivy all afternoon, yesterday. If you want to bash a head, choose his. Besides, what makes you think this has anything to do with you? Was it the word, stubborn?"

Jade tried to pull her hand from the three-way clasp, but neither he nor Emily would allow it.

The curtain parted. Children clapped and cheered.

Hector the Hungry Hedgehog was in love, so lovesick, he couldn't eat. Why, he could barely sleep, and when he did, he hardly snored, a serious affliction for a hedgehog. He gave a demonstration of his weak snore for the children and told them he forgot how a real snore should sound, so, "If you please," said he. "Can you snore and help me remember?"

The little ones snored louder and longer than Hedgehog could bear. He put his hands to his ears and swung his head from side to side, as if the noise was driving him mad.

Marcus laughed aloud.

Jade was charmed, he believed, though she'd hardly admit it. The stubborn bride, indeed. Between Garr and Ivy, he wondered who'd come up with this one.

Hector's love was Merry Mouse, and though it was apparent, from her sighs, that she loved him as well, she declared that they could never wed.

"We live in different worlds," said she. "We even look different."

"I *love* the difference," said Hedgehog in a sly scoundrel's voice.

"But my skin is soft and velvet smooth and yours is covered in spines. And I know for a fact that hedgehogs eat mice, and I'm a mouse!" The mouse puppet squeaked to prove her point, setting off a fit of giggles from the audience.

"But we both live in underground burrows," said Hector, "and that must count for something. I would never eat you, or any of your relatives. You know me better than that, Muffin mine."

"But you need a bigger house than mine. You collapsed our family's little underground burrow while you were building your great big one. Now all my baby cousins need me, because they have nowhere else to go. If I go off with you, they'll have no one to care for them."

Hedgehog puffed out his chest. "We can care for your cousins together."

"My burrow's not wide enough to fit you."

"I'll make it wider. I can do anything," bragged Hedgehog with a swagger that tickled the children.

"No," Merry Mouse wailed. "That's impossible. You'd have to destroy your home to make mine bigger. What would happen to your brother?"

"He's a big boy. He'll go and make a new burrow somewhere else. He cares about me and wants me to be happy. He wouldn't hurt your mouse cousins. Don't you trust me? Don't you want to marry me?"

"I do," admitted Merry, "But my cousins need me, so I can't."

"You're afraid," said Hedgehog, "that you'll like my spines. Afraid that someday Sergei the Wolf will come along and I won't win the fight. You think it's safer to care for your cousins than make a life together with me." Hedgehog sighed. "There's nothing keeping us apart but you. I'm going away. Forever." And he did.

The children moaned in disappointment.

The indignant mouse paced the stage. "I'm a strong mouse. Merry as the day is long. All the mice need me, and I never needed any . . . critter . . . until Hedgehog."

A blush rose up Jade's neck. Marcus looked back at the stage, hoping she didn't realize he'd noticed.

Merry Mouse wept, and some of the children yelled, "Don't cry. Please don't cry." One of them cried too, until Sergei the Wolf chased Hedgehog back onto the stage. "Mice are more delicious than spiny Hedgehogs," said Sergei. "Give me that one for dinner tonight." The wolf puppet pointed to Merry. "And I'll never trouble you again."

"Never!" shouted Hedgehog.

"Then I'll take her!" Wolf lunged toward Merry and Hedgehog wrestled him in a dramatic fight, drawing gasps and warnings from their young audience, until Hedgehog won the day and toppled Sergei off the back of the puppet stage, his wolf cry fading as he fell.

The children cheered. Hedgehog bowed.

Merry Mouse, with a flowing white bridal veil and flowers in her hand, agreed to wed her Hedgehog Hero, and they were married by the Pompous Parson. Then Glory the Fairy Queen made an appearance in a burst of fairy dust and granted them a "Happily Ever After."

The children sighed in contentment and applause broke out. Jade rose as the performance ended, able to pull her hand away only because Emily's hold had slackened when she fell asleep.

Marcus called her name, but Jade looked straight ahead as she left.

Garrett and Abigail had left the performance before her and she'd promised Abby to help her change for her wedding trip.

When she got to Abby's door, however, she heard Garrett's voice and stopped short of knocking.

"Money doesn't matter to me, Garrett," she heard Abigail say. "Stop the blasted railroad. We don't have to live in a castle on a cliff. We can live anywhere, here even, as long as we're together."

"If it were just about me, I would have stopped it already to help Jade, you know that."

"Who else is involved, then? Marc certainly wouldn't care if it meant helping Jade."

Jade was horrified to be the subject of their discourse, but she couldn't seem to move away.

"A hundred families are involved, the entire population of Tidemills, as a matter of fact. The villagers there depend on their flour mills for their living. But they need to ship the flour more efficiently, or the village itself is at risk, which is why they *need* the railroad. If it doesn't reach them—and it has to go through Jade's property before it can, as soon as next week to satisfy Parliament—Tidemills will become a ghost town. The villagers will lose everything."

Jade felt hope slipping away and panic rising up to take its place.

"But those people can move, live and work elsewhere," Abigail said. "Can't they?"

"They could move, if they could afford to, but that wouldn't solve anything. The only trade they know is the flour mills they're trained to operate. Their mills are powered by the tide and can exist nowhere else."

Jade fell against the door, all the fight drained out of her. A hundred families.

Garrett opened it, responding to the sound, and she nearly fell into his arms. He helped her to a chair.

"I'm sorry . . . I didn't mean to . . . intrude," she stammered.

Tailcoat off, cravat hanging loose, top button open, Garrett chafed her hand. "It's all right. I was about to go and find you. I'm going to stop it, Jade. The railroad, I mean. Neither of us—he indicated Abigail—cares about the income, or the house in Seaford, as long as we have each other. We might have to live here for a while, though." He chuckled halfheartedly.

"No," Jade said, her fight gone. "I wouldn't mind taking you and Abby in; I'd like having you around. But an entire village, Garrett." Jade swallowed her panic and forced a smile. "I haven't the room to house a hundred families."

Abigail bit her lip as she handed Jade a glass of water. "I didn't know myself until now. Jade, tell us your problem. We'll help you. Marcus will too. All the girls would help, if you'd let them."

Jade shook her head. "Merry Mouse concedes. Let the railroad go through. My stubbornness was a foolish determination to grant a dying old lady's unreasonable request. Think no more about it. Go to Seaford and take some time alone. I'm only sorry it will be cut so short. If I'd have let the railroad go through sooner, you could have a proper honeymoon."

Jade touched Garrett's hand. "Forgive me, Garrett, for all the frustration and expense I've put you through. It's a wonder you didn't have me arrested."

He chuckled. "Forgiven and forgotten, and Marc wouldn't let me have you arrested. I tried."

Jade responded to his tease with a weak smile and kissed both their cheeks. "Abby, you don't need me to help you change, do you?"

Abigail blushed and Garrett chuckled.

Jade got to her room down the hall like a walking corpse and winced at the analogy.

She'd know soon enough what a corpse looked like, if not what it felt like to be one, because she had no other choice now but to dig one up. Tonight.

Twenty-One

Jade lay on her bed in her darkening bedroom realizing dusk had already fallen. It had been a long day. Garrett and Abby were leaving late. The puppet show had delayed them. She wiped the tears sliding down the sides of her face with the backs of her hands. She and Marcus had *never* been destined for one of Glory's "Happily Ever Afters."

If she got caught tonight, she'd be hauled off to Newgate. If she didn't get caught . . . well, she still wouldn't be free to relinquish herself to Marcus. The women in her care must remain her prime concern, which was neither here nor there at the moment.

She rose and sat on the edge of her bed. For now, she must concentrate on the task ahead, not the nebulous future. At least she needn't worry about Emily, tonight. Marcus and Ivy had promised Em and Molly they could sleep in the puppet wagon as a special "wedding" treat. Ivy would stay with them and Emily had talked Marcus into sleeping there as well.

He'd winced and agreed while Jade laughed. She knew he'd wanted to clear the night so he could try to wheedle his way into her bed. She found the notion as charming as she found him. She might have let him in, given today's happy nuptials, if not for this disastrous turn. But if she thought too much about the only choice left to her, she'd make herself sick. Yet she couldn't get on with it, until the bridal couple went on their rice-strewn way, so she put on a smile and returned to the celebration.

Three hours later, Jade drove a dray cart pulled by a sturdy dray horse.

She crossed the open field, turned onto the wide path at the eastern side of the beech wood, and headed toward the parcel of land that Neil 'Blasted' Kirby had optioned to the South Downs Railroad.

She knew exactly where to find the wall that led to the grave.

Once she arrived, Jade followed a legacy of directions. She started walking at the end of an unmortared stone wall to the right of a path and took six paces from the hedgerow toward the far left of a stand of white pine.

There, she drove her shovel into the earth.

By the time she'd dug a hole approximately six feet long and two feet deep, she began to marvel at her grandmother's strength. Gram had always been a frail, wiry creature. Then again, she'd endured enough beatings to toughen a mouse.

Merry Mouse, Jade thought, on a bubble of hysterical laughter.

She dug another couple of feet, and still no body.

Suppose a stone wall stood now where none stood before? She might have started from the wrong place and ended at the wrong stand of pine. But looking around, it didn't seem possible.

She released an unwitting cry of frustration and continued to dig from inside the hole, deeper and deeper still.

When she hit something soft, she stifled a gasp . . . as if she might have hurt the bloody wife-beating cadaver. Her heart's thumping calmed only when she discovered that Grandfather was wrapped in a cover of sorts. She lowered her lantern to better observe beetles and such skittering in and around the rotting fabric.

On a gasping shudder, Jade placed the lantern up on the edge of the grave and began to pull the wrapped corpse by what she hoped was its feet.

She giggled at the ridiculousness of the scene, should anyone come upon her, aware that if she didn't release her trepidation in some way, she'd scream.

She had ended so deep in the earth, she wondered not only how to get Grandfather out, but herself, as well, when a wave of dirt came flying over the top, snuffing her lantern, stopping her heart, and making her drop Grandfather. When that organ started pumping again, it knocked fast and hard against her ribcage, cutting her breath. Had she back-tossed the dirt? Had it come from above? A hedgehog, or another animal, might have tossed it out while digging or scampering.

No matter her mind's logic, her heart continued to race. Heeding it, she raised the shovel like a club, peered into the darkness and listened to every night sound.

"Need some help?"

Jade screamed, tossed the shovel at the bodiless voice, and tried to scramble from the grave, aware suddenly that the solid step she'd used to gain purchase must be Grandfather's head. She had no control over the demented sounds coming from her throat. She scared *herself* with her nightmarish scream, but she couldn't seem to stop.

Something dropped into the grave behind her, accelerating her wild panic. *It, he, someone* tried to keep her there, immobilize her.

She fought for her life.

"Jade. Jade, stop."

Reason tried to intrude but she couldn't seem to check herself.

"You're hysterical, Jade. Stop . . . sweetheart."

Her captor's hold loosened. Soft kisses blessed the back of her neck. She stilled, like a roe deer in lantern light, captured, but not.

Marcus turned her. The moon, momentarily free of the clouds, shed light on his concerned face.

She cried in his arms.

She wept for a battered woman forced to murder or die . . . for months of ravaging fear, all for naught. Then she wept for her and Marcus, for all they would never share, and all she'd kept from him, all that he would now know anyway.

With worry, he gazed at her as if she were daft. And she must be, because now she laughed through her tears as she tried to tell him she wasn't. And somewhere along the way, she forgot which to do, laugh or cry, and she laughed at the absurdity. "Step aside, Sir. You're standing on my grandfather!" Her mirth over her foolish words ended in sobs.

"I'm here," Marcus said. "It's time to let me help you." He held her, without judgment, without words, for a long, long time.

She welcomed his silence and calmed.

He lessened his hold, held her at arms length, examined her face. "Why are we digging the old boy up?"

She had to use his handkerchief before she was able to talk, then she found it necessary, in a flash of topsy-turvy awareness, to get off Grandfather's chest.

There, inside a grave, beside a corpse, Marcus kissed her brow. "Do you feel better? Are you ready to tell me about it," he asked in the same way he might were they strolling across the lawn.

Amazed by the incongruity, Jade nodded, and Marcus hefted her by her waist to sit her at the edge of the grave, her legs dangling, a little like Ivy sat his puppets.

Marcus jumped up to sit beside her. "Odd time for a treasure hunt, Scandal."

"Odd time for a saunter, Scoundrel."

"So . . . that's Grandfather."

Jade looked into the grave. "Poor old bastard."

Marcus's lips twitched. "Beecher said he went missing; you said he died, but I was too caught up in *you* to realize the significance of the discrepancy. Who planted him?"

Jade sighed. "Grandmother. She told me she ruined her favorite jade figurine doing it."

"Hard to dig with a figurine."

"She might have used a shovel for that part."

Marcus nodded. "Self-defense, I'd wager, 'cause he beat her?"

" 'Twas murder—in her mind."

"The magistrate might have seen it differently."

"Or not."

Marcus nodded. "Or not. But she's gone. She can't be punished now. Why not tell the magistrate and have done with it? Why the delaying tactics with the railroad?"

"To keep it from meeting its deadline, thereby stopping it from exercising my land option, and digging up Grandfather, of course."

"Another company would have tried soon enough, you know. They're lined up, three deep, to get a charter for this route in the hopeful event we fail. Coastal routes are prime property. Again, why not summon the magistrate and be done?"

"Giles Dudley," Jade said on a sigh.

Marcus sat straighter. "I should have myself shot."

"I think not."

"Dudley's the cousin trying to have your grandmother declared insane, right?"

"You knew about that?"

He waved away her question. "If Grandmother's . . . peccadillo . . . comes to light, she's got to have been insane, therefore, he succeeds in wresting Peacehaven away from you, and your girls lose their refuge. I am so dense. I had all the pieces, but I was too love-struck to put them together."

Marcus punched the ground with a fist. "Damn, I just remembered another piece. Your pirate ancestor who beat a dog to death and buried it out here." He pointed downward, a question in his look.

Jade nodded. "Gram's big old Newfoundland." She looked into the grave again, as if searching. "He should be down there somewhere. He was there first. Grandmother was trying to make a point."

"I doubt your grandfather understood that."

Jade sighed. "I know. Too bad."

"Wait, your grandmother named you after a murder weapon?"

She laughed. "My mother named me after my grandmother's favorite jade figurine before the . . . momentous event."

"That doesn't bother you?"

"Gram told me about it on her deathbed, the same day I discovered the family skeleton might very well be dug up by the railroad. Did I have time to be bothered?"

"Do you still have that figurine?"

Jade nodded.

"Can I have it as a wedding present? I love Jade."

Jade stifled a sob. "You know I can't marry you. And you can't still want me, after everything I've done to you."

"Some of the things you've done to me have become memories that console me." He hesitated. "Guess they're going to have to last me a lifetime." He sounded hurt, re-signed.

Jade swallowed the sorrow that rose in her throat to choke her. "Damn it. You don't want me. My family tree is riddled with wife-beaters and murderers."

"All you need is some aristocratic blood injected into your vermin-riddled—Ouch!"

Jade rubbed his arm where she'd pinched it. "Sorry." They regarded each other solemnly, sitting at the edge of a grave at midnight, lantern light once again casting a glow across a certain dead branch of her tainted familial tree. "Marriage is impossible for me, Marcus. Gram was right. If I relinquish myself to you, to passion, I forget all else. I cannot afford to lose my purpose. If I give my heart or my hand, I'm living proof I'll lose my focus, my very self."

"You've already given me your heart, but you're afraid to admit it, so that argument's useless. You've been caring for your girls as well as ever, despite your love for me, I'd like to add."

She ignored him. "If I lose the Benevolent Society for Downtrodden Women, the women in my care will lose as well. Being attracted to you makes me weak and . . . needy. A woman must remain alone and invulnerable to remain strong."

"Balderdash!"

"I must think and do for myself, Marcus. I need to be strong. About that, Gram was right. But about one thing, I believe she was wrong."

"Which is?"

"Men. Not all of them are created equal. Some of them are good."

"If I'm so bloody good, why won't you keep me?"

"You know I can't—"

His brutal kiss stopped her words. She allowed it to distract her for less than a minute, before she pulled regretfully, but forcefully, away.

Anger turned Marcus hard, dispassionate. "Let's finish what you started. What next?"

"Relocate Grandfather. Garrett's railroad crew is going to cut a course through here in a few days, to prepare the land for track. I told him he could."

"Garr and Abigail turned their coach around to come back and tell me that. That's why I'm here. They were worried about you."

"They couldn't have known—"

"No, but we all know you well enough to know that no small thing kept you fighting. Giving up was so out of character for you, we knew something else must be afoot."

Jade huffed, put out to have been so easily read. Then she stilled. "Where's Emily?"

"With Ivy, of course. He heard why Garr had returned and promised on his life to keep Em and Molly with him while I came to find you. The girls were sound asleep when I left. Molly was tucked up with Sergei the Wolf and Emily had Hungry Hedgehog and Merry Mouse. She didn't want to separate them on their wedding night."

Jade smiled sadly. Emily wouldn't appreciate her separating herself from Marcus, either. "I'll bring the cart closer. Can you get Grandfather out of there? That hole's deeper than I am tall."

"Having a little trouble with that, were you?"

"Not as much as I'm going to give you, if you don't start moving."

Marcus jumped into the grave and got moving.

By the time he filled in the old grave and dug a new one, about half a mile nearer Peacehaven, on non-optioned

Smithfield property, two additional hours had passed.

"You should have brought two shovels," he groused as he climbed out of the new grave and wiped his brow with his sleeve.

"I didn't expect company."

"Still and all, you got your slave to do most of the work."

"I'll show you how to be my slave," Jade shouted as he went toward the corpse-laden cart hidden in the woods.

He wasn't taking her final marriage refusal at all well. Neither was she, if truth be told. "Marcus?" she called, because he'd failed to respond to her tease, though she supposed she shouldn't expect him to be happy about it.

"Marcus?" Jade started forward as pin-pricks of alarm assailed her.

A gunshot broke the burgeoning silence.

Marcus! Jade ran, but stopped short when she came face to face with a pistol.

She looked up. "Where's Marcus?"

"You should be relieved. There'll be no more talk of marriage now. You seemed to find it so distressing, I almost laughed and gave myself away, hearing the two of you discuss it earlier."

A sudden pounding invaded Jade's head. Bafflement vied with a rising crest of despair, but confusion was more welcome. She embraced it. "Kirby, what are you doing here in the middle of the night? Is this why you're trying to blackmail me?"

"Blackmail? My poor deluded relative. You don't know, even now, do you?"

When she gave no sign of understanding, her former man of affairs mocked her with his laugh. "I made up the name Neil Kirby, you little fool. I'm Giles Dudley, cousin on your grandfather's side."

Awareness came to Jade like a slap.

"That's right," he said. "You're beginning to understand. Yes, I'm the man who should have inherited Peacehaven, but for that batty old woman's foolish notions."

Jade could barely comprehend the depth of the man's avarice, unless he was driven by something more dangerous. Like madness.

"I posed as your man of affairs to get on the old bat's good side. Not that it worked, but it did fill my coffers while allowing me to sell that land option as a nest egg. I set my own man up in your employ, as well, to keep me posted, as it were."

"Your man?"

"Dirk, in the stable. Came for me tonight, as a matter of fact, the same way he did the night your lover kept another of my men from shooting you. After that, I knew I'd have to take care of you, myself. The night I blew up that rail shipment, I planned to get you put away for killing the guards, except they weren't there. But you were and I knew that blowing you up, as if you'd killed yourself with a final attempt to stop the railroad, was masterful. But I failed," he said with disgust. "And I thought my luck had run out, but it's back."

Evil, and yes, mad.

"Imagine my surprise to discover the old bat was insane after all. A murderess, no less." Dudley laughed.

Jade refused to believe Marcus was . . . gone . . . except, he would be rescuing her if . . . she fought a rush of rising panic. "What will you do now?" she asked, to give herself time to think.

"Plant you and your dead lover with your grandfather.

I'll inherit quite easily when you go missing."

Bile rose up, threatening to make her retch. "You won't inherit for years," Jade said, trying to appear calm. "There was a long tie-up with grandfather's money, if I remember, correctly, because *he* went missing. I wonder how the law will appreciate a second family member coming to a questionable end?"

Dudley got anxious and rushed her, backed her toward the new grave. He raised his arm to strike. "Don't give me—"

A growling caught their attention. Mucks lunged and attacked Dudley's leg, fused to his flesh by her teeth.

As Dudley raged and tried to shake the pup off, Jade knew that Emily couldn't be far behind. She ran in the direction the pup had come, but the dog's painful yelp stopped her.

"Papa? Papa?" she heard Emily wail.

Em had found Marcus.

Tears spilled down Jade's cheeks. A darkening cloak threatened to engulf her. How could she have brought Marcus to harm when she loved him so much?

Emily called to Marcus again.

Jade fought the darkness threatening her, a half-hearted fight. With Marcus gone, if not for Emily, Jade would welcome oblivion.

The determined pup rose and went back on attack.

Dudley kicked Mucks aside.

Emily shot from the woods in her pup's defense and got herself caught in Dudley's crazed clutches.

Jade tried to pry Emily free of the viper, but he cuffed her and knocked her to the ground. "Let her go, Dudley," she said. "You can have it all. I'll sign it over to you."

He laughed. "I don't need a signature. I need a shovel to

plant the three of you." He closed his hand around Emily's tiny throat.

"Mama," she called.

A body flew at Dudley and knocked Emily free.

Marcus, bloody of face, pummeled the bastard as Jade swept Emily from the fray. But Dudley got the upper hand, battering Marcus about his injured head, his fist slipping in Marcus's blood when knuckle met bone.

Jade held Emily's face against her neck, and for her sake, she did not cry out, but her silent tears fell free as she watched a fight only one man could win. The stronger one.

Emily tried to look. She called for Papa. Jade pulled her face back against her. "It's all right, baby, it's all right. Mama's got you now. You're safe."

Jade wanted to shout to Marcus that she loved him, that she'd marry him, but she was afraid to distract him. Except, he should know. He should know before . . .

Dudley beat Marcus senseless.

The man she loved hit the ground. Unmoving.

He would not rise to fight again.

Dudley had won. He swiped blood from his face and retrieved his pistol. Standing beside Marcus, Dudley trained his pistol at Marcus. "One shot and he's gone," he said watching her. Dudley grinned and cocked the trigger.

A shot rang out and Dudley doubled over, and lurched forward, his pistol slipping from his hand.

Jade stopped screaming when Em's little hand touched her lips, not certain what happened, except that Dudley lay face down across Marcus.

Beecher rushed from the woods to kneel beside them, tossed aside his pistol, shoved Dudley aside, like a piece of trash, and gave Marcus his full medical attention.

Jade carried Emily toward them. "Is he . . ."

"Alive; he's alive." Beecher placed two fingers against Marcus's neck. "Good pulse. Lost some blood. He'll bruise." He pried open an eye, probed a head wound. "Gonna have a headache like the roof's coming down."

"But he'll live?"

"Expect so. Stubborn as you, unless he doesn't care to live. If a body gives up, it's finished."

Emily scrambled from Jade's hold. Jade knelt beside her as Em touched Marcus's hand. "Papa?"

Marcus opened his eyes, ate them up with his gaze, impaled Jade with his look and begged for . . . something.

She made to speak but Marcus regarded Beecher. "What took you so . . . long?"

"Wedding guests." Beecher rolled his eyes. "When I heard Ivy's tale, I come running. Found the old grave easy enough, but I had a bit of trouble finding the new one."

Jade let out a shuddering breath, kissed Emily's brow. "Where is Ivy?"

"Sleeping," Emily said.

Beecher chuckled. "Out cold when I got to him. He overheard Dirk telling your black-hearted cousin how things stood. Ivy tried to stop your cousin. Told me all about it when he came 'round. I moved some fast when we found the little one was gone."

Jade covered the old retainer's hand. Beecher had always been there for her. "Thank you."

He nodded as he worked. "Time you knew something about your grandmother, young lady, before you make any more foolish mistakes. Don't get huffy, now," he said, bandaging Marcus's head. "Listen for a change."

Marcus chuckled but groaned at the pain the chuckle cost him.

"Serves you right," Jade said, cupping his cheek, before

returning her attention to Beecher. "Tell me, then."

"Your grandmother wanted the world to think she hated men so much, she made them servants to keep them in their place. But the fact is, she rescued most of them, me included."

Jade took her gaze from Marcus and focused on Beecher.

"Don't mistake the hard edge she showed the abusive men in this world for the kind heart she showed humanity, man and woman alike. You think she chose a lonely solitary life, so you're dead set on following her. Fact is, she didn't choose to be alone." Beecher gazed openly at her. "Constance had a man in her life."

"When?"

"From the day your grandfather died 'til the day she did."

"She did n—"

Marcus touched her face, silencing her. She covered his hand with hers, held it against her cheek, unable to speak, seeing for the first time the man who had always been there for her and her grandmother. "You," she said to Beecher.

"Me." He nodded toward the hidden dray. "I tended her often, after that one, justifiably dead, roughed her up. We fell in love. Jade, your grandmother knew enough not to equate love with weakness. She wouldn't want you to make that mistake." He frowned. "Not anymore than you already have."

"But you never married. You remained a servant in her employ. How could she—"

"I remained her servant to be near her, because her husband was presumed living. There was no other way. Much as Constance flaunted scandal, and loved every minute of it, by God, living openly with a man not her husband would have destroyed her ability to help downtrodden women.

275

That, she could not abide."

"But you didn't; I mean you couldn't have—"

"We weren't celibate, if that's what you're implying, though I don't suppose Constance would approve my telling you so."

"I love you, Beecher," Jade said. "Did I ever tell you that?"

"No, Jade, darlin'. No, you never did. But I always knew."

Emily yawned. "Take Papa home now? Mucks?"

"Yes, Emmy-bug," Marcus said on a wince. *Home.* He put so much emphasis on the word, hope blossomed in Jade's breast.

Beecher checked the panting pup and bandaged her middle. "Ribs," he said to Jade.

She nodded. "What about Dudley?"

"Gone. I'll take care of everything. You get Marcus and the little one home. I'll be along in an hour or so."

Beecher helped Marcus lie down in the dray. Emily sat beside her papa, taking his hand, Mucks beside them. Jade drove them back to Peacehaven.

Because they were worried, Garrett and Abigail had stayed, so Garrett helped Jade get Marcus to his old room on the main floor.

"Fancy that," Marcus drawled as Garrett helped him along. "You helping me walk."

"Stuff it, Marc." Garrett's voice broke. "Why the devil did you put yourself in jeopardy like that?"

"Jade," he said, simply. "Emily. I'd do it again."

Garrett cursed. "Aye. I'd do it as well."

"Jade," Marcus called, seeking her hand as she turned down the bed.

She gave it and waited. "I'd help you with your Downtrodden Society. Did I ever tell you that?"

"No, love," she said, kissing his raw knuckles. "You didn't, but you showed me in so many ways that I should have known."

Garrett urged Marcus to lie back.

"Good," Marcus said on a sigh and closed his eyes.

Jade remembered Beecher saying much the same thing to her. It was easy to take love for granted, and she promised herself to be careful in future not to.

Abigail took Emily and Mucks to see Eloisa, who also awaited news of them.

Garrett helped Jade undress and bathe Marcus, who passed out when she washed the grazed gunshot wound on his head, as Beecher had instructed her to do.

Jade covered Marcus with a sheet and walked Garrett to the door, leaning into him when he put an arm around her. "You're a good brother," she said.

"You're a good sister."

Jade shook her head, unable to think of anything except Marcus. "I hurt him every time I refused to marry him."

"He understands. Let him ask again?"

She smiled. "I think I'd like having you for a brother."

"I think *I'd* like having a honeymoon." Garrett's grin discharged the emotional moment. He claimed Abigail and her bedroom upstairs for what was left of the night. Emily would spend it with Eloisa, as she already slept in her bed.

Jade went back to sit by Marcus. Why did it take her so long to realize he was her missing half, that she couldn't live without him?

He slept for a good while as she sat watching to make sure his chest rose rhythmically. He nearly gave his life for her and Emily, and he'd do it again.

277

"Oh Gram, I have a rare one, and so did you. Why did you never tell me?"

"Because you were an innocent, that's why." Beecher came up behind her and placed his hands on her shoulders. "By the time you were a woman grown, her mind was muddled and she didn't have it in her to tell you. And I . . . I was a coward, I think, and sick over the thought of losing her. I didn't consider anything or anyone in those dark days but my own grief."

"Would you have died for her?"

He smiled and placed the back of his hand to Marcus's cheek, nodded. "Was a day I almost did, but like your young man, I kept fighting. That was the last time your grandfather hurt anybody."

Jade read the truth on his face. "But, just before Gram died, she told me *she* killed Grandfather."

"Did she?" Beecher's eyes filled and spilled over. "Her last rational thought, her last words, were to protect me." He wiped his eyes. "I didn't know. And she didn't know about that land option, you understand, or what she would put you through. I wasn't certain what you thought. Might have been you were protecting her land because she wanted it so. Didn't know she told you about your grandfather, much less that she did it." Beecher shook his head in wonder.

"If your grandfather's . . . irregular . . . death came out, Constance's knowledge of the circumstances would have come out as well. That alone would have certified Dudley's quest to declare her insane. When I realized you'd started fighting the railroad, I decided to protect and help you, whatever your reason or course."

"So why were you so mad that time I borrowed some of Lester's clothes without your knowing it?"

Beecher shook his head in exasperation. "I heard about that body on the tracks and knew right away it was you. You could have been hurt, blast it." He inclined his head. "I still don't understand how Lester's clothes figured in with that stuffed yellow dress, though."

Jade grinned. "I wore Lester's clothes over my own breeches to make me look bigger, more robust, and to fit into that big old yellow dress Hildy left behind when she married that peddler, remember? When I got to the edge of the woods near the track, I took off the dress, stuffed it with leaves, and left it on the track. If anybody saw me put it there, they would have seen a heavyset man."

Beecher sighed, his look a mix of pride and aggravation. "I should have known."

"I did wonder," Jade admitted. "Why you climbed up on that railroad car, after giving me the devil for being there, and helped me throw that lumber in the river."

"I did it for you, and for Constance."

Jade stepped into his embrace. "I miss her."

"Me too." Beecher took a breath that shuddered out of him. "Life's short, darlin'. Don't waste it."

Jade regarded Marcus, face bruised, head bound, more handsome than ever. "He is going to be all right?"

"The bullet just grazed him. After a day in bed, he'll be champing at the bit and you'll be fit to tie him to the bed. You set to stay with him tonight?"

"Try and stop me."

Beecher kissed her brow. "He's a good man."

"I already figured that out. I'm a slow-top, I know, but late is better than never."

"*Never* was a near thing."

"I'll keep that in mind and appreciate every moment."

After Beecher left, Jade knelt by Marcus's bed and held

his hand to her cheek. She wept for the love she had with-held and for the time they had lost already because of her. And when she tired, and finished with self-flagellation, she climbed into bed beside him and laid her arm gently, but possessively, around his waist.

"Jade," he called, frantic. "Emily!" He tried to rise.

She pushed him gently back against his pillows. "We're safe. I'm here. Em's asleep in Eloisa's bed. Done in."

He sighed in relief, touched his brow, felt the bandage, then he feasted his eyes on her.

"You're nibbling on me in your mind again."

"You're in my bed. That gives me nibbling rights."

"That's a hard head you've got there."

Marcus chuckled and winced. "The pot calling the kettle black."

"Yes, and I'm truly determined on one particular point at this moment, so there's no hope for you. You'd best give in."

"All right," Marcus said with wary concern. "I give in . . . I think."

"Heal fast," Jade ordered, "because I have plans."

"Do you?" Relief and pleasure replaced his wariness as he read her. She saw the smile in his eyes. He brought her hand to his lips, nibbled a finger with tiny distracting kisses. "What kind of plans?" he asked. "Mind, I'm a sick man."

Jade laughed. "Not too sick, I see. But if you must know, I'm planning a wedding . . . ours . . . because I love you and you love me."

"Aye," said he. "I do. And I'm up for a wedding." He gave her his cocky half-smile. "But right now, headache or no, I'm up for a honeymoon more."

Epilogue

July 5, 1847

The wedding day of Marcus Gordon Fitzalan and Jade Elizabeth Smithfield burst bright upon the dawn, the sky clear and blue.

As sunlight filtered through an honor guard of stately stained-glass windows, scattering rainbow ribbons throughout, Jade marched down the aisle of St. Wilfred to meet her destiny.

The sexy scoundrel she adored, resplendent in dove-gray trousers and black frock coat, winked when their eyes met, tripping her pulse, filling her heart.

When Ivy escorted her to the single triple-arched gothic nave of the church, Marcus took her hand in his and whispered, "I adore you." Then he placed it on his sleeve and covered it with his own.

As life beckoned, radiant with promise, Marcus escorted Jade up six stone steps to kneel before God and His minister.

Amid a profusion of multi-hued chalk orchids, the likes of which Jade had not seen gathered in one place, ever, they pledged their vows, voices sure and fit to reach the stars.

As with the last Fitzalan nuptials, the wedding breakfast at Peacehaven Manor bore the same guests, but perhaps a louder celebration, since this union had been such a near thing.

The cries of kittiwake and herring gulls serenaded the guests at tables on the lawn amid the murmur and approval of the rolling sea.

Marcus was called from the table to meet a stranger waiting in the house. Then, to the shock of one guest in particular, Marcus escorted Stephen Hawksworth, Duke of Somerset, out to the celebration.

Eloisa screamed and wept as she threw herself into her husband's arms, and he kissed her enthusiastically enough to draw grins from Marcus and Garrett and sighs from every female present.

"I thought you were dead," Eloisa kept saying.

"I was found halfway across the world, days after the ship went down, starving and ill, on a floating barrel of molasses. Once I came to, it took forever to get well and sail home to you."

Stephen kept his arm firm around his wife, his eyes suspiciously bright. "Then I feared I'd never find you. I know what Arthur did. He's been dealt with. He won't hurt you again."

The news spread through the gathering. Eloisa was the Duchess of Somerset and her husband had returned from the dead.

Since she seemed too overcome to realize she had a surprise for Stephen, Lacey and Jade fetched Mac and Garth.

When they brought the twins 'round to the group, Eloisa's handsome Duke looked surprised at the sight of a bride and her attendant, babes in arms. He smiled but seemed unsure of what to say.

Eloisa squeaked and took the babies. "Stephen, this is little Marcus and little Garrett. We call them Mac and Garth for short."

Her Duke chucked one under the chin and ruffled the other's wayward thatch of hair, though it was clear he had no notion of why.

Jade laughed. "I'm very sorry to say that they're not

ours, because we love them, but they happen to be yours."

The handsome man looked thunderstruck. "But I thought . . ." He regarded Eloisa. "I was told that you'd lost—"

She shook her head. "I lied to protect our sons, and just now, in the face of your return from the dead, so to speak, I honestly forgot you didn't know they existed."

"Our sons," Stephen said, a grin spreading across his features, brightening his eyes, making him appear more handsome.

Eloisa placed them in his arms, and Stephen joined the wedding guests at the table.

Jade and Marcus returned to their seats to await the next course. Jade leaned close to Marcus. "Stephen still has Mac and Garth on his lap," she whispered. "Do you think we should tell him about their unfortunate tendency to piddle at unexpected moments?"

"I think he needs to be . . . baptized in the knowledge."

The bride and groom's laughter set the pace for the day.

As the South Downs Railroad had reached Tidemills by its June 30th deadline, the members of the wedding party were not only celebrating a marriage long overdue, they were jubilant over surmounting impossible odds. They also stood to become wealthier than they had dreamed, for Parliament, the day before, had granted them a charter to finish the trek to Dover. The East Coast route would be theirs.

Beecher gave them additional reason to celebrate. The day after Grandfather's relocation, he turned himself in to the magistrate for the deaths of Jade's grandfather and cousin.

Within the week, because his actions had saved the lives of others in both cases, Beecher was exonerated.

The wedding feast lasted three hours, but the celebration continued, in high spirits, long after.

Late in the day, Ivy came to sit beside Lacey. "Why so sad?"

She smiled serenely, belying her sadness, as she watched Eloisa speak her tearful good-byes, her Duke beside her. "I'm not sad, Ivy. I'm happy. Glory the Fairy Queen's been granting 'Happily Ever Afters' all over Peacehaven lately."

"Time you had one for yourself, little girl."

"Me? I'm beyond fairytales."

"If you're so set on facing the real world, then, why don't you come back with me to Arundel?"

"There are those who would not be pleased to have me home."

"It's time you thought of *you* for a change." Ivy slapped his thighs. "You're coming. That's an order, and I'll have no argument. It's time."

Lacey smiled in a way that made Ivy grin. "I'll be ready, my friend," she said, "whenever you are."

He kissed her brow. "I'm looking forward to our journey. But for now, I have a date with two little girls and a second attempt at a puppet-wagon sleepover. We'll give Jade and Marcus a late morning, and leave for Arundel around noon, shall we? I'll have a difficult enough time as it is getting Emily to sleep tonight. She attended her parents' wedding today and she's going on her first honeymoon tomorrow." Ivy chuckled as he walked away.

Jade and Marcus stood in the Peacehaven forecourt at the top of the drive and said their final good-byes to Eloisa, Stephen and the twins.

"I feel like crying," Jade said as their coach departed. "I'm going to miss little Mac so much."

"I will too, love, but they'll visit, and we're married now.

You do know what that means?" He raised a roguish brow.

Jade grinned. "What?"

He leaned near her ear while he dallied with the ribbon at her bodice. "It means we can make a little Mac of our own now."

Jade's smile turned soft and her eyes bright.

Marcus took her into his arms and waltzed her onto the lawn. "No tears on our wedding day, not even happy ones," he said, tightening his hold and spinning her in widening circles, until she laughed aloud.

Then he caught her close and compounded her dizziness with a stallion-ready kiss.

"You're as beautiful and sleek in white silk as you were in black leather, Jade Fitzalan. A scoundrel's perfect swan." He spanned her waist with his hands. "And you're mine, every sinfully-delicious inch of you."

Jade gave him a knowing smile as she tossed her silk tulle veil over her shoulder and began to circle him in a way meant to intimidate—like a buyer examining a stallion's fine points—not entirely unaware that her perusal afforded him the same seductive opportunity.

"You're not nearly as perfect as I first thought," she stopped to say. "But I think, perhaps . . ." She took another turn about him. "Yes, perhaps I'll keep you."

Watchful and eager, Marcus laughed, noting Jade's fine little bottom as she passed, and because she was his now, he *did* introduce it to the palm of his hand. Her perusal made him feel like that stallion, agitated and vigilant, as if something momentous were about to take place.

He whisked her into his arms and carried her toward the house. By God, he would *instigate* something momentous.

Their guests applauded.

Jade kicked as if she were being abducted.

Marcus slowed to feast his eyes on her.

All cream porcelain, and soft, willing woman, she raised her defiant chin and leveled him with her sparkling ebony gaze, and he was transfixed. Those eyes gave her skewering power, and that hint of a widow's peak added sorcery to the blend.

Heart tripping, blood rushing through his veins, Marcus Fitzalan inhaled his wife's lavender scent and stepped up his pace.

"Where are we going?" she asked.

"To prepare for our honeymoon."

Jade laughed. "We're not leaving until tomorrow."

"Right. We have to practice."

About the Author

Annette Blair is the Development Director and Journalism Advisor at a private New England prep school. Married to her grammar school nemesis—and glad she didn't know what fate held in store—Annette considers romance a celebration of life.

Among her career achievements are: a Beacon Award of Excellence, a Southern Magic Award of Excellence, RIO Awards, Booksellers Best Awards, Lories Awards, Blue Boa Awards of Excellence, and an RT Reviewers' Choice Award Nomination. She won the HRC Bravest Heroine of the Year Award, and made finals twice for the prestigious Holt Medallion and the Aspen Gold.

In bookstores now are Annette's Contemporary Romantic Comedies, *The Kitchen Witch* and *My Favorite Witch*. You can find her comedic novella, "You Can't Steal First," in Berkley's *Hot Ticket* anthology. Also available now is *The Butterfly Garden*, her Amish historical, another Five Star Publishing Expressions Romance.

Always happy crafting a new romance, Annette loves hearing from her readers, antiquing, and collecting glass slippers.